THE GORDIAN KNOT
A Modern Tragedy

Steve Herman

GRAVIER HOUSE PRESS

An Independent Publishing Company
New Orleans, Louisiana
1999

Library of Congress Publication Data:
Herman, Steve.
The Gordian Knot / Steve Herman.
ISBN 978-1-7335181-6-1
(Original GHP Paperback ISBN 0-9671179-0-9)
Fiction.
            Library of Congress Catalog Card Number:
99-94313.

First Edition
June 1999

Revised Edition, for E-Book
August 2018

For Karen

BOOK ONE

But that which must be healed - we must use medicine,
or burn, or amputate, with kind intention, take
all means at hand that might beat corruption's pain.

AGAMEMNON

CHAPTER ONE

The days last silver light was now retreating quietly from all the rows of broken glass and rubber-metal shards, the tangled pipes now rusted, some of them, in the eastern part of the sky. Alexander Thealah was kneeling on a pile of speakers, phonographs, and radios, to an old blue eight track tape machine, unearthed and exposed. Then he stood, surveying. The junkyard rose for miles, it seemed, up from the smaller rows of rubber tires and bent machines to the layered squares of crushed and rusted autos in between. Alexander stepped into the path where dented pots and pipe were forming barricades that walled the javelin dead expanse of crippled motors, engines, old converters; the strips of glass and broken fiberglass; the rubber hose; the iron tires; the copper, steel, and tin.

Alexander was making his way to the out-house shack that formed a cartoon silhouette beside the sky, when he stopped to inspect an old meat grinder that was lying next to a few dead carburetors and a stale black michelin. He lifted the grinder and examined the metal folds. "Hold it right there, fella." And the same red guarded voice was saying "slow-ly" slowly, as Alexander slowly turned. His hands were lifted in the air, and he was facing the two-shot barrel of a ten-gauge gun. "What you doin here boy?"

"I'm just lookin for someone" Alexander said.

"Yeah?" The man was wearing an ARCO baseball cap with the bill turned down over his eyes. Alex reached for his pocket and slowly peeled the coat from its lapel. He waved the blazer gently so the man could see that he carried no gun. The man nodded, and Alex drew a photo from the inside pocket of his coat and held it to him. The man shrugged.

"Do you know him?"

"Maybe."

"I hear he hangs out in the warehouse over there sometimes," and Alex pointed off behind the gate. "Thought you might have seen him around. Thought you might be able to tell me where he is." The man lifted his chin: "You're dressed pretty nice to be diggin around in my garbage."

"Do you know him?" Alex asked again.

"Not sure" said the man. "What's his name?"

"Stiles. Jeffrey Stiles."

"I might know him" said the man.

"Have you seen him around?"

"Sometimes."

"Have you seen him lately, by any chance?"

"Twelve bucks."

"Twelve."

"Twelve bucks. I'll give you the grinder and tell you everything I know."

Alexander pulled a leather wallet from his pocket, and handed the man some five dollar bills. "Fifteen then" the man said, as he gestured to the meat grinder, and Alexander lifted it again from the pile. "I saw him about two weeks ago" the man said. "Down by the warehouse. A week before that, I sold him two chandeliers. Some candle holders. Stuff like that. One of those jew torches. You know. Stuff like that."

"What else?"

"That's it."

"That's all you know?"

"That's all I know."

"Thank you" said Alex. "Take care."

"Wait" the man said. "One thing more - no, two. More. One, Stiles, he sometimes hangs out in a bar down on Conicose. It's called Fred's, I think. Or Red's - something like that. Jed's. Yeah, that's it. Jed's, on Conicose. And two, don't come around here again after workin hours. You might just find yourself dead."

Alexander nodded. "Take care."

"Susan" he called, "Susan" as he opened the door. He threw his keychain onto the mantle and set the grinder on a small wood table next to the phone. "I'm in the kitchen" she called, and Alexander went to the television and turned it on. "Smells good" he said, as Susan Thealah was saying "glad you're home."

Alex folded his navy coat and olive tie across the chair, and stepped into the kitchen where the red clay tiles were splayed with lettuce and oil. "I dropped the salad."

"Just didn't feel like cleaning it up?"

"Nah" she said, "it'll be there tomorrow."

"I guess it will then," and he leaned smiling to kiss her. Alex then stepped to the pan. "Looks good" he said, and he was spooning mushrooms with his fingers, nodding with approval as he chewed. Susan had grabbed a brown paper trash bag. She was kneeling on the floor and placing the pieces of lettuce into the bag.

Susan's locks were deeply red like sunburned shades of black that fell about the shoulders of her eloquent frame. Her eyes were as brown maple olives, rouge cheeks, lips of red. She swept her tongue and fastened the sash of her robe. "Got a postcard from Jim."

"What's it say?" he asked her, spooning the mushrooms and picking leafs of lettuce from the floor.

"Thanks" Susan said, handing him the trash bag. Then she dried her hands on a hand-towel and lifted the postcard from the bar. "'Alex'" she read aloud, "'and Susan too. The smell at low tide is enough to knock a chicken off a chicken cart. It smells like a fried-egg salt-water fart. Other than that, it's pretty neat. We saw this big church and this other church which had this really cool picture of this guy with his head chopped off. Then we went to this palace with a lot of big Tortolinis, (Karen calls them Tintorettos), and some swords and helmets from the fifteenth century. Take care, Jim.'

"'P.S. the pizza sucks.'

"Then there's a note from Karen which says, 'We are having a wonderful time. Don't eat steak. Love Karen.'"

"Jim's wit, I see, finds international success" was Alexander's response, as he was looking at the cool reflected brown Venetian gondola beneath the clotheslines that were strung with shirts and tablecloths across the card above. "So did you find him?"

"This stuff couldn't feed a starving pigeon" he said when he opened the oven door, "and no."

"Pigeons don't get heart disease."

Alexander shrugged, biting into a mushroom, and Susan said "you should just give up."

"I'm gonna check out this last bar tomorrow" he said. "And if he's not there...."

"What bar?"

"Jed's."

"Where's that?"

"I don't know. I went there today. He wasn't there."

"You should just give up" she said again, and Alex shrugged as he was forking a piece of roast beef onto a dinner plate. "Two things" she then said. "The Judge called. He wants to see you tomorrow at four."

Alexander nodded, and "Doctor Ridgefield called. She wanted to talk to you about Helen, for some reason. Said it was nothing, even though she wouldn't tell me what it was - bitch - and she is going out tonight, so call her tomorrow."

"Is that all there is?"

"You can only have two ounces I'm going to bed" she said without taking a breath, and placed the iron pan into the sink.

"So soon?"

"Yeah" she said, "I gotta be in early tomorrow. You gonna clean this up for me?"

"Sure" he said. "Goodnight Sue," and kissed her on the forehead as she placed the dry pan into the wooden rack before the stove. Susan kissed him also, and stepped into the bedroom, closing the door.

Alexander slumped into his leather gray recliner and took a Smith & Kendon candy from its tin. He placed the tin back onto the table, where the light from the television coughed and hummed, imbued with reds and indigos: the sound there droning on with Peter Jennings, who was subtly warning us about the jews; and Homer Simpson, who was telling Bart that cheaters always win if they're not caught; and Coach, who was singing about Albania; and Aliens[3]; and Coke is It; and all-temperature Cheer.

Alexander lighted the bedlamp and lifted the Twice Told Tales from his living-room stand. He read there watching tv, and then (having turned the lights and the television off) stepped lightly into the bedroom opposite Sue's, and closed the door.

The only sounds were singing crickets quilted with the blades of alternating air-conditioner compressors, and the only lights were those of alternating streetlamps over all-deserted pavements that were hollow where they shone.

CHAPTER TWO

The morning light was splintered through the tree leaves, breaking over all the sills of Alexander's home. Inside the pan, the quiet sun was as a new-life circle floating in the glassy waves of egg - not yet white. Alex was sipping from a large round mug of fresh squeezed orange juice, flipping the spatula in the palm of his hand. The egg turned slowly white beneath the glassy surface, and the sizzling from the butter mixed with dull cold noises from the tv where the news reporters spoke of passing currency.

Alexander slid the spatula beneath the egg and slipped it onto the face of a dry brown piece of toast. After four bites, he wiped the yolk from his mouth across a paper towel and threw the pan, still hot, into the sink.

Alexander quickly dressed in khaki pants and a hard white oxford, draping a tie and blazer over his arm. He stepped to the phone and dialed 1-411, gripping the cold receiver in his hand. "Doctor Kim Ridgefield" he said, "on Cambridge Way."

"No, office" he said. "Thank you," and after hanging up, then punched the seven digits into the phone.

"Hello" a woman answered finally.

"Is Doctor Ridgefield there?"

"She's out of the office. Can I take a message?"

"Is she at home?"

"No, she's at her daughter's piano recital."

"Oh, then I won't bother her."

"Would you like to leave a message?"

"Yeah, can you tell her that Alex Thealah called please? Thank you."

Alexander left his home, and drove down through the lush green rows of sycamore and through the lanes of oak trees to the bridge, where on the other side were concrete walls and benches scarred with brown graffiti, (Def Leopard, Def Con 4, Def Generation, and the other deaf entreaties of the many lusts and loves of Amy, Jennifer and Jim, of Robert, Dave, and every name on down to Zachary, deaf portraits, deaf red sickles, deaf brown lines). The bus stops were strewn with half-torn motion picture posters, and the street lamps were stapled with ads.

Alex slowed approaching Jed's, and turned into a shell lot in front of the bar. There were two small cars parked beside the entrance, as Alexander stepped in through a broken door. Alex blinked four times, adjusting his eyes to the abrupt and sleepy dark. There was a stain-wood bar, not quite lighted by five orange bulbs.

"Hey" he said to the bartender (very nicely), "I was in here yesterday looking for a friend of mine."

"Yeah, I remember. He's not here." The bartender wiped his lazy eye and scratched his beard. "You want a drink?"

"No thanks. Was he in last night at all? Have you seen him?"

"No, I told you.   Not since last Tuesday or Wednesday. Like I told you." The bartender took a cigarette from his shirt pocket and offered it to Alexander, who said no. "You know Jeff Stiles?"

"Jeff Stiles?"

The man was wearing a baby blue and white striped bowling shirt. He massaged the edge of his straw with indelicate fingers, while resting his tattooed forearm on the bar.

"He's about five-five" started Alexander, "one-seventy, dark hair, dark eyes. Hangs out sometimes in the warehouse over by the junkyard..."

"Jeff Stiles..." said the man, and took another sip through the straw. "Jeff Stiles. Jeff Stiles, yeah, I know Jeff Stiles. Aint seen him though."

Alexander made one last survey of the bar. "Thanks a lot" he said. "Take care."

"He win the lottery or somethin?"

"I don't know" said Alex turning, "maybe so."

Several hours later, Alexander Thealah was standing in a third floor courthouse phone booth, where just beyond the plastic door a man was saying "fuck that shit" to another who insisted "take the deal".

"Is Doctor Ridgefield there?" Alex was saying into the phone.

"No, she's not here right now" answered her secretary.

"Well, if you're gonna get up on that stand and give the jury some more of that I didn't do it bullshit, you might as well just keep your sorry ass down in your chair."

"Okay."

"Wait" said the woman, "is this Alex Thealah?"

"Yes it is."

"Well I guess I will just sit my sorry ass down then."

"Doctor Ridgefield was called away due to a family emergency, but she left a message for you - a note, that she wanted you to read since she couldn't get in touch, and she said she would talk to you as soon as possible."

"Okay. Is everything all right? I mean with Doctor Ridgefield's family?"

"Well Mister Ridgefield's mother had a stroke. And they don't know, they are not sure, if she will be, you know, lucid, again."

"That's awful" he said. "Tell Kim to give me a call if she needs anything."

"Well that's very nice. She thanks you, I'm sure."

"Okay, thanks."

"Have a nice day."

"Wait!"

"Yes?"

"Your offices are open until five-thirty?"

"Yes sir, they are."

"Thanks."

"Goodbye."

"Bye."

Alex set the phone into its place and stepped past the two men who were arguing and several nervous witnesses who sat beside the door with folded palms between their legs (like prayer) and faces drooping over them. He passed the bailiffs smoking in the hallway, and the water fountains and the coke machines; past the two young lawyers talking, and finally into the chambers of The Honorable Cleveland Walsh.

"Hello Eloise" said Alexander to the receptionist.

"He's in session, Alex. You can go in."

When Alexander opened the door and was seated in the back of the courtroom, one of the attorneys was questioning the plaintiff from the stand. "It was a Thursday" he was saying, "I remember cuz we had to get back for Sheila's macaroni special at the grill."

The Judge was stalwart from the bench, with silver hair and pelican eyes that captivated the courtroom in his stare. The robe fell gracefully about his arms, and his red tie folded down on the v of its neck. His expression owl-like, Judge Walsh twirled a rubber band about his thumbs.

"Thursday, the seventeenth?" asked the attorney.

"Correct."

The attorney was tall, with a slippery black moustache that formed an m across his upper lip. The plaintiff was fat and featureless, but for the titian mole beside his nose. "So Frank likes I should go out to the airport" he continued, "and pick up this load of fish comin in from Chinktown."

"Chinktown?"

"San F."

"San Francisco?"

"Correct. So these niggers start loa-"   "Mister Hamtrell" interrupted the Judge, "this is a court of law. And before the law, all men are equal, and are to be treated with a common amount of decency and respect. And if you use another derogatory epithet concerning a race or any member of any race, I will hold you in contempt of this court."

"What?"

"Don't say the n-word."

"Correct. So these coloured guys are loading up the truck with all these fish, right? And I'm driving back from the airport and I gotta stop and roll down the windows, cuz it's smellin like a two-ton pussy. Pardon, Judge, pardon. So I'm rollin down my windows, and bam, right outta nowhere, right in the fuckin ass-phalt, you know?

"So I jump outta the truck and the fish go everywhere. I mean everywhere. And all of the ni- I mean all of these folks is jumpin out from everywhere to get their free set of gills. And this bastard is yellin at me - can you believe it? A lotta nerve, huh?, this guy. A lotta nerve."

"Did you know that you were injured at this point, Mister Hamtrell?"

"No, I had no idea."

"When did you discover that you had been injured, sir?"

"Well they was drivin me back to the office, and I noticed that I had this pain, like up in here."

"Please note for the record that the witness has testified to pain in his third and fourth thoracic ribs, on the left-hand side."

"Yeah, and in my chest."

"When you felt the pain, did you know that you had been injured from the accident?"

"No, I thought I had gas."

"Why did you think that?"

"I had it before."

"When did you discover that the injury was more severe than that?"

"Well the pain started to get real bad. Real bad. So I took a thumbfull of rolaids and let mother methane take its course. But when I lifted my leg, like to fart, nothin came out, and I said, 'Oh shit, I musta torn somethin!'"

"That's when you went to see the doctor?"

"Yeah, but I didn't want to see no company doctor."

"Why not?"

"I don't like no company doctor."

"How come?"

"Well, I mean, the company doctor is like bake-um and soak-um. That's what we call them, bake-um and soak-um, because all they want to do is bake you with a pad or soak you in a tub. Like last year, we was jackin this pipe, and, when all of the sudden, Tommy yells I should look out. So I look up, and a piece a two-inch pipe was headin straight for my nuts. So I - catlike reflexes - bop the pipe with my arm. Like that. Broke my arm, but I saved my balls."

"Thank you."

"So Frankie likes I should go see the company doctor, and he sticks me in a pool with a gook there soakin his foot in it. I said, 'I can't go for that shit.' I mean, I'm an American."

"Thank you, Mister Hamtrell. Now, if you could tell the court what happened when you saw the company doctor about the pain in your ribs?"

"He likes I should take off my shirt, and I got this big trapoisle of purple in my chest."

"Trapoisle?"

"You know: like a square, but a v."

"You mean a trapezoid?"

"Sure, I guess so, it was purple."

"So then what happened?"

"So he pokes around a bit. 'Does it hurt?' It hurts, no shit it hurts, it's purple. So he asks me if I hit it on the steering wheel, and I say maybe. Then he asks me if I was wearing my seatbelt, and I say maybe. Then he likes I should drop my drawers. He likes to stick his fingers up in there. He says I'm too fat, he can't feel nothin. He likes I should jump up on the table. He sticks his fingers up in there. Then he likes I should jump off the table!

"I said, 'You no good son of a bitch! You stick your hands up in my nuts again, I'll punch you from here to Westwego!'"

When Mister Hamtrell was finished testifying, his face was red. The bailiff and all the attorneys were laughing, and the two or three observers shook their heads. Slowly the courtroom quieted and looked to the cypress bench and marble great facade that rose behind the Judge, who looked to Alexander, winked, and smiled. "Recess, everyone?" The attorneys nodded. "The court will resume at eight-thirty tomorrow morning. Thank you, Mister Hamtrell, you are a credit. Finis."

"Please rise" said the bailiff, and all did, as Judge Cleveland Walsh proceeded from the gallant courtroom and Mister Hamtrell floundered from the stand.

The Judge stood pouring two small glasses of scotch beside a desk of great mahogany, and Alexander sat in one of two black leather chairs. The shelves behind the desk were lined about the cd/tape deck and the crystal-lead decanter with Aesop's fables, Shakespeare's plays, the Testaments, Confucius, the Koran, and the Art of War; Homer, Virgil, Plato and Saint Thomas; Sir Gawain, Beowulf, the Song of Roland, Morte D'Arthur. The higher shelves were filled with tiny statuettes, hand-crafted from abroad in jade and marble, alabaster, ivory, with some in bronze, and bound between two (two on each shelf, six in all) bookends formed like pyramids and painted black with silver plaques - small plaques - of Themis and her scales of justice on the side.

"So what do you think, Alex?"

"Always an adventure."

"Indeed."

"Congratulations-" "thanks" "on your honor. I read about it in the paper."

"Thanks" said the Judge. "But you know how honors go. They are more often for the benefactors than for the beneficiary."

And Alex grinned in accord.

"Have you seen the paper today?" asked Judge Walsh as he turned.

"No, I generally wait til I get home."

The Judge and Alex lifted their glasses, "salute", and the two men emptied them both. The Judge brushed his lips with the backs of his fingers, and poured another glass for Alexander, saying "Yankees in the race for pennant, Orioles acquire Boggs."

The Judge placed the glass of scotch for Alex on the cold mahogany and receded to the leather depths of his chair. Alexander took the scotch in hand and the Judge said "you look good."

"Thanks" he said. "So do you."

"What are you down to, two-ten?"

"Two-o-seven."

"One-ninety-one."

"That's good" said Alex, "you look good. What are you running now, five a day?"

"Six on weekdays, ten on Saturdays, Sunday off."

"That's not bad for a man of your years."

"A man of my years?"

"You're getting up there, Judge."

"Everyone ages, Alexander. Even you."

The two men sat for a moment, and the Judge said: "Yankees in the race for pennant, Orioles acquire Boggs." And after a moment: "Do you want some ice?"

Alexander, who had begun to roll the glass between his palms, answered no, and the Judge tapped on the cold wood with his fingers playfully.

"What sign are you, by the way, Libra?" Alex nodded. "Libra... let me see..." as he surveyed the living section of the paper. "You have to be strong" the Judge recited, "both mentally and physically strong, and do what you know to be right. A surprising turn of events goes to make this a memorable time. Plans will be put into action. Ideas will be sculpted in the world around you. Be ready, be aware. Jupiter will fall in the seventh circle, and your love life will slightly improve."

"Hmn" said Alexander. "Yankees in the race for pennant, Orioles acquire Boggs...."

"Yes" confirmed the Judge. "Indeed."

"I don't know, Judge. I'm not on the ball today. I'm pre-occupied."

"We are all pre-occupied, Alexander. That is the point. Focus."

"Chrysler in the race" he then offered, "GM acquires Perot."

"Exactly" said the Judge, "precisely so. Athens in the running for Byzantium, Sparta acquires Troy. Deutschland in the race for Albion, the New World acquires..."

"Rita Hayworth."

"The bomb."

"Bomb, bombshell."

"Six of one, half dozen of the other."

"Two for the price of one."

"If the Germans had Rita Hayworth.... who knows."

"Okay" said Alex. "Mercy. I give."

"I was never afraid of communism" said the Judge. "It was a doomed system from the very beginning. And that's what John said, (Richard Lion, factually, but as the story goes): it's a bad system, it's a doomed system, it's an unworkable system, and so. Yet he was for some reason compelled to do something about it. Isn't that strange? You see, he did not believe it himself - which is quite different from not believing in himself, rather believing himself. (Which is the mark of all King Johns and Richards, Lionhearted as they be, that they do not believe in their own selves, quite tragically so.) Hence, the proposition: Yankees in the race for pennant, Orioles acquire Boggs. Which is to say that prospects of the New York Yankees as contenders have urged the Orioles into this undertaking. For battling with a nation doomed proves quite an unwise undertaking indeed. No one, it seems to me, would wage a war against a cause which he in truth believed to be futile."

"Which is to say" concluded Alex, "you say, that the people who were afraid of communism were not afraid because they believed it unworkable, impossible, and doomed. They were afraid it might succeed."

"Yankees in race for pennant, Orioles acquire Boggs. Clark hits homer. Ryan no hitter. Rose strikes out. Finis."

"Yes, well," and Alexander placed the glass upon the cold mahogany, "it's getting so the right can't scratch its ass without the left putting up a no ass-scratching sign."

"I'm afraid that's true" said the Judge. "In this age of ghostly terms and metaphors. The right, the left, democrat, republican, liberal, conservative: such terms mean nothing, nor should they, in this day."

"To the independence of the judiciary" saluted Alex, raising his glass.

"To independent minds of all ages" toasted the Judge. "Finis with all of this, politics. Finis."

Alexander finished the scotch in his glass accordingly.

"I tried to reach your father earlier, but he was somewhere, doing something."

"I don't keep track."

"A seaman in a pilot's world."

"A mate, no less."

"To your father."

"A mate."

"A mate."

"Query" then said Alexander. "What good is a skiff to an astronaut?"

"What is odyssey without home?"

The Judge leaned back onto the rest of his chair. His cheeks were full and rosy, and his grey eyes glistened in the light. "Query then" said the Judge. "There is a man running home. There is another man, wearing a mask, who is guarding home. Please explain."

Alexander sat for quite some time. He placed his index finger on his lip. The Judge wiped his eyes. "There is a man running home" he confirmed, and the Judge said "correct".

"And there is another man at home."

"Correct."

"And he's guarding home."

"Correct."

"And he's wearing a mask."

"Correct."

"Let me think about that for a minute, while you tell me why you have so graciously invited me here today."

"We are holding - actually we are not holding, he is out on bond - one Richard Samuel Stone for two counts of grand theft auto. The key witness in the case is one Jonathan Rembrandt Gish, who is currently serving a sentence of eighty to one hundred years in our fine penitentiary for two counts of rape and three counts of sexual assault."

"He's not a criminal of any kind, is he? The man running home."

"No."

"Please continue."

"No one can tell whether Gish is telling the truth. If he is, then Stone will plead it out. If not, the district attorney will drop the charges. The determination is yours."

"A human lie detector?"

"I thought that was your specialty."

"Why not just give him a polygraph?"

"Won't take one" said the Judge. "Mister Gish can be difficult. Not physically, I don't think, but strong-willed, and according to his own set of rules."

"Are they rules, or just edicts?"

"Very good. I stand corrected. Edicts. You are correct."

"What is his motive?"

"Gish?"

"Oh, Judge, you are quite replete with baseball images today. It's a baseball game."

"Excellent" said the Judge. "Exactly."

"That's a good one."

"Anyway, I don't know what motivates Mister Gish" continued the Judge. "That is for you to decide."

"I'll take a ride out tomorrow morning. Are you coming for dinner tomorrow night?"

"I'll be there."

"Good, I've got a friend coming in tomorrow who wants to meet you."

"Trevor" said the Judge, "is his name?"

"Yes."

"Splendid."

"Well I have got to get going" Alex said, but "do you remember a guy named Jeffrey Stiles?"

"The man with the will?"

"Yeah."

"Of course."

"He's disappeared."

"Hmn."

"What should I do?"

"I don't know Alex. Keep your gun loaded and hold onto your checkbook I guess."

"Okay" he said. "I'll call you tomorrow afternoon and tell you about this guy. Stone?"

"Gish. John R."

"Right, and I'll see you tomorrow night." The two men stood and embraced as Judge Walsh said "thanks for coming" and Alex said "always a pleasure" and was gone.

It was twenty minutes later, and Mary Stewart was punching double holes into the doctors records and placing them neatly into the files, when Alexander stepped into the offices of Doctors Isaac Kirshman, Reggie Schnieder, Kim Ridgefield, and Terry Kahn. "Hi."

"Hello" Mary said, "how may I help you?" Mary was delicate and demure with short hair and persian blue eyes. "I'm Alexander Thealah" he said. "I believe we spoke earlier."

"Yes, but I am surprised to see you," and she brushed her blond curls gracefully.

"You don't have a note for me?"

"No, I mailed it."

"You mailed it?"

"To your post office box."

"The post office box to my office?"

"Yes sir, I believe so."

"I thought I was to pick it up here?"

"Oh, I'm sorry."

"I asked you what time the offices close."

"Yeah, I was wondering why you did that."

"Yeah."

"I'm sorry."

"That's okay" said Alexander. "I guess I'll get it tomorrow."

"I'm sorry" she said again.

"Let me ask you something?" he then asked her.

"Yes?"

"Has Helen Thealah come to see Doctor Ridgefield recently?"

"Yes, she was in two or three days ago, for a bronchitis I believe."

"Can I see her records?"

"I'm sorry, but that is confidential."

"I'm her brother."

"I know, but you have to be a parent."

"Okay, well, thank you very much."

"I'm sorry again" she said as he was leaving. "Goodbye."

"Goodbye."

The light was fading to the north where mountains formed a barrier between the city and a deep expanse of olive marsh and forest waters ebbing softly into night. The sky above was as a purple melon dripping from its bent flesh over streets below, and on the streets were all the children playing football or jumping rope with all the babies being strolled out of the parks and to their homes. Alex drove among the autos filled with businessmen and businesswomen that were smoking cigarettes and listening to news or post-rock on their radios. Twice young children dropped their footballs and ran out to the car with buckets and squeegees, as Alex politely told them no.

"Hello" he said, "I'm home" as he opened the door. Alexander placed the keychain and his wallet on the mantle, and folded his coat and yellow tie across the stool among three others at the bar. He found a note from Susan saying that she went to dinner with Leslie and Rob, and they were meeting up with Jane at Hullabaloo's if he wanted to meet her there. He was reading this note and he pressed the button on his answering machine and a voice said: "Alex, it's Kim. I'm sorry I keep missing you. I'll try to call you later. Hi Sue. Bye."

Alexander found some spinach in the freezer which he threw into a pot of boiling water not yet boiling, and was examining the roast left-over that was sitting in the cold refrigerator by some fish when the telephone started to ring. He closed the door to the refrigerator and answered hello.

"What's up buddy?"

"Hey, I was just about to call you."

"I just got home."

"Well actually I wasn't about to call you; I was gonna call you later; I was trying to decide between roast, which I want to eat but shouldn't, and fish, which I don't want to eat but should."

"Do this" the person said. "Throw enough butter and garlic on the fish to make it as bad for you as the roast and it will taste as good."

"Yep" he said. "That was my plan."

"So what are you up to?"

"This guy disappeared. Been trying to find him."

"Probably turn up dead somewhere."

"Probably."

"Anyway" said Trevor, "I just handed my first check to my first client."

"Fifty million."

"Fifty thousand, more or less."

"Was he molested by a greedy corporate marauder?"

"Pretty much" he said. "They fired him for some bullshit eleven days before his pension was vested."

"Well, I'm glad you jacked them up a bit for it."

"Yeah. So what have you been up to?"

"I watched this trial for a while. Workers comp case. Right out of a movie. You would have loved it."

"Really?"

"Yeah, it was something. And then I talked to the Judge for a while. He's gonna be at dinner tomorrow night, so you will be able to talk to him for a while."

"Great."

"And we talked for a while, and he asked me to do a favor for him tomorrow morning, before I go to pick you up. Then I tried to get in touch with this doctor who wants to talk to me about something, but I couldn't reach her. So..."

"Consultation?"

"Nah, well maybe" Alexander said. "But I think it's something about Helen."

"Oh" he said. "Helen is your youngest sister?"

"Yeah."

"How old is she now, like fourteen or fifteen."

"Thirteen. So how are you guys?"

"Pretty good" Trevor said. "Julie is at a meeting right now, and I'm home watching the baby."

"Don't you have like a nanny or something?"

"Yeah, she comes during the day. She left when I got home."

"And how is the baby?"

"Fine" he said. "He is just getting to the age where it seems like he is actually communicating with you, you know? He smiles, and laughs, and makes faces."

"That's good."

"Much cuter than he used to be."

"I bet Julie is looking forward to taking care of him by herself all weekend."

"Well, her mom is coming in from Albuquerque."

"That's good."

"So anyway, I'm coming in on Delta, flight three-ninety-seven, from Atlanta. Gets in at four-fifteen."

"Okay" said Alex, who was taking down the information. "I have to go out to the penitentiary tomorrow to do this thing, and then I've got a few appointments in the afternoon, and then I'll pick you up around four-thirty in baggage and we can go over to my folks for dinner. The Judge will be there."

"And Sue?"

"And Sue."

"Okay. I'll see you tomorrow."

"Take care."

"Bye."

Alex took the cold fillets of snapper from the icebox and placed them on a bed of olive oil in the pan. He set the oven to BROIL and BROIL, and took the lemons and the I Can't Believe It's Not Butter from the refrigerator door. He squeezed the lemons onto the fish, and added some bay leaves, some onions, cut garlic, parsley, and two thin I Can't Believe It's Not Butter squares. Finally he sprinkled some pepper over the fish and tossed the squeezed half-lemons into the pan. He threw the pan into the oven, and waited.

The room was very busy and loud, with people crowding the dance floor beneath a revolving crystal-metal ball. There was cigarette smoke rising from all the tables, which were crowded with bottles of beer and glasses of soft drinks and mixed drinks and wine. There were blue and yellow and red balloons that were hanging throughout the bar, and the bar itself was round (like a big half-balloon) made of glass and painted steel.

Susan was seated with two other women at one of the tables. She was wearing a grey two-piece business suit, and a silky white blouse. Her friends were both wearing dresses. One was drinking from a bottle of beer, the other smoking. "So this guy Trevor is coming in town tomorrow?"

"Uh huh" Susan said. "Tomorrow around four."

"Where did Rob go?" asked the other woman.

"Are you excited?"

"Nah."

"Have either of you guys seen Rob?"

"I think he went to the bathroom" Susan said.

"I'm gonna go look for him."

"Okay."

The woman was wearing a white cotton dress, very casual, with a candy white headband in her hair and a pair of creamy white shoes. "Hey Leslie" Susan said to her as she was standing, "take my wallet and get us another coke and seven-up, would you? Thanks."

"Okay" Leslie said, and took the wallet from Susan's purse before stepping down into the bar. "So this guy is married now?" asked Jane.

"Yeah."

"Did you ever?"

"No" Susan said. "God no."

"Sure?"

"Yes, I'm sure" she said. "Of course I'm sure. And he has a kid."

"He has a kid?"

"Yeah."

"Oh." Jane put the cigarette into the ashtray, still lit, and exhaled the smoke from her mouth out behind her and away from Sue. "Is it yours?"

"You're terrible."

"There is little profit in sobriety."

"Maybe not, but you've really got to quit smoking. I mean not only is it unhealthy, but it's also just really disgusting and gross."

"Disgusting and gross?"

"Yes. Both."

"Yeah, well..."

"There is little profit in clean air, clean hair, clean teeth, and lungs?"

"There is little profit in life without the quick and ever-satisfying stimulus of nicotine." And with that, Jane took another drag on the cigarette and tapped the stale ashes onto the floor.

The two women chewed on the last pieces of ice that were left in their glasses, while surveying the dance floor and the people who were standing directly across from them. They were laughing, as the shorter of two men was trying to rest his left hand on the seat of the girl sitting next to him. "So when are you gonna ask someone to dance?"

"I do not, Susan, ask men to dance. Men, Susan, when I am ready, request to have the privilege of dancing with me."

"Well when are you going to have them ask you, because I want to dance, and I don't want to go out alone."

"Okay" Jane said. "But lets wait for Leslie and Rob."

"You should really think about going out with my brother."

"Nah."

"You two would be perfect for each other."

"What's he like?"

"He's very... I don't know" Susan said, "he's hard to describe."

"Is he good looking?"

"He's gorgeous."

"Come on."

"No, seriously, I mean I know he is my brother and everything, but objectively, he's gorgeous. Ask Leslie when she comes back. Ask Rob. He's really good looking."

"What's he look like?"

"He's got these really blue, grey blue piercing eyes. And this very straight, roman nose. Strong features. Beautiful cheekbones, strong chin. You like that."

"How is his hair?"

"He's got hair to die for" Susan said. "Really. It's dark brown, and curly, but not perm curly, just wavy. Not long. Kinda long, but not pony-tail offensive long."

"Tall?"

"He's a good height. I mean I don't know how tall he is, in inches or anything, but he looks the right height to me."

"Is he athletic?"

"Very."

"Cuz I don't like those guys that are good looking, but they're whimps" Jane said. "I like athletes."

"He was the state wrestling champ in high school" Susan said. "And he did the, what's that thing, with the ten events? The decathlon."

"Hmn" she said, and nodded as she lifted the cigarette.

"And he's a genius" Susan added. "I mean a real genius. He finished high school a year early. College in three years. Med school."

"He's a doctor?"

"Yep. He has his own practice and he's only twenty-nine years old."

"Wow" Jane said. "Why isn't he married already?"

"I don't know" she said, and then, (after thinking about it). "He's very traditional."

"Is he gay?"

"No" she said, "he's not gay."

"Well there must be something wrong with him."

"No there's not" Susan said. "He's perfect. It's just that he has this whole, original, philosophy, and psychology, about women, and marriage, which he has tried to explain to me several times, which I still don't fully understand. But he basically has a very clean, idealized view, unpolluted, about women. And the woman. And he is really not interested, I don't think, in pursuing a relationship, or a fling, or anything else, with anyone who is not the woman. And you, my friend, just might be the woman."

"You're so full of it" Jane said, "trying to pawn off your brother onto me..."

"I think" Susan almost whispered, "I think he might even still be a virgin."

"You are so full of it Sue."

"I'm serious."

"No one is our age, and still a virgin. Especially not a high school wrestling champion with a roman nose and grey blue piercing blue eyes."

"He's very traditional."

"I think you are suffering from family delusions" Jane said. "He probably has this whole life that you don't know anything about, where he is either this huge stud, going out to strip joints and banging cocktail waitresses two at a time, or he's impotent, or has aids or something, or he's gay."

"No" Susan said, "you're wrong. See my brother, he's not like other people. He can be. I mean, sometimes, he can be like other people. Cool, or with it, or funny, and personable, sometimes. But he has this whole other side to him, (and he can switch gears, like that!), which is very serious, and traditional, and religious. Magical almost. Almost charmed. You know? He has this genius to him. Not just intellectual genius. But vision. Magic. Religion. Like, like, like when we were young my parents took us to the water. And he had disappeared. And we went crazy looking for him, all over. My mother was in tears. And then we were outside, on the beach looking for him, and we came over the top of these dunes, and there he was. Sitting there, with his arms folded, in the center of this great circle of birds. Like cranes, or pelicans or osprey or egrets, and terns, just perched there sitting on his arms. Like he had entered their world or something. And summoned them there."

Jane rolled her eyes.

"It was amazing."

"So what does he do? What are his hobbies? Where did he go to school?"

"In Baltimore, at Johns Hopkins."

"Was he in a fraternity?"

"Yeah. Alpha Chi. He was in the fraternity with Trevor. That's how they know each other. They're brothers."

"He's not a drunken frat guy, is he?"

"No" Susan said. "He drinks some."

"And he's a doctor?"

"Yep."

"What else does he do?"

"I don't know. He likes movies, I guess. He likes books. He likes to watch tv. And sometimes he also likes to go shooting. Bows and arrows, and guns. When we were little he used to love to go sailing. Him and my father would spend hours making those little wooden ships and sailboats out of wood, and he used to go sailing all the time. But then one of his friends drowned."

"Oh" Jane said. "That's sad."

"Yeah, he tried to save him, but..." Susan took another piece of ice and held it against the roof of her mouth with her tongue. "He has a coin collection" she then said. "A really big one, with mostly old greek coins. He has this coin from Rhodes that my dad gave him from like the thirteenth century."

Jane dug into her purse for a moment and pulled out a compact, touching up the faded spots that encircled her eyes.

"He gets Newsweek every week" she continued, "but he only reads the overheards."

"Really?" Jane perked up. "Me too."

"See. I told you you would be perfect together."

"At this point I would try almost anything" she said. "What else?"

"Um, let me think..." And Susan searched for a moment. "He's a sky watcher" Susan then said.

"What?"

"He's a sky watcher."

"What do you mean? He's not a granola, is he?"

"No" Susan said, "not at all. He is just one of those people that has his eyes fixed always on the sky. Whatever he's doing, wherever he is, he is very conscious of the sky. The sun, and the moon, and the colors, and the clouds. He's just always, aware of the sky."

Jane made a face. She was snubbing her cigarette into the ashtray and wiping her forehead to the left of her brow. Her nails were painted red, and her dress fell nicely about her neck, which was bronze in the warm spanish light of the bar. Her curls were thick and black, and long, with a braid that danced on the edge of her bronze sleeveless arm. "So invite me over to dinner or something" she said.

"I will."

"Good."

"Maybe he's great in the sack."

"Jane."

"What's up?"

It was Leslie, who had returned with Rob. With a coke and a seven-up and two more bottles of beer. Jane was lighting another cigarette. "Susan is trying to set me up with her brother" she said.

"Oh he's gorgeous" said Leslie.

"See, I told you."

"Who is gorgeous?" Rob was asking.

"Is he gay?"

"Who's gorgeous?"

"No, he's not gay."

"You guys wanna dance?"

"He might be gay."

"Who's gorgeous?"

"Yeah, lets go dance." The two girls took two more sips from their soda glasses, and Leslie took one last sip of beer from the dark brown bottle. Then they placed them on the table and headed for the dance floor. Rob was lighting a cigarette. He took another sip from his beer bottle and placed it down on the table. "Who is gorgeous?" he wanted to know.

CHAPTER THREE

The next day Alexander washed his face beside the cactus that was growing on his bathroom window sill. He cupped his palm beneath the flow of sink water and sprinkled the drops across its needled leaves. The sounds of children meeting at the schoolbus stops were climbing over gates and wind-blown portals where he listened as he brushed his teeth:

"Mom said-" "I've got a He Man lunchbox." "Mom said-" "so? I've got a Teenage Mutant Ninja Turtles." "Mom said you have to sit next to me." "Where is it?" "Jeff..." "at home." "So? He Man is better than Teenage Mutant Ninja Turtles." "Jeff...(!)" "no he can't." "Mom said you have to sit next to me on the bus," "and not only that, but he could kill Splinter too." "Not Michelangelo." "Yes too Michelangelo." "Jeff, mom said-" "no way." "But mom said you have to." "Nothing can kill Michelangelo." "Jeff, mom said you have to...."

Alexander placed the razor into the mirror-cabinet and wiped the shaving cream from his ear. He stepped into the bedroom where his clothes, the dark grey suit, white shirt, red tie, were lying neatly on the messy bed. The outside doors were open where the sunlight poured in through the iron balcony, drenching the flowers warmly in its hue. The block of light that fell across his floor and stopped before the bed was warming his cold toes, where to the left his desk was filled with wrestling trophies to the shelves with six from the decathlon. Beside the stereo, in shelves, were hanging frames of Caravaggio (reprints) and the plaque and flag from his sixth and tenth grade science fairs.

Alex quickly dressed and stepped into the kitchen, where Susan sipped warm coffee from a mug. "Good morning" he said, "how was last night?"

"Pretty fun. We went to Templeton's for dinner, and then went out dancing with Jane at Hullabaloo's."

"Yeah, sounds fun, I just felt tired."

"You know, I like her more and more" Susan said. "She is really nice, and really funny, and very intelligent," and after taking a sip from her coffee mug, "I think she is beautiful."

"Leslie?"

"Jane."

Alexander said nothing, while Susan took another sip of coffee from her mug. She was wearing a summer dress that hovered lightly on her slender legs above a pair of almond espadrilles. "I see you ate my fish" she said, brushing some of her curls behind her ear.

"Sorry, was it yours? I thought you left it for me."

"That's okay" she said. "How was it?"

"Pretty good." (He was kneeling into his shoes.)

"When is Trevor coming in?"

"Gotta pick him up in baggage at four-thirty."

"How many you got today?"

"Two" he said taking her coffee, "and one con."

"You want me to pour you a cup?"

"No, just a sip," and he handed the mug back to her. "Well, I'm off."

"Bye," and the two kissed, "bye."

Alexander locked the door behind themselves and they parted to their separate cars. "Dinner at six" he called to her, "at dad's", and she nodded to him from her red Spider. There was a sunlit stream that cascaded from a leaky hydrant and ran down through the cement gutter from the curve. Two birds had stopped there, pecking drops out of the pavement. Alexander smiled to Sue and watched her drive off into morning, which was losing fresh green colors to the noon.

"Come on, Tex, you got company."

The ochreous man was seated by a guard across from Alexander. His eyes were as red rubies through the bars, and a scar carved out a leather Σ beside his ear. His skin was dark and filthy; his hair like wiry wet straw. He scratched with dirty fingernails his neck and chin.

"You ever been to Nebraska?" Alexander asked him.

"Corn" said the man, "lots of corn."

Alex possessed an impenetrable gaze. His lips were dry and still, and all his playful curls were dark and silent at his brow. He lifted his shoulders and then settled, so that his tie was briefly as the wild tail of some poppy-red wrasse of the Caribbean.

"You ever eat monkey brains?"

"Once" Gish said. "I was fishin with the Dali Lama in Pittsburgh once. He had this red-ass sent over from the zoo. Bashed it, sipped it, threw it in the dump. Then me and Lama went out chasin bird. I caught a sweet young honey jay. Lama got stuck with the hawk, and did she have some claws on her!"

"You ever-" "Yeah old Lama went and took the grenade."

"You steal any cars before?"

"No" the man said. "Who are you?"

"You ever play chess?"

"No" the man said, "but I played polo once. Doc Livingston said he would set me up with Catherine The Great. All I had to do was play a half a round of polo and she would eat me up. Made it for about five minutes fore I fell off; when I woke up I was lyin in the kitchen, and Doc Livingston was off with Catherine in the next room."

"You ever met me before?"

"No" the man said. "We in high school together?"

"You ever meet Bruce Springsteen?"

"What high school did you go to?"

"What high school did you go to?"

"Newberry."

"You ever meet Bruce Springsteen?"

"You do look familiar" the man said. And then: "Sure, the Boss? Shoot I was in a bar one time, Bruce was singin back-up and I was shootin up at the bar. I went to take a piss, and he was in there pissin beside me. He said I'm gonna be famous one day and I said yeah, but you still got a little pecker."

Jonathan Gish was lighting a cigarette while Alexander noted answers to his questions in a pad. His eyes were white like hollow diamonds alternating through the bars, the convict wiping thirsty fingers over his own yellow-madder orbs. "You on speed right now?" asked Alexander. "No" the man said. "I just like to converse. You know?"

"Cocaine?"

"No."

"Pot?"

"No."

"Heroin?"

"No" he said. "Only the black fellas can get horse in the joint."

"What about alcohol?"

"No."

"You ever beat up on your mother?"

"Hell no!" the man said, "my mother. Who the hell are you anyway?"

"You know Joe Patrossi?"

"Who told you that?"

"You know Joe Patrossi?"

"About my mother."

"You have brothers or sisters?"

"One brother. He's in San Quentin. Raped some broad."

"You ever-" "didn't rape her. He just fucked her and they called it rape cuz she was only sixteen. She wanted it though."

"You ever read Westward The Tide?"

"That the book about Barbara Streisand screwin that guy that got raped in the ass with some tiger?"

"No."

"I saw the movie" he said. "Wasn't too good."

"Have you ever seen a bullfight?"

"I saw a cockfight though. Crazy George said bet on Flipper, I said I aint bettin on no cock named Flipper - sounds like a fish. So I say all my money on Lightnin and that goddamn fish-bird won. Last time I ever go to one of those."

"When was the last time you ate turkey?"

"Christmas."

"What was the last thing you remember before you were taken to jail?"

"I was in the courtroom, right?" He paused for a moment, "and I saw the face of that girl that said I done what I did, and I said to myself for a second I wish I wasn't like I am. But I aint never been nobody else, so what the fuck. And I turned to that door with my hands down and I just said 'take me, what the fuck.'"

"You ever breakdance before?"

"Who do I look like, Michael Jackson? No but I do the pretzel, you know. The hustle. All that."

"You know Rich Stone?"

"Yeah" the man said, "met him in Vegas."

"You guys kill anybody?"

"Naw" he said. "He asked me if I wanted to hotwire a couple cars with him. Said he would give me a ride back home - wanted to see my mom before she died. So I said okay. But I didn't do nothin. I just went along. Got back. He said you want to go out stealin? I said, 'Shit man, I'm a rapist, not a thief.'"

"You ever drink fifty beers in one night?"

"Yeah, all the time."

"You ever been to Trenton?"

"No."

"You ever seen an Irish wedding?"

"Yeah, my sister Katherine. They did it up. Looked like Finnegan's Wake or somethin." Suddenly he lost his smile. "He killed her though."

"You ever meet Trevor Green?"

"Nah" he said. "Don't think so."

"You ever been in the merchant marine?"

"No way man. Those boys all got aids."

"You ever been to Las Vegas?"

"Yeah, once, for a few weeks. Won a thou off this fella playin poker on a pair of eights and an ace. He had the other two."

"You ever kill anyone?"

"Not yet that I know of" the man said. "Not yet, anyway."

"You ever been-" "what about you?"

"Not yet" said Alexander. "You ever been to a football game?"

"Yeah man, I'm an American. In high school I played flanker - like a wingback in the slot at our school, cuz we ran a six and nine and everything. And you know me and Joe Montana have been hangin out for years. We play basketball on Sundays. Takes me out to all the games. Candlestick man is cold. But he's gonna take me out to meet the team one of these days when I get outta here. Eddie D. Everyone."

"You know what a trial is?"

"Sure man" he said. "You think I'm crazy. But I aint crazy. And I aint dumb. Sure I know what a trial is."

"What does the judge do?"

"He says your sentence if the jury says you're guilty."

"What-" "Except murder one" Gish added. "Murder one, the jury decides."

"What do the attorneys do?"

"One tries to get you off, the other tries to fry you."

"And what do you do?"

"Try to get off man" he said. "Maybe you can get off on a technicality."

"How much money do you have?"

"Bout twenty-three dollars I got saved up in a Christmas account, and I know how I'm gonna spend each and every penny when I get outta here man, Merry Christmas!"

John Gish looked around the room. "Naw, but I got millions" he whispered, "stashed away. I'll cut you in man. What do you want?"

"Okay" Alex said, "I'm finished here," and he stood. The guard took John Gish by the arm and lifted him to his feet. "You take care man" he said to Alexander. "Don't drink the water."

Alex nodded, placing the black fountain pen into the corner of his notebook and turning to the empty hallway. A man was standing in an olive suit beside the door. "So what's the story, doc? Is he lying or what?"

"Is Stone from Trenton?"

"I think so."

"Has he ever been to Vegas?"

"I think he got a collar there a few years ago. Why?"

"This guy Gish, is his mother living?"

"Let me see." The man flipped through the pages of a manila folder he was holding. "No. Died two weeks before he was incarcerated. Got a dead sister too. Husband beat her to death."

"Let me see that," and Alexander was reading from the folder. "Yep."

"Lucky like thirteen, huh?"

"So it seems."

"So what do you think?"

"Nothing to gain? No time off?"

"Nope. Just telling to tell, I guess. I really don't know."

"He's a storyteller" said Alexander, "but the stories are true enough. Essentially factual."

"Can we get a report?"

"Sure" he said, "you gonna pay me for it?"

"I'll take you to lunch." The two shook hands as just then one large guard with tattooed wrists and blue eyes rushed in with his night-stick wrapping against the outside of his leg. "Doc" he said. "Doc Thea-The-a-Thealah?"

"Yes."

"They need you at the tenth ward right away." The man was catching his breath - he placed his hands upon his thighs - while Alexander drew his keys from his front right pocket stepping quickly to the door.

Forty minutes later Alexander burst into the ward with one male nurse and a guard. The room was painted white with colours flushed in at the windows from the trees and brightly painted walls outside. The beds were drawn in rows descending from the door, and there was a television in the corner of the room where four men were sitting patiently. Across the way two ladies played dominoes. The child was crying in his bed. "Did you call his mother?"

"She's tied up" said the nurse. "She will be here as soon as she can."

"He's been crying all morning" said the other. "Louder and louder."

Finally Alexander reached the bed. The light was breaking in amongst the bars through the window, where the child was wrapped in white pajamas and a light blue sheet. The child was gripping at the cardboard edges of a book. His cheeks were red and his entire face was full of fierce and wild tears. His hair was a stringy mess, unwashed and damp from his crying.

Alexander touched his forearm gently with his fingers. The boy closed his eyes more fiercely and tightened his grip on the book as he let out an awesome cry; "please" he then whispered, "please".

Alexander held him, the small boy, in his arms. The book folded and dropped to the floor. And Alexander tried to wipe the tears. "Shhhhh..." he said. "Shhhhh, it's okay."

The silent pictures on the television droned on as the old men watched them. The pair of women stacked their dominoes, while the nurse and orderly were summoned off to other places on the ward. The men were lying peacefully. And through the silence Alexander's voice came singing. First a whisper. "Tu ra lu la lu-lah, tu ra lu ra lie. Tu ra lu ra lu ra, it's an Irish lullaby." Then a song, "ra lu la lu-lah, tu ra lu ra lie. Tu ra lu ra lu ra, it's an Irish lull abye." Alexander stroked the child's head as he chanted, hugging the boy's face in his bosom, and stroking gently the child's damp hair. "Go to sleep my child" he sang, "ease your tortured soul. When you wake tomorrow, you'll be resting safely home.... Tu ra lu la lu-lah, tu ra lu ra lie. Tu ra lu ra lu ra, it's an Irish lull abye."

CHAPTER FOUR

That afternoon the room was filled with pleasant village watercolors, Alexander standing at his desk beside the phone. He pressed the flashing button on his answering machine, and went to the window where two women dressed in nurses clothing were waiting for the bus. "Hello, you have reached the offices of Alexander Thealah. I am not here at the moment. Please leave a message. Thank you.... Hi, it's Sue, don't forget airport four-thirty and dinner at six.... Hi Alex, this is Doctor Ridgefield. I hope you have read my note and gotten a chance to see her. I'll try to call later. Sorry I've been so out of touch, but Bob's mother is sick, and we have been in the hospital here around the clock. Take care, good luck, be careful with it, and I'll try to call you back later, bye.... Hi son, it's dad. Your mom and I were just calling to make sure that you and your friend Trevor were coming to dinner tonight. Give me a call at the office. Bye.... Hello, this is Shelly Mayfield, and I wanted to talk to you about seeing my son, who is about, well he is thirteen. My name is Shelly Mayfield and my daytime phone number is seven six three, one four eight six. Thank you." Alexander wrote down Shelly Mayfield 763-1486 on a notepad, and lifted the receiver to the phone. He dialed seven numbers and a woman said "Thealah, Wicker, Clark" over the line.

"Is Mister Thealah there please?"

"May I ask who's calling please?"

"Alexander."

"Hello Alex. Hold on a second. I thought that was you...."

"Victor Thealah's office."

"Can I speak to Mister Thealah please?"

"Alex?"

"Yes."

"Hold on...." Alex looked around the room where the grandfather clock was ticking-tocking and the shelves of books were stacked beside two chairs that half-way faced each other, forming a very flat v. Opposite the desk against the wall a couch sat prone between a rug from Persia and the wall, the watercolors hanging gingerly. Alex tapped his pen against the pad in polyrhythms, and a deep voice said hello through the phone.

"Hi."

"Hello son."

"We are, uh, coming for dinner, right?"

"I hope so."

"Yeah, we are coming. Six o'clock?"

"Yep, sometime around then. You can come by earlier for a drink and your friend Trevor can talk to the Judge while we help your mother."

"Okay. I'll see you then."

"Great."

"Wait, is Helen's chest okay?"

"Yeah, she's fine."

"Is she at school?"

"Yeah" he said. "I think so. I think she has a soccer game at four."

"That's good."

"Okay son. Bye."

"Bye."

Alexander stepped out of his office and across the street where an old man watered trees while kneeling on the sidewalk with a hose. Two young women passed in flowered dresses smiling - one was fixing her hair. Alex crossed another building where a For Sale sign was slapping gently in the breeze. Then he came to the post office. He drew from his pocket a keychain and stood before a wall of boxes, reaching for 119. "Is that your box?"

Alexander turned to find a withered old man who was hiding beneath two grocery bags and sipping Mad Dog from a third. "Yes" said Alexander, as the vagabond was nodding to him and taking a last gulp of the wine. Alex opened the door and sorted through the People and the Newsweek and the Sports Illustrated magazines from the bills, a sort-mail, a Uniceff, and a postcard from Jim.

"Damn" he said, and turned the postcard over:

Alex-

The bread sucks, the pizza sucks, and Pisa sucks. The leaning tower is a piece of crap. And the people here, they don't smile, they do stare, they bump in line, they push you, they don't move! they all smoke, and none of them speak any English. The phones suck, there aren't any sidewalks, and every other person you see is some punk skinhead Nazi on a moped with a cigarette in one hand and a marble staff up his ass. How's work?--I thought I'd brighten your day. Karen says "hi". We're in the room. Just finished The Firm. It sucks.

Take care,

Jim

Alexander took the correspondence in his arm and returned to his office where the phone was ringing and a small brown spider dangled beside the front door. Alex turned the key and pinched the spider's lifecord, watching it fall as he answered the phone. "Hello?"

"Hi, it's Kim."

"Hey, finally."

"Have you... done anything about it?"

"About what?"

"About Helen!" she whispered loudly. "Did you get my note?"

"No, your secretary mailed it to me."

"What?"

"I don't know."

"Well it doesn't matter. Listen, there's something important that I have to tell you."

"Yeah... (?)"

"Well... are you sitting?"

"No. Do I need to?"

"I don't know how to tell you this."

"What?"

"I think Helen has been molested."

"Molested? Sexually?"

"I believe so."

"Why didn't you tell me?!"

"I've been trying to."

"I know, I'm sorry. Tell me what happened."

"Your mom brought her in to see me, her chest was congested and such. So I asked her to take off her shirt, and she was very bashful. Extremely bashful, violently so. You know what I mean. So I struggle with her for a while and finally give her one of those gowns so that I can examine her, and she is clutching her breasts the entire time. And then I - well I have encountered this kind of extreme bashfulness only twice, and both times this was the case - so I decided to try to examine her privates, and that! was a struggle. So I, finally, got her to take her panties off, and... she has been penetrated-" "oh god" "-I'm ninety percent sure. When I looked up, the poor child was in tears."

Alexander was silent for a moment, (the "oh god" had been a whisper), and he was wiping his eye. "Why not me?"

"I know you, Alex" said the doctor. "I know you."

"Yes" he said, "you do."

"I'm so sorry."

"Thank you Kim" he said. "Give my best to Bob."

"Thank you, Alex. Be careful" she added. "Bye."

"Goodbye."

CHAPTER FIVE

Alexander quickly wrote 'NO Appointments Today - EMERGENCY! - All APOLOGIES - WiLL CALL - Alex' on a piece of paper and taped it to the front door. He leapt into his car and sped through the streets to his home. The air was very humid-heavy and the wind was very hard as he was passing all the hobos, children, businessmen and cocker spaniels barking where the light was wrested from the clouds and a telephone repairman was on a wooden pole beside his drive.

He hurled the door on its hinges, and rushed into the bedroom opposite his own. The walls were dressed with framed balloon prints - watercolors, photographs, and oils - depicting clowns and trapeze artists sadly flaming dutch orange marigolds and dandelions, spanish greens and indigos. He turned the doorknob to her closet door and searched beneath the dresses where her many shoes were stacked with boxes on the floor. The heavy breeze from outside crept into the room and Alexander wiped the anxious sweat from his forehead and brow. He found some photo albums and some scrapbooks, and went to the shelves beside the door. The shelves were filled with photographs with all her friends, and some with family, beside her old diplomas, stamps, certificates, awards. The books - in shelves and on her desk - were legal textbooks, manuals, and hornbooks; and there was also a Williams vs. Kramer file. He flipped through the pages and opened the desk drawers where he found some checks, a watch, some rings, some pens and paper, playing cards, lightbulbs, staplers, paper clips, and coins. "Damn" he said, and stepped to the bedside table where a kleenex box sat next to The Grapes of Wrath. Alex opened the upper drawer and found the three white diaries he was looking for.

The books were locked, and Alex wiped his forehead one more time and went into the kitchen for a knife.

He opened the last diary first. The entry was about a dream, where she was floating and they arrested her boyfriend and she was trying to break him out of jail. Next, a short poem. A letter to Kathy Montgomery about law school. And Alexander flipped through the pages, catching glimpses, phrases: "Dream 51" "Letter to Kathy Montgomery" "Letter to Judy Blume" "the fire was really red" "dead like leaves" and he read where she wrote "Autumn is falling dead like leaves with all of these newfound pressures, lost dreams, hopes now losing time," and skipped to the next page "Nightmare Four" and he read where she wrote "On a boat and Mom is there and they are making us walk the plank into the sea of stormy burning tar and Sylvester Stallone is trying to talk them out of it (like he does all calmly with his glasses on Arsenio Hall) and I'm saying, 'Get your gun, Mother Fucker!' And some other guys are there and they are sneaking up on the Captain, with this patch over his eye and this stubble and these rotten yellow-black teeth, and he is trying to get Mom and Mrs. Walsh (before she died - she just came), and I am tied up where these swabbies are trying to grope me and the Judge and Dad are leading parties of men with machine guns around these parts of the ship to save me, and Mom is still on deck but I am at the plank, and then I jump."

He read through more of the pages, finding nothing of significance, and then turned to the last entry, which described some guy at Hullabaloo's that she had danced with, or wanted to dance with, several nights before.

Alexander took the knife and opened up the next book, which was filled with Susan's dreams and nightmares, letters, law school quotes, college quotes, life quotes, stock prices, prices of movies ("so that I can tell our kids that when we were growing up we could see a movie for four and a half dollars and two bucks for popcorn and a dollar-fifty for Coke, the way Mom always tells us that when they were kids they went to a movie with twenty-six cents, a quarter to get in and a penny for popcorn"), letters to Mom from college, a letter to Dad, a letter to Sissy Happlinger, and a letter to Bobby McGee; she also had some sketches of kittens and puppies and hands - sketches and sketches of hands and a Leonardo postcard of his hands, (drawn by him, as if an exercise), and also notes from her trip to Europe and a ticket to the Louvre.

Finally, Alex opened the oldest diary. The first three entries depicted lists: "Boys that I want to marry: 1. Mike Coleman, 2. Clark Griswold, 3. Shane Turnbull, 2. Bjorn Borg, 3. Clark Griswold, 4. Shane Turnbull, 5. maybe John Travolta? (if he's nice)," and she had gone back and scratched out Mike Coleman with a blue pen and written "NOT Mike Coleman!!!" in the margins.

"Boys that I want to Marry: 1. Clark Griswold, 2. Bjorn Borg, 3. Shane Turnbull, 4. Rusty Stahl, 5. Jonny Cooper without braces."

And finally:

"Boys that I want to marry: 1. Clark Griswold, 2. Bjorn Borg, 3. Rusty Stahl, 4. George Chambers, 5. Shane Turnbull."

The majority of pages were filled with first dates, first dances, first kisses duly noted, and Sundays spent with Becky Shelter at the park with Becky Shelter's dog. On one page, however, Alex found a paragraph that said: "I think Daddy likes me best. He is nicer to me than Alex and Theresa, and he does more things for me. I'm not gonna tell Alex because he might get mad."

Alexander tore furiously through the pages and pages of dances and dates, and finally found one page that started "Something Happened"--that was the title. "Something happened" Susan had written. (Alexander didn't know the date because none of her entries were dated, but she must have been about fifteen.) "It was very terrible, and I am very very sad. I don't know if I can write about it now. I just want to remember that this is the saddest day in my life. And I never want to forget."

Alexander read on, furiously, through her dates and dreams and nightmares, quotes and letters, several sketches, where she wants to go to college, how she will apply, the day they all went fishing with the Judge, the time she went to Florida for spring vacation, and the time they went to San Francisco for her Daddy's case. In the back of the book he found a page that was titled "I lied". Alexander read where Susan wrote: "I lied to Daddy. He wanted to go to Summerset, just the two of us, while he investigates and gathers records so I can see what he does. I told him that I couldn't go because I had a tennis match, which I do. But I just didn't want to go."

The rest of the diary was filled with stories from high school: tennis tournaments and dates, the Senior Prom, which was to be her first time, but she threw up and he passed out. And Graduation: "Mom looked beautiful. She had this pink dress on with her pearls. And Alex was there with all of his friends trying to hit on Maria 'The Fantasy' Fontaine. Theresa was in this cute dress, but it was too short. And I had this beautiful bouquet of roses, and Jeff went to pin on my corsage, and poked my chest by my neck so mom had to do it.

And Keith made a funny speech. And Karen won an award for special honor student. And afterwards, Dad told me he was really proud, and Mom was crying, and she gave me the necklace that Mammy had given to her, but I told her to take it home so nothing would happen to it. And me and Jeff got really drunk, and we had a great time. And when the sun came up, we all went outside to watch it come up and everyone was very happy and sad all at the same time, but mostly sad. And no one said anything. Jeff kissed me on the forehead, and then everyone started hugging everyone else, and then we came home. When we got home it was 7:00 but I wasn't tired, and I just sat up all morning drinking coffee with Mom while we read the paper, and finally I fell asleep while we were watching the <u>Price Is Right</u>. And that is today, the day after I graduated from high school. And I feel much older. I really do."

The phone rang, and Alexander answered hello.

"It's Cindy, you bastard."

"What's the problem?"

"You canceled me, Al. What the hell is going on?"

"Look, I've got a family emergency here, Cindy. I'm very sorry."

"I don't give a shit about your family. What about me?! What about my problems?! What the hell do I pay you ten thousand dollars an hour for?! Now, you hang up this phone, and you get--"

Alexander hung up. Then he went to the bedside drawer, and placed the diaries where they had been discovered. He opened the second drawer, where he found only headbands, gloves, and scarves. He closed the drawer and stepped into the living room, where again he answered the ringing telephone.

"Yes?"

"Hi, it's me again. I'm sorry."

"Where are you?"

"I'm in my house."

"Are you okay?"

"Um-hmn."

"Good."

"Look, I'm sorry Alex, but I really need you, I do. I really want to see you."

"I told you, I can't see you right now."

"But I'm all alone here."

"Where is Alvin?"

"He's at work, and I'm all alone--in this great big house, all alone by myself, with no one to be with. Just waiting for you, Alex. Please."

"Look, I want you to go into the bathroom, and I want you to run the water, and take a nice long bath. And then you get into bed, your nice warm bed, and sleep this whole thing off. And when you wake up, Alvin will be there, and you will be just fine. Okay?"

"God dammit" she said, and hung up the phone.

"Bye."

Alexander went through the kitchen to a large room walled in cement with a dirty old potter's wheel and a Kenmore washer/dryer next to a bunch of metal shelves. The shelves were filled with tools and cleaning instruments and liquids, and in the corner of the room were tennis rackets, golf clubs, weights, and boxes, records, books and trophies, magazines, and trunks. He went to the bigger of two trunks and opened the lid to find a stack of papers by Susan Thealah. The first were law school papers: appeals briefs, motions, memorandums, and such; the next were papers from college: The Ancient Mariner, Budd, The Cold War, Tyger, The Marshall Court, Nixon and the Price Controls, U.S. Foreign Policy in the 50s, Klimt's Women, Television Advertising and Coca-Cola, O'Keefe's Bones, Samson Agonistes, Cancer and Cure: How Much Should the United States Invest in Medical Research, *Roe v. Wade:* Is the Right to Abortion Guaranteed by the Constitution?, Jelly Roll Morton:

American Jazz and the Beginning of Rock and Roll, Hamilton vs. Jefferson: The Jury System in America, and several more. Next were papers from high school: The Golden World, Metamorphoses, Plato and the State: Is His State the Perfect State?, Mercantilism, To Be or Not to Be: Hamlet in the 21st Century, Ranidaes, Sharks, Animal Farm, A Woman's South: Alice Walker and Eudora Welty, *Roe v. Wade:* Is the Right to Abortion Guaranteed by the Constitution?, Greece: Mother of Civilization, Sting, A Biography. There were several more.

Finally Alexander came across her many hand-written pages with poems and stories and prose. He began to read her account of fifth grade summer camp when the ringing started and he got up to answer the phone.

"What's up?"

"Trevor?"

"Yeah, my plane got in early."

"Shit, I'm sorry, what time is it?"

"Bout four thirty."

"Shit, I'm sorry, I'll be there in ten minutes."

Twenty minutes later, Alexander arrived at the airport where Trevor was standing beside a leather bag. Alexander shook his head I'm sorry, and popped the trunk from inside the car. He opened the cardoor, and he and Trevor embraced. "I'm sorry man" he said. "I was totally caught up in something."

"No problem."

"I can't believe your plane got in early. I've never heard of that happening."

Trevor shrugged, closing the trunk, and the two climbed into the car. Trevor was tall, but he did not have the mass nor the definition of Alex. His waist was round (though not quite fat), and his legs were thin and white beneath the hems of his dark blue shorts. He was wearing an oxford, which was tucked into his leather-belted shorts, and a pair of Bass top-sider shoes. His hair was sandy brown with waves that fell to the upper brow of his face, and his face was slightly freckled, with pink lips and light brown eyes.

"So how was your flight?"

"Fine, fine."

"And Julie?"

"Good. Man, you got to see this baby. I love this kid."

"Your mother-in-law's here?"

"Yeah, she's staying with them."

"And you're meeting Bill Davis tomorrow?"

"Yeah, at two."

"Okay, I can take you."

"So how have you been?"

"Okay. I - well, I just got absorbed in something this afternoon, and this patient called up and..."

"It's okay" Trevor said, "don't worry about it." Alexander nodded, and "so anyway" Trevor continued, "I was waiting for the plane and the most bizarre woman comes up to me. She is about sixty years old with this pink straw hat with a banana in it, and she says, 'I've got three bazookas for Johnny and an ace in the spades for Tim.' I say what? - I think she's a spy or something, and she says, 'I've got three bazookas, I have to go to the bathroom' and she left."

Alexander's eyes were focused on the road, and he did not at all respond. "So then I get on the plane" Trevor continued. "You know what I hate? Safety instructions. You know? Cuz you've heard them a million times but you feel compelled to pay attention cuz no one else is. I feel bad for the stewards."

"Hmn."

"Anyway" Trevor said, "so tell me about this guy, this guy you're looking for?"

"He was a patient of mine. Just disappeared, stopped coming a few weeks ago. Can't find him anywhere."

"Probably out killing people or something."

"Yeah" nodded Alexander. "So how's work?"

"Pretty good, pretty good. We have this case here, and then we have - well I was going to get to try my first case, real case, last week - I think I told you...."

Alexander's eyes were on the road.

"So but we settled. I haven't gotten to argue before a jury yet. I just did some direct once. But no cross, and no opening or closing."

"That's good."

"Something wrong man? You seem a little out of it."

"I'm sorry. I feel bad. I'm just so preoccupied, with, some things."

"Sue okay?"

"Yeah, she's fine" he said. "As far as I know."

"So you're surrounded by lawyers for the weekend, huh?"

"Yep, guess so. My dad doesn't really practice all that much though. Most of his business is in shipping still."

"Yeah, how is that going?"

"Pretty good. You know. Oil prices are up; that always helps."

"How did you guys and the Judge's family get to be such good friends? Your dad saved his life or something?"

"They were in their twenties, going to law school, and the Judge had come into a lot of money on some kind of fly-by-night long-shot commodities deal or something. And these guys came for him one night, and they had the Judge tied up and were slapping him around to see where he had the money. My parents lived in an apartment across the way, and they could see what was going on through the window. And my dad knew him; they had grown up together, and lived across the street since they were kids, but weren't real close. And but anyway, they can see what's going on, and my dad wants to go help him out, but he didn't have a gun or anything, and my mom won't let him go. So my dad pulls out his bow and arrow from the closet - he was always into archery - and he opens the window, and shoots an arrow into the Judge's apartment; and the guy had this telephone book that he was using to beat the Judge with, and the arrow went straight through the middle of the telephone book. Scared the shit out of the guy, who pissed in his pants, and they ran away and never messed with the Judge again. Then my parents went over and untied him, and they have been close ever since."

"That's neat."

"And in fact my parents are the ones that introduced him to Jessica, his wife, because she and my mom were friends."

"I didn't know he was married."

"He's no anymore" said Alex. "She died."

"That's too bad."

"Yeah."

"So these two guys are driving - no this guy and his wife are driving down the road, in a convertible, and she says, 'Slow down, Stanley, you're gonna hit something.'

"And he says, 'It's fine, don't worry.' So he gasses it up to eighty, and she says, 'Slow down, you're gonna hit something.'

"He says, 'I'm fine, don't worry, got it under control.'

"She says, 'I gotta put my coat on, I'm freezing. And she starts to put her coat on, and bam!, they hit this thing and they pull over to the side of the road. And so they get out and he has hit this big skunk. And there is this little baby skunk curling up next to its dead mamma on the side of the road, and the woman says, 'Oh my god, you have orphaned this poor little animal. I'm gonna take him home with us,' and he says 'okay, get in.'

"So she gets in with the skunk and they start tearin down the highway, and she says, 'Slow down, Wilbur, it's cold.'

"Stanley."

"Oh, was it Stanley? I always do that. Anyway, Stanley. 'Slow down, Stanley, it's cold.'

"So he says, 'Put your jacket on.' So she puts her jacket on. 'But this poor animal' she says, 'he's freezing.'

"'Put him between your legs' Stanley says, 'that will warm him up.'

"'What about the smell?' she asks him.

"'Just put your hand over his nose' he says, 'it won't bother him none.'"

Alexander smiled and Trevor was laughing as they pulled up to a red light and watched an old woman walking her cat and a paper grocery bag across the road. "So, you have a good year?"

"Yeah" said Alexander, "pretty good."

"That's good."

"What did you make last year, forty?"

"About that" Trevor said. "What about you?"

"I did okay."

"How has it been trying to establish your own practice."

"Okay" he said. "I still get a lot of clinical type patients. Through the courts, jails, rehabilitation, mental homes..."

"Yeah."

"I have very few, only two or three really, private patients."

Trevor nodded. "I got this case with this guy who - listen to this - the guy was driving his car down the interstate, when he started to pass a kidney stone."

"Oooo."

"I know" Trevor said. "And so the pain was so great, he crashed into the rail, bounced off and hit two cars. Fortunately, no one was injured that seriously. But."

"That's quite a defense huh?"

"Yeah, well, the standard of reasonableness drops pretty goddamn far when you're passing a kidney stone."

"That is one thing I never want to experience."

"They say it's worse than childbirth."

"Maybe so" he said. "Who would know?"

"That's true" said Trevor. "Hey, how do I avoid that?"

"Pick good parents."

"Genetic?"

"Yeah that's a big part of it, but moderation is really the key, in terms of what you can do. You can eat pretty much any thing you want, just don't go overboard with anything."

"Yeah, I guess that's true of pretty much anything."

Alexander and Trevor arrived at Alexander's house and put Trevor's bag down in his room. Trevor took a shower, and the two men sat in the den drinking gin and tonics and watching the news until it was time to go.

CHAPTER SIX

An hour later Alexander was ringing the doorbell at his parents home. The house rose gently from the soil where planted flowers grew out of the broken bark and shreds of wood that covered the dark damp earth. The walls were forged of brick, the doors of wood, and many windows all around the first and only floor. Catherine Thealah was a tall and gracious woman. Her high cheeks formed two tea-rose swells beneath two eyes of hickory. Her strands of soft black hair were interwoven with a rare white few. She kissed both Alexander and Trevor, leaving cold lipstick impressions on their cheeks, and invited them inside. "How have you been?" she had said to Trevor.

"Fine, fine."

"And the baby?"

"Fine, fine."

"Hi" came Susan from the kitchen with a big red smile and hugged him. Trevor kissed her on the cheek and took her cold wrists at his side. "You look great."

"So do you."

The two parted (but for their eyes) and Susan went to kiss Alex who was standing at the door. Susan was wearing a black dress cut about the neck so that her longer curls fell onto the whiter curves of her breast. She took Alexander's hand in hers and kissed him quickly hello. Then she immediately turned to Trevor, taking him by the wrist and saying "you have to meet the Judge."

Alexander followed his mother Catherine into the kitchen and asked her if he could help with anything. "You could slice the mushrooms" she said. "Thanks."

"How have you been mom?"

"Fine."

"How is Helen? I heard she had some lung trouble or something."

"Oh she's fine. Played soccer this afternoon. She almost scored two goals."

"She in her room?"

"Yeah, she's taking a shower."

"I'm gonna go tell her hello."

"Wait a minute" his mother grabbed him with one hand as she was cleaning the lettuce, "give your old mom a kiss, and then you can go and tell your sister hello."

Alexander kissed his mother and stepped into the bright solarium where his father was fixing two drinks for himself and for Trevor, who sat opposite the Judge. The sun was pouring in through the windows and striking the leaves of all of the flowers and plants with great force, as well as the glasses and statuettes. Victor Thealah was not as large as Alexander, but handled himself well for his age. He had dark hair and dark eyes, and he wore a dark moustache which covered the crooked scar on the right side of his lip below his nose. He was dressed in an autumn suit, and had loosened his electric tie. The Judge was wearing a knit blue Izod shirt and a pair of blue jeans that were tucked into the ankles of his Nike running shoes. "Yeah, there is a little path out behind my house" he was saying to Trevor as Alexander was kissing his father hello, "and I try to go every day around dusk. Hello Alexander."

"Hello Judge."

The Judge took a sip with his left hand and shook Alexander's with the right. His father asked him if he wanted a drink. He said in a little while. "So I was telling Trevor about my little jogging path" the Judge continued. "And when you get up there, you are on this ridge, as it were, with the city on one side, and the wilderness on the other, and the two seem to me equally profound."

"How far do you go?" asked Trevor while taking the glass from Victor over his shoulder and saying "thank you very much, Mister Thealah."

"I try to get in about six miles during the week and then ten maybe on Saturday. Take Sunday off."

"That's great" said Trevor. "I usually do about forty minutes on the stairmaster."

"What's that?"

"Indoor exercise" answered Victor.

"It's a meat market is what it is" said Alexander's mother from the kitchen. "All of those little teenie boppers and second wives in their little bathing suits and little pink leotards."

"I don't know about all of these youthful urban profession gimmicks" said the Judge. "They warm the body, but not the soul, if you ask me."

"Which no one did."

"Touche."

"Where are you going?"

"Helen."

"You're talking clichés Judge," and Alexander was in the hallway and approaching the door. He knocked three times. "Come in."

"Hey pumpkin" he said.

"Don't call me that" she said, as he kissed her cheek hello.

Helen was combing her wet hair and trying to wring the water from her delicate curls. Her eyes were as the first ocean; and her wet lashes curled gently about them, so that Alexander could not tell whether she had been crying. She was wearing a summer sun dress, with her feet in a white pair of shoes.

"How was your game?" he asked her.

"Fine."

"Did you win?"

"Yeah."

"What did you play, left half?"

"Yeah, and center."

"Center?" he said. "Wow. That's good."

"It was okay" she said. "I like left better."

"Oh" he said. "How is your coach this year?"

"Fine."

"Is your coach a guy or a girl?"

"Girl."

"Oh that's too bad" he said. "Girl coaches are always much harder than guy coaches."

"Why?"

"I don't know."

"I never had a guy coach."

"Oh."

"How are Blinky and Twinky?"

"Good" she said, "I have to feed them."

"You want me to do it?"

"Okay."

Alexander stepped to the desk where two small soccer trophies flanked a water tank and in the tank were two small turtles slowly crawling about two large rocks. Alex took the food and shook the flakes lightly into the aquarium. "You have to clean this out" he said.

"I know" she said. "I'm gonna this weekend."

"Oh." He sat on the bed and she sat beside him. Her hands were folded onto the top of her lap and her eyes fell unfocused on the floor. "How is your chest?"

"Fine."

"That's good."

"I don't like Doctor Ridgefield."

"Why not?"

"She was mean."

"Well, you know, sometimes doctors have to do things that are unpleasant so that they can help you feel better."

"I know, but..."

"What?"

"Nothing."

"Do you wanna play a game?" he asked her.

"Yeah."

"Name your three favorite animals, and three things that you like about each one."

"Okay" she said. "Um..."

"Take your time."

"I like the dove. Because it's pretty, and because it's white, and because it can fly. And I like rabbits, because they are soft, and warm, and cuddly. And I like... oh, the turtles. I love the turtles because they are cute, and they like the water, and they have a pretty shell to protect them."

"Neat" he said. "So how is school?"

"What's your favorite animal?" she asked him.

"The lion."

"Why?"

"I think probably because it seems pure."

"I like lions too" she said, "but I like cheetahs better, cuz they are fast. And they can beat anything. And if anything tries to catch them or to eat them, they can just run away and no one can."

"You gonna set the table?" he asked her.

"I guess so."

"Well we better get moving" he said. The two stepped through the hall and into the warm aquatic room of absinthe blades and indigos where Trevor and the Judge were speaking, the sunlight shawling down over Helen's wet bangs and flushing her sensitive eyes. She stopped to wipe them, and started walking to the kitchen where her mother was cleaning a drum. "Do you remember my friend Trevor, Helen?"

"Hi" she said bashfully, wiping her eyes.

"Hi there" he smiled. She stepped into the kitchen and opened the silverware drawer. "One must make exception" the Judge was saying, "not free license, but exception, for drug companies and other medical research companies who are making good faith efforts to improve the standards of care. But for most goods, the producer must be held strictly liable."

"You're a communist, Judge" called Catherine from the kitchen.

"Not so" said the Judge. "Quite the contrary. If you create a product that is good, you profit. If you create a product that is harmful, you do not. This is the foundation of a free market. Socialism is what we have now, because we are subsidizing companies with profits undeserved."

"You're gonna run everybody out of business, Cleveland."

"One percent, Catherine. Those are the new statistics from the General Accounting Office. Litigation accounts for one percent of retail sales. But assuming the point, arguendo, of what value is a business that is doing more harm than good?"

"The problem is" offered Trevor, "when you have a company that is not at fault. Why punish a corporation that hasn't done anything wrong?"

"Because they are reaping the rewards. It's not a matter of punishment, but equity. If Mister Wolf is reaping the profits of its good products, why should he ask Misses Lamb to bear the costs of the bad products that cause harm?"

"Accidents happen."

"They do indeed" said the Judge. "And let us say that Bestrubber Company is the greatest tire manufacturer in the world. And they do research, and they do testing, and they use the finest rubbers, the finest steels, the most skilled and astute employees, and engineers, and they produce nine hundred thousand, nine hundred, and ninety-nine exceptional tires. And here comes Misses Lamb, into the tire shop, and she says I want Bestrubber Steel-Belted X-Five-J, with white walls and the gold plated rims. And Mister All-Too-Helpful Salesman gives her the one millionth tire, and it's defective.

"Now Bestrubber was careful, of course. They did the tests, and they used all the finest hobnobbery, but accidents happen, and this one just slipped through the cracks. And Misses Lamb gets on the interstate with her husband and her brand new golden retriever, and bam, all of the sudden, there is a blowout, and they hit a concrete slab, and Rusty is at the vet with two thousand dollars in vet bills and Mister Lamb is in stable condition in General Hospital's intensive care. And Susan's friend, Mister Wolf here, wants the Lambs to pay for this? Now, now. Bestrubber has profited from the nine hundred thousand, nine hundred, and ninety-nine tires that have proved beneficial, should the law not require them to also account for the one that does harm? Yes. And that is the free market, as you say, social darwinism and survival of the fittest and capitalism and all of that: if you sell something that is good, you profit; if you sell something that is harmful, you don't. Quod erat demonstrandum. Finis."

"Won't that lead to prices that are so high that no one can afford anything?"

"That kind of thinking is socialist, my friend. The courts are here to redress harms. Was this person harmed? Was he harmed by this defendant? To what extent was he harmed? These are the dispositive questions in all matters of law. There can be none else. Justice, in this way, speaks to no one, and to everyone equally. Justice does not tell Misses Lamb that she is out of luck because we don't want people to have to pay seven cents for a stick of gum rather than five. A liberated economy is expensive, in more ways than one. It demands excellence. And justice demands even more."

"It just seems" Susan started, and the Judge said "yes, of course. So often then, what seems to be is not what is. And in this way such terms, as communism, socialism, special interests, capitalism, free market system, society's interests, good, are mingled and maimed - and then nothing. Finis."

"Whatcha doin, sport?" Victor then asked of Helen who was picking at her fingernails.

"Come here darling" said the Judge, and Helen glided in his direction across the floor. He took her shoulder in his hand and smiled at her, but she was looking to the ground and picking at her nails. "You know what?"

"What?"

"I bet Susan will teach you how to paint those pretty nails. Then if they are dirty, no one will be able to tell."

"She's adorable" Trevor said.

"Say thank you."

"Thank you" Helen muttered, her eyes still on the floor.

"So" the Judge said then to Alexander, "what did you think of the amazing Mister Gish?"

"Interesting" Alexander said. "Very compelling."

"Is this the man that raped that woman?"

"Yes."

"So have you talked to Kelly lately?" Trevor asked of Susan, "or Melinda?"

"No" she said.

"How does a man do such a thing?" asked Cleveland Walsh.

"The last time I saw Melinda was when I went to Seattle two years ago" Susan was saying. "I haven't seen her since."

"I don't know Judge" Alexander said.

"I still talk to Kathy every couple of weeks" Susan continued.

"To look into the heart of such a man" said the Judge. "A man capable, of doing, such a thing that all would cry in rage to see him dead."

"I heard Kelly got married" Trevor was saying.

"No."

"To stand up on two legs and meet that man face to face" the Judge continued, "to face the wild conflicting deep abyss of that."

"To some salesman from Connecticut."

"No, she broke it off."

Alexander stared into the depths of Cleveland Walsh's eyes. The sun was lower now, dissecting onto horizontals all the limbs of flowered plants and trees. The pelican reflections of grey-green light were soft and quiet in his irises. And spines of hardback books and shelves were cut and shafted through the sunlight as it danced among the sills and pane. Susan's tresses were as auburn splashes in some fairy neverland, while Trevor sipped the last of bourbon, Victor taking the empty glassware in his hand. Helen sat against the armchair by the Judge, picking at her fingernails and scratching at her eggshell forearm skin.

"I heard that Roger married Josephine Richards" Susan continued.

"He did" said Trevor. "He married her at school."

"Do you want white wine with dinner, or white and red?"

"So, Alexander, what is your evaluation? Is Mister Gish an honest man?"

"I wouldn't say he's honest" said Alexander, "but he tells the truth." The Judge nodded. He was grinning. "So Stone will plead it out I guess" concluded Alex.

"White is fine."

"She was a lesbian" Susan was saying, in the meantime, to Trevor.

"No she wasn't."

"Come now, Alexander. Is that justice? A jury of one."

"She got together with Amy Griswold."

"No."

"Junior year."

"A bargain?"

"I never knew that."

"A trade?"

"It's true" Susan told him. "Amy confessed it to me, point blank."

"Those twelve people in the jury box" continued the Judge, "is all that stands between chaos, and this."

"I agree" said Victor. "I agree."

Alexander was looking to the Judge.

"Well Jeff Simonds came out of the closet" Trevor was saying.

"I heard that."

"So you weren't sending me to be a human lie detector."

"I can ask you to do me a favor, Alexander, but I cannot ask you to care."

"He was in the army" Trevor continued, "and came out, and they kicked him out."

"Maybe he was just saying it to get out."

"He must have really hated it."

"It is very easy to persuade one to participate" the Judge continued, "but only he may, of his own volition, get involved."

"I want to go back" Susan was saying.

"Well, next year, for the tenth."

"Yeah I know" she said, "but you just never know what you're gonna be doing."

"Yeah."

"How is Danny?" she asked him.

"Fine" he said. "We still go out every Tuesday night."

"So will you, Alex?"

"Will I what?"

"Get involved?"

"You mean with Mister Gish? Sure."

"So what do you get when you cross a penis and a potato?" then interjected Victor. "A dick-tater."

"Cute."

All inside the sunlit room were smiling but for Alexander and his sister, who was curling the damp black tendrils of her hair. The Judge's hand was resting on her hip and Susan sipped her glass of ouzo in the day's last sunnier part of the room. "So we eat?" the Judge asked. "Catherine?"

"Just one minute" she called, and they stood to fill their glasses one last time before entering the dining room where dinner (all but shrimp and salad) lay before them on the table spread with linen tablecloths and glasses and plates and dishes and silverware.

"See what Covalt's wife said in the paper yesterday?" asked Victor of Cleveland Walsh as they were sitting. "Said living with him is like living in the zoo. Sometimes he's a tiger. Sometimes he's a lamb. He's a monkey on occasion, and he's a jackass a fair amount of the time."

"They had this judge in California - thank you Catherine, looks wonderful - Ninth Circuit Court of Appeals I believe, and he was discussing in his opinion this case concerning a sexual assault statute, and he said, 'As a matter of common sense, the penis without the scrotum is like a flintlock rifle without the flint.'"

"Do you want some more salad honey?"

"No."

"This judge last week" Susan started, and was stirring a mix of catsup-horseradish on her plate, "he was filling in for Arnold, and Jimmy Maxim from Cranston Stone came in wearing a seersucker suit, and he sits down, and we put up our witnesses, and we recess for lunch, and he puts up his witness, and he is being ridiculous with all of these stupid objections and his little very surprised about that voice and all that, and we give our closing arguments about four. So the judge starts to instruct the jury and he is going on and on, preponderance of the evidence and master servant and all that, and I charge you this and I charge you that, and I charge you that you must be impartial, and you shouldn't decide the case according to the lawyers but according to the facts. Then he says, 'I charge you that you should not take into account that the defendant's lawyer is wearing a seersucker suit, nor are you to hold it against his client, nor are you to take into account the fact that he is an asshole.'"

"I heard about that."

"I can't believe it."

"Matlock wears seersucker."

"Exactly."

Everyone enjoyed the quip and ate quite generously from the succulent mounds of shrimp in butter-garlic sauce and salad soaked in caesar dressing, loaves of bread and kalimari fried with remoulade. "This is terrific, Misses Thealah, thank you very much."

"You're welcome, Trevor."

"The kalimari is excellent, honey" added Victor.

"Thank you."

"You fried this yourself?"

"Um-humn."

"It's terrific."

"Where did you get it?"

"Just over at Bazaelon's."

"It's delicious."

"The Taj Mahal has very good shrimp I hear."

"Oh I can't stand that place" Catherine said.

"It's this great giant supermarket with twenty thousand of everything" Susan explained to Trevor as Victor was saying "that's the only way to do business these days."

"I just want to go to my little store" Catherine said, "and I know it has exactly what I want, and I know exactly where it is and what it costs."

"But you know that Taj Mahal has it at half the price" said Susan. "You're just throwing money away."

"It's worth it" she said. "No amount of money is worth that god-forsaken place."

"That's crazy" Susan insisted.

"I don't want all the choices. There's too many choices. It's very taxing."

"I don't think you really save money in those kinds of places" added Trevor, "because they force you to go down the rows and pass all of their products at all of these great prices and you end up spending ten times the money you wanted to spend in the first place for things that you didn't really want or need."

"But you have ten times the things mom" Susan said.

"It's not just that it's taxing" she said, "it's overwhelming. It's revolting, all of that stuff. You step into the place, and you are bombarded with brands and brands and brands and brands... of crap!"

"Would you please pass the bread" asked Victor. "Thank you."

"And it's not just that" Catherine continued. "It-"

"And the butter, honey? Thanks."

"They just stack those boxes and boxes and boxes" Misses Thealah continued having passed the butter to her husband, "so much stuff, that you just can't tell what's good anymore, because there is just no way to sift through all of it. And it just lowers our standards, lower and lower until nobody knows what's good anymore, and even if they did, there is nothing good left."

"I agree with you whole-heartedly Catherine" said the Judge, "and the meal proves excellent."

"Thank you" Catherine said. "We may not be rich, but we are well enough off that we don't have to cater to that garbage."

"Okay mom," and Susan looked to Trevor, quietly amused. "Speaking of garbage" she said, "did you see Whitney Shears at Elaine's party? She looked like fifty pounds of shit stuffed into a ten pound bag."

"She is going to buy Mitchell's."

"There goes one more quality store."

"Did you hear about the spontaneous twenty foot tidal wave that hit Florida yesterday?"

"It's not a tsunami. They don't know what caused it."

"I can't believe that she is buying Mitchell's."

"It hit Daytona."

"Where did she get so much money?"

"Daytona? Maybe it's the work of God."

"Is Daytona that bad?"

"Did you get your lottery tickets?"

"Yeah I got them."

"Daytona is just about the worst place you can be, other than Los Angeles."

"What do you spend a week?"

"Maybe He could get Los Angeles with an earthquake and Daytona with a tidal wave all in the same day."

"Just five bucks."

"Like Sodom and Gomorrah."

"You're just throwing your money away."

"I know, that's what I said."

"No, you're getting something" Victor said.

"You don't have a chance."

"Yes, but you're part of something. You have something to look forward to. I mean, you have three less dollars, but now you're a part of something. It's worth it."

"And you always think that you are going to win."

"What's the psychology of that, Alex?"

"You just imagine that those numbers will be yours." (Alexander ignored the invitation, quietly eating shrimp and salad mixed together in his bowl.) "I mean you can just see your numbers coming up and know that it's going to happen, even though you are all the time perfectly aware of the odds and that you have no chance of winning at all."

"But it's fun."

"It's something, you know?"

"Exactly."

"Have you ever played that scratch four game?"

"Nah."

"Guy Tollintree won two thousand bucks playing that."

"What is the state's take in that?"

"About fifty percent" he said, and Victor added "ten points more the way they pay it out. So it's really about sixty or seventy, depending on the bond."

"And it goes into some general fund?"

"I think it all goes to education."

"Yeah it goes to education, and it also goes into the lottery board's checking account, the gaming commissioner's passbook, and the governor's pocket."

"No, actually, they say that it's ear-marked for education. But whatever they make, they give to education, and then they decrease the education budget by that amount. So it's basically all a lie, and, effectively, it all goes into the general fund."

"Minus the kickbacks."

"And the payoffs."

"And the bribes."

"What's the difference between a kickback, a payoff, and a bribe?"

"A kickback is an arrangement between two co-conspirators who agree to share in the proceeds of an enterprise after it gets developed, while a payoff is made before the project gets off the ground."

"Is that the legal distinction, Judge?"

"There is no legal distinction."

"Remember the Swallows?" asked Catherine.

"Of course."

"Swimming Swallows."

"He's in prison."

"Really?"

"What did he do?"

"Had some kind of insurance fraud scheme."

"Alexander had a crush on Misses Swallow."

"She was the first one in the neighborhood to get fake boobs."

"Were they plaintiffs or defendants?"

"Both."

"Both?"

"Yes, the bank was suing them for breach of a joint venture agreement and they had asserted a quite yet ultimately spurious counter-claim."

"Lost?"

"I believe they settled while the jury was out, if I recall correctly, and then proceeded directly into bankruptcy."

"To think we had those people over to dinner."

"I know. We let them play with you kids. What bad parents we are," and then: "did father tell you?"

"We are going to move all of my stuff into the new lake house when it's done, and we are going to buy a kiln-" "really?" "-and I am going to have my own little studio."

"That's terrific."

"I'm excited."

"Well Catherine, this was wonderful. Wonderful."

"Um-hum."

"Delicious, dear."

"Thanks mom."

"Thank you Misses Thealah."

"You are all quite welcome. And If you just help me clear the table" she said standing, "I will take care of the dishes."

"I'll help you mom" offered Susan.

"No you go on ahead and talk to Trevor, I'll do it."

"So what's on tv?"

"You sure?"

"Yeah."

Alex stepped into the kitchen where his mother washed the dishes humming Guantanamera as she scrubbed a wetted plate. Alex took a sip of orange juice from the white container and wiped his mouth with the side of his palm. When he returned to the room where everyone was sitting, Susan was telling Trevor about a college friend and Victor was talking to the Judge about a shipping contract that had been proposed. Helen was sitting on the Judge's lap, and he was caressing the silky strands of her hair. Alexander sat beside his father, who was saying "then we now have plans to finally start building the house on Lake Croce."

"When do you start construction?"

"I don't know. They are processing the loan, which takes about ten days, and then we have to make sure that Friedman can design it."

"You should get Winchester. He designed Jane and Bill's house on Lake Maybelline."

"Oh he is excellent, but Catherine has this thing for Friedman."

"Well do you and Catherine want to come over to the lake house, uh, not this weekend, but the following weekend? Go fishing and canoeing."

"We would have to bring Helen."

"Of course" said the Judge.

"Oh, shit, I think that is the weekend we are gonna be in Houston."

"I thought Helen was staying with me and Sue?"

"She could come out by herself" said the Judge. "I'll take her fishing."

"She can stay with us" said Alexander.

"Do you want to go fishing with the Judge?" asked Victor, "when we go to Houston."

Helen shrugged.

"I'm just saying that she is welcome to stay with us" said Alexander again.

"Let her go out to Cleveland's, Alex" said Susan. "Maybe she'll find another turtle. She can go fishing and stuff."

"Last time Helen and I were at the lake house we had a ball. Right honey?"

"That's when I found Blinky."

"Yeah."

"Great" said Victor. "She will have a ball."

"Well if anything comes up, Judge" said Alexander, "she can stay with us."

"Okay pumpkin" said Catherine, the sink water dripping from her hands, "time to go to bed."

"I think we are gonna send Helen with Cleveland to the lake house while we are in Houston for that weekend."

"That's great" said Mrs. Thealah. "Come on, honey, kiss everyone goodnight so I can tuck you in."

Helen kissed her father and the Judge. She kissed Alexander on the cheek and Alex whispered "I love you" with some reservation into her ear. She said goodnight to Trevor, and kissed Susan who hugged her warmly, and she was off to bed. "Well it's time to get going" Susan said, and everyone said goodbye and thank you and nice meeting you and dinner was delicious and parted, all save Catherine, Victor, and the Judge. The three were sitting on the couch and chair and watching T.V. Jawbone on the television when Alexander finally closed the door.

CHAPTER SEVEN

Hours later Susan sat with Trevor shooting ouzo on their balcony. The soft and sooty shadows fell amongst the leaves and sidled down across the gardens rolled beneath them on the hill. The crest of air that formed a mountain ridge before the moon was lagging as the fog rolled in from the north, engulfing outer edges of the city where the rats and night policemen crept on swift legs through the cloistered allies of the night.

"So who is this Cindy?" asked Trevor.

"Alexander's?"

"Yeah" he said, "I guess. She left a message for Alex earlier. Sounded kinda hot for him."

"Yes, well, Cindy Jessica Skinner went to high school with Alexander. She was what every girl wanted to be. Beautiful, rich, smart, elegant, nice, and fun. Cum Laude, Yearbook Editor, Homecoming Queen. Then she went off to college, got drunk, hooked up with some guy in a fraternity, got pregnant, and married the bum. She gets married, goes on her honeymoon, and the very next week, she has a miscarriage."

"No."

"Yep."

"God."

"She has a tipped uterus or something" she said.

"That's terrible."

"Yeah, they're still married" Susan said. "He's a rich doctor. She's crazy."

"Do, did, did her and Alex ever... (?)"

"No," and Alexander stepped in through the door and filled his glass. "Alex used to have a crush on her in high school, now he just... pities her."

"Whom?" asked Alexander, appearing.

"Cindy."

"I don't pity Cindy" said Alex.

"Well, I do" said Susan, "and I'm going to bed."

"Goodnight" said Trevor as she was standing, and leaned to kiss him. He kissed her on the cheek, and she kissed Alexander "night" and went to bed.

The sounds of crickets rose and then descended in a faroff doppler. Alexander looked away to the moon. He rubbed his sticky fingers to his eyes, and yawning, arched his back, and fell into the lawnchair on the balcony.

"That true?" he asked, "what Susan said."

"As one would know."

"Do you know more?"

"That's confidential" he said.

"Is it confidential whether you have taken this young beauty to your bed?"

"No" he said, "and no."

"But everybody else has, huh?" (Now he was poking at him.)

"She is not so young as her years" said Alexander.

"You find some nobility in that."

"Yes" he said, "Cindy is very noble in her own way."

"I mean you."

"What's that?"

"Nevermind" said Trevor standing, "I gotta use the head."

Trevor left Alexander, who was staring through his shot glass at the moon. The light moved in an oval through and about the edges of the glass as malformed faces, balloons, and balls. "Your little sister is really cute" he said when he returned to the balcony.

Alexander said nothing.

"She reminds me of that little girl in Withachoclata. You know?"

"Yeah" said Alexander, "I know."

"Yeah" Trevor said.

"I don't know" said Alexander, "I feel old."

"So?" he said. "What's so bad about getting old?"

"Well, it's not so much that I feel old, but the fact that I don't know how I became old. It's like, I woke up one day, and all of the sudden I felt that I had become old."

"It's like these people, like on tv, these celebrities, that are famous, without ever having gone through the process of becoming famous. You just turn on your tv one day, and there he is. And you say, 'Who the hell is this guy?' And someone says, 'You don't know? That's Johnny Domino. You've never heard of him? He's famous.'"

"Johnny Domino?"

"See" he said. "Exactly."

Trevor stood, and circled the perimeter of the balcony. His eyes were wet and joyful. He was raising the cup to his lips. But when the ouzo touched his mouth he did not drink from it, but let it wash his lips and circle there as he surveyed the loud and motionless spaces below.

"You still have all of your soccer trophies around?" asked Alexander.

"Yeah" he said. "I keep them around to impress Julie's friends when they come over."

"I'm sure you do."

"What about you?"

"Yeah."

"Decathlete, wrestler, olympiad."

"Olympiad is an event, not a person."

"You could have gone to the Olympics."

"No."

Trevor now took a gulp from his glass and swallowed. He was measuring the distance with his eyes to the earth below. Alexander was staring at him from behind, and played with his fingertips on the arm of the chair.

"So did you and Susan ever... (?)"

"No" said Trevor, "god."

"Sure?"

"Yes."

"Whatever," and Alexander looked away. "It's true" said Trevor. "You want to go shooting tomorrow?"

"Sure" he said. "I haven't been in a while."

"You still got that forty-five?"

"Yeah."

"And that... Winchester?"

Alexander nodded.

Trevor returned to the table, filled his shot glass, and raised it before them. "Evette-" he started chanting, "Corvette - Fifty Seven to Sixty One-" and Alexander had joined him in the chanting, "Sting Ray - Ray Boom Boom Mancini - Boom Boom - Bam Bam - Pebbles - Pebble Beach - Beach - Bitch..." and Alexander was coughing, "...Back in the Butt - Boogie in the Butt - Booger!"

The two toasted glasses laughing and drank.

"What was the other one?" asked Trevor, "Back in the Butt - Back Zits - Spitz (?) "

"Yeah."

"Man, do you remember when Kindergarten took a dump in the dogbowl at Phi Delta Psi?"

"Yeah. But that wasn't as funny as when Dancer took a dump on the bus."

"Was that coming back from Camden Yard?"

"Yeah."

"That was funny."

"Yeah."

"Now you're making me feel old."

"It's not just old" said Alexander. "It's responsible."

"Come on, man, you were always responsible. You have your own practice, and you're only twenty nine years old. You're practically Doogie Howser, PSD."

"Y" he said. "Psy."

"Whatever" he said. "The point is, you were always responsible."

"I was always active" said Alexander. "That is not the same as responsible."

Trevor returned to the edge of the balcony and was looking out at the moon. He had set his glass down on the table, and was resting his chin on folded arms. The sound of crickets hummed about his ears and all his body lingered in the beauty of the night.

"Where is your friend Jim?"

"He is in Italy" Alexander said, "with his girlfriend."

"Have you ever been there?"

"No" said Alex, "I never have."

"When I was young, you know, in high school, I used to think how in the hell can they do that? Thousands and thousands of peasants, barely starving to death, all through the middle ages. And but the church has all of this wealth, and just about all of it, everything they had, went into the building of the cathedral. You know? And I thought how terrible. How utterly ridiculous. But then you go there, and you walk inside of these great structures, and just the magnitude, of the stone, and you start to think, maybe, that if you feed a peasant today, he will just be starving again tomorrow. But if we build a cathedral, it will be there for men to appreciate for thousands of years."

Alexander rubbed his eyes blankly.

"They arrested a priest back home" Trevor continued. "Embezzlement. A pillar of the community for twenty years. Helping people. Youngsters. They gave him a year in jail."

"Was that just?"

"I don't know" Trevor said. "If the law says you can't do something, then a year in jail may be a just penalty, regardless of who the priest is. You know? That's what justice is. It speaks the same to everyone" he said. "So, really, when you think about it, the law is not just or unjust. Only the application."

Trevor shrugged, and took a sip from his shot glass. Alexander was serious, and the two remained silent for a time. "Did you see that new movie about the Hermitage?" asked Trevor.

"No" said Alex, "I didn't see it."

"It was good" Trevor said. "It reminded me of those old carpets, you know? Those old persian and oriental carpets - if a movie can remind you of a carpet. Which I guess it can."

Alex did not respond. A black cat had leapt up onto the balcony and was quietly sidling along the rail. When he got to the other end, he settled into a Sargent still-life, gazing at Trevor with his wild yellow eyes. The cricket sounds were dying in the distant parts of the sky.

"Man, you should fuck that Cindy chick" said Trevor then after a time. "You are way too tense." Alexander took a deep and sober breath, and he was looking again to the sky. "Yeah, man" said Trevor, "you've been really out of it tonight. What's up?"

Alexander took another sip of ouzo, and then turned his eyes briefly to the deck. The cold ceramic seemed as it were baking slowly from the yellow light. He took brief sip, and stared at Trevor with his eyes. "You cannot tell anyone of this. I probably wouldn't even be telling you if I were sober. But I think, I just found out today, I think, that Helen is being molested."

"Molested, sexually? Helen your sister? Christ."

Trevor shook his head from side to side, "that's terrible". He put the shot glass on the table and looked back at Alexander. "Who do you think it is?"

"I don't know" he whispered. "I mean, I first thought, I mean you have to think, my, uh, my father."

"Nah."

"Just objectively, you have to.... So I came home and started to read through some of Susan's things."

"No (?) "

"I found this one thing, that made me think.... I have to find something. I know she wrote this down, whatever it was, she wrote this something, that happened, unless it's been destroyed."

"Wow."

"So I thought it was my father" he continued slowly, whispering, "you know, and I was considering teachers and coaches and things; but, for some reason, I just started to think..."

"The Judge."

Alexander looked at him.

"Right?"

"Why did you say that?"

"Just popped in."

"The Judge is like a father to me" said Alexander. "He's my godfather. I've known him since I was old enough to know. Christ, I was pallbearer at his wife's funeral. I was only thirteen years old."

There was a short pause between them. Alexander's eyes were caliginous and damp. Trevor swept his straw hair over his brow. "You can't let her go to that lake house with him until you find out for sure, man."

"I know."

"That's only two weeks away" Trevor said. "What are you going to do?"

"I don't know."

The moon was sinking on the horizontal treeline as the sounds of distant engines rose and fell. Alexander sipped from the glass. Trevor brushed his eye. The two men were as night-owls perched in olive branch beside the dark and deep terrain. And Alex stood. "Have you ever heard of Orestes?"

"No" said Trevor, "who is he?"

"He was the son of Agamemnon" explained Alex. "He had to kill the king."

CHAPTER EIGHT

The next day he and Trevor pulled up to the lot of Jackson's Mid-City Firing Range and Shooting Club. The building rose of hardwood cedar out of gravel dirt surroundings; it was accessed by the Interstate 4-12 Service Road. The cars whizzed by, and the distant smell of gunpowder was resonating faintly with the stronger smells of cedar, pine, and gum. The two men opened the large wood door, and were greeted at the desk by two young women who said "hello Mister Thealah" in almost unison. One of the women was wearing a blazer and a bra. She whizzed her stringy hair with painted fingernails, and the other pursed her lips. "Hello ladies" said Alexander. "May I present the fabulous Trevor Green."

"Hi."

"Hi-i."

"Nice to meet you" Trevor said.

The second girl rubbed her nose. "You wanna take seven?"

"Sure."

"Here you go," and she was making eyes at Trevor. "You want me to sign him in?" asked Alexander. "No, that's okay."

Trevor followed Alexander down a cement hallway. The thunder-popping sounds were bouncing in from the six dark rows where men and women pointed guns into the concrete darkness echoing. The two men stopped at seven, and Trevor fixed the thick gray plastic headphones firmly on his lobes. Alexander fixed a human shadow target to the clothesline, and drew it back to a fair distance, handing Trevor the gun.

"What's this mark?" Trevor asked, examining the checkmark on the handle of the gun where paint and outer lead was carved, or burned, or scarred.

"It was there when I got it" Alexander said, and Trevor nodded. "It's cool."

The shots rang out as guarded thunderbolts, and when the smoke cleared, Alexander had begun to reel the beaded paper on the line. "Pretty good" said Alex, "pretty good."

"You gonna shoot?"

"Nah, that's okay" said Alexander, "have another."

"No" he said, "I wanna watch a pro."

Alexander reeled another shadow figure on the line and with his right arm aimed and fired. When Trevor cranked the sheet in, he had formed a perfect hole. Trevor took the canvas, and threw his fist inside the paper where the shredded fiber edges brushed against his forearm hair. "Damn."

"Give it a couple more tries" Alex said as he was loading, "and then I'll take you to meet him."

"Hello Mister Thealah."

The man who spoke had great thick tendrils falling from his cheeks and chin. His eyes were cobalt blue, and the taller hairs cut into the wrinkles of his aging skin. The man wore a red button-down shirt that was tucked into a pair of faded old jeans. One of the pockets was ripped, and there was an iron buckle with an eagle marked Anheuser Busch and BUD.

"Hello Rich" said Alexander, taking his hand. "This is my friend Trevor Green. Rich Johnson."

"Hi."

"Nice to meet you."

"You going to Chattanooga next month?"

"I don't know yet" Alexander said. "How bout you?"

"I think so" he said. "I'm gonna make it if I can."

"Yeah" said Alexander, "will see."

"Well I'll see you later, Alex. Nice meeting you."

"Nice meeting you too."

"Ready?" he said. "Give it a few more tries and then I'll take you."

"Yep" said Trevor, "sure thing." Trevor sighted the barrel mark against the target, squinting his eye. "Well shoot em up fella" said Richard Johnson, (who was still next to Alexander). "Let them roar."

An hour later Alexander was back in Susan's room and looking through her drawers. The light was creeping in like water through the room, and the shadows of the sill and pane-lines formed a set of thin grey bars on Alexander's lap and arms. He found an old red leather book with parchment sheets. The writing was script and beautiful, where Susan's first and shortest poems were centered on the leaves. A trinity of parchments then sketched three dream homes in desert, on a hill, in woods. The script took up again the page where Susan wrote of the Olympics, and a young girl who had dreamed her whole life in a colored bottle full of sands that fell for less than just one minute, and another fallen. "A miracle" she had scripted, "even more."

Alexander turned the page, where he found the "Something Happened".

I am writing about the worst two days of my life. These forty-eight hours occurred from 8:30 p.m., Fri. Sept. 12, 1977 to 8:30 p.m., Sun. Sept. 14, 1977. It starts around 6:00 when the Judge called to ask if mom and dad if they wanted to come out to the cottage. They didn't go, but Carol was over and we were watching TV. At around 7:10, my parents got a call and went running out of the house. Mom started to cry. Carol and I thought that something happened to Grams. I kept imagining Grampee finding her in her chair because she had a heart attack, but she would be okay. But I was wrong to the utmost unfortunance. At 9:45 my dad came home and told Carol that there had been an accident and she had to go home. We thought that they were mugged and I kept imagining that the Judge got shot in the arm or the shoulder and that he had a white sling over his clothes but that he would be okay. At 11:15 my parents came home. My father was almost crying. Mom went to put Theresa to bed and dad came to talk to Alexander and I. He said that Jessica was dead. I was crying harder than I ever cried in my whole life. My mom came in and she was crying and Alexander was crying and my father was crying. It was the first time I ever have seen him cry. He said it was a mistake. He said Judge brought the fish in he had caught and she was cleaning them, while he went in to take a shower. He said that something must have happened in the woods. That she must have heard something that surprised her like a wolf or a skunk or a bear, and when she was startled she tripped and fell back and hit her head on the corner of the brick bar-b-que pit. He said the Judge came running and she was lying on the deck. And when he leaned to her, she was dead. Before this, I was feeling pity for both of them, but after I heard this, I could only think of my best friend. How unfair it was to her. Dying when Carol was only fifteen. She would never see her prom. She would never see her graduation. She would never see her wedding. And I thought of the great oil painting of a lighthouse that Carol was painting for Aunt Jessica as a present for her birthday and how she would never get to see it. She spent so much time on it and she has the most artistic ability of anyone. The next day we went to the Judge's and we all sat there crying and thinking about the past and the future. Carol asked if she could break the glass table and he said no but she could go outside and break a brick. And I went with Carol outside and she broke a brick on the sidewalk. The next morning was the funeral. It was the saddest event that I have ever been to. Mom tried to speak a eulogy but she started to cry. So dad had to finish it. That afternoon we went over to Aunt Jessica's mother's house. Carol, Alexander, Dad, Rena & I were sitting at a table, trying to cheer ourselves up. We told stories about Aunt Jessica and about when we had been bad, and jokes, and about Louie, who causes all of these accidents for other people but never gets into them himself. Then we built the big bonfire and told all of the legends. Arthur, and Roland, and Samson, and Prometheus and Lamia, the snake, around the fire. And then we came home. The two worst moments in these two days, and in my life, were when dad told me on Fri. night, and at the funeral on Sun. when they rolled the casket out and Alexander said "Goodbye Aunt Jessica."

The shadow had crept up over Alexander's chest and arms. A stray tear rolled his noble cheeks and all the curls of hair had fallen down across his ear and brow. Alexander wiped his eyes and closed the book, setting it gently into the drawer.

CHAPTER NINE

Two mornings later, Alexander stepped into his office. He was alone. The pastel watercolor prints were glowing, and the sun was striking his green wet spider plants at the edge of the room. A slender woman was standing in the doorway with her child. Her eyes were deep mahogany, on cheekbones high and lips that turned deep red. The child had curly hair and was wearing a white striped shirt that he was tugging at with one hand while the other was pawing at his mother's gentle skin.

"Hello" he said. She said "hello, I'm Shelly Mayfield, and this is my son, Gerald." The woman was wearing a cream print blouse with flowers. The blouse folded over the hem of her skirt, where two long legs fell into the high heels of her shoe. "Hello Gerald" said Alexander. "Hey."

"I'm going to let you two get acquainted" said the woman. "You be good."

"Bye."

The woman turned and skated slowly through the sunlight and into the hall, her ebony skin there forming a marked impression on his eyes. The boy was watching him, and he smiled. Then the boy jumped onto the couch and said "what's the story, doc, you like to quiz me or what?" Then he yanked his shirt down over his legs, and brushed his eyes. "What should I quiz you about?"

"I don't know" the boy said. "Show me some ink stains or something."

"Do you like being quizzed? Taking tests?"

"Yeah" the boy said, "that's why I came."

"To take tests?"

"Sure. I'm smart. My IQ is a hundred and thirty-five. That's just thirteen away from genius you know."

"I know" he said. "That's terrific. Did your mom tell you that I would be giving you some tests?"

"Yes."

"And you like tests?"

"Yes."

"And you like school?"

"It's okay" said the boy, "sometimes."

"I didn't like school."

"Maybe you're not smart. My mom said that you were smart, and that you would test me. She said you would tell me my fortune, and my sign, and my chart, and my IQ, and hypnotize me, and all that stuff. Are you gonna hypnotize me?"

"Okay" said Alexander, "here is a test."

"Okay," said Gerald, as he moved to the couch and sat down. "Now" said Alexander, "first you have to tell me how old you are, what grade you are in, and how many brothers and sisters you have."

"I have two brothers and one sister, and I'm eleven, and I live on Streeter Avenue, and I go to Rogers and Clark sixth grade Junior High School."

"Your parents aren't divorced, are they?"

"No."

"What does your dad do?"

"May dad is a businessman and my mom manages a hotel by my house."

"Where do you live?"

"On Streeter."

"Okay. Good."

The boy possessed a joyful smile, his round cheeks forming not quite dimples as he grinned. He had dark and quiet eyes. "Now" said Alexander, "you have to tell me first your three favorite animals and three reasons why you like each one."

"I like the tiger, cuz it is fast and fearful and strong. And I like the eagle, cuz it can hunt, and cuz it can see everything, all the land, and cuz it can fly. And I like the dragon, because it's mysterious, and wise, and because it can make fire."

"Okay," and Alexander was finished what he was writing into the hand-pad. "Now, for the most important question, what is your favorite thing to drink, and why?"

"I like a nectar snowball, because it is sweet, it's cold, and you can put it in the freezer and eat it later."

Alexander laughed a bit.

"What's so funny?"

"You want to know what it means?"

"Sure" he said, "let me have it."

"You want others around you to see you as a tiger. Fast, fearful, and strong. You see yourself as an eagle. A hunter, who can see everything around you, and who can fly. But you are really like a dragon. Wise, mysterious, and you can make fire."

The boy nodded, approvingly.

"And Gerald" he said, "you like sex, because it's like a snowball. It's cold. It's sweet. And you can put it in the freezer and eat it later."

"Naw, man, that's pretty neat." The boy reached into the pocket of his jeans and pulled out a stick of gum. "Want half?"

"No thanks" said Alexander, and Gerald was brushing a piece of lint from the gum. "You gonna hypnotize me and everything?"

"Maybe some other time."

"Okay."

"See what we do here is you tell me things. Whatever it is that is on your mind. Whatever you want to talk about. Football. Gymnastics. Music. School. Any stories you want to tell me. Things that happen. Vacations that you took, or take. Everything."

"And then when I tell you everything like that, then you tell me the future?"

"Something like that" said Alexander. "No, Gerald, by the time we are through, you will be able to read your own palm. And the future will take care of itself."

"Okay" the boy said. His eyes were dark and wide, his lips so soft that as the gum was folding on his tongue it could not be distinguished from them. Alexander rubbed his cheek and asked him "what's your favorite sport, Gerald?"

"Basketball" he said, "I like to watch. Like to play baseball or pool."

"Pool?"

"We have a table."

"At your house?"

"In the back. We have a back house, like an apartment. My brother lives there."

"Oh yeah? What's his name?"

"Bobby."

"That's a good name."

"What's your name?"

"Alexander."

"Like Alexander the Great!"

"Yeah, somethin like that."

"He was god of the sun."

"Really?"

"He went to Africa and conquered all of Asia" the boy said, captivated. "His teacher was Aristotle, and he died when he was only thirty."

"Thirty three" said Alex. "I think he was thirty-three."

"Oh" the boy said, "and but you know what else?"

"What?"

"He cut the Gordian Knot."

"He did" said Alexander. "That's right. He did."

The two sat silent for a while. The boy was marking rhythms on the carpet with his shoes. He wore a pair of Nike Airs, with the laces purposely untied. Alexander was wearing a blue suit with a white shirt and a paisley tie. His eyes were in shadow, and his teeth were like pearls as he smiled.

"I think your mom should be coming back soon."

"Yeah, she will be around soon."

"You got a lot of homework for tonight?"

"Nah, not that bad. Gotta practice though."

"Oh yeah? What?"

"Trombone."

"How long have you been playing?"

"Three years."

"Play in the band?"

"Yeah, and this guy Russell gives me lessons sometimes."

"Who's the midget?"

A striking woman was standing in the doorway. Her hair was sandy bleach blond falling over two blue eyes and button nose between her high cheeks thick with rouge. "I'm no midget" the boy said, "who's the bitch?"

"Gerald" said Alexander, "I would like you to meet Miss Cindy Skinner."

"Misses" the woman said.

"Enchanted" said Gerald, "I'm sure."

"Cute kid."

"Thanks."

The woman wore cotton leggings and a too small blouse that gripped her chest. Her fingers were lithe with painted scarlet on long nails. She pursed her lips and lit a cigarette.

"I'm sure you're aware that that's not healthy" the boy said.

"I'm quite aware," as she exhaled. The stale dead scent of ash was blending with her foul aromatic perfume drowned like rubbing alcohol on unexcited flesh.

"For me neither" Gerald said.

"I'm quite aware of that too."

"Hello" said Gerald's mother, Misses Mayfield, at the door. "I'm Shelly Mayfield."

"Nice to meet you. Cindy Skinner."

The two shook hands and Gerald rose to meet his mother in the doorway. Alexander stood behind his desk and nodded, "he was fine, I'll call you."

"Thank you. Goodbye."

"Goodbye Gerald."

"Bye doc."

"Goodbye."

"Nice meeting you."

"My pleasure" Cindy said.

"Have a seat" said Alexander, as Gerald and his mother closed the door. Cindy sat opposite Alexander, crossing her legs and taking a sip of nicotine. "You got anything to drink?"

"Nope" said Alex. "Have you?"

"Nah" she said, "not today. What's up with little Stevie Wonder there?" asked Cindy. "His mom looks like Helen of Troy."

"Jealous?"

"Make that Cleopatra" she said mischievously.

"Are you jealous?" he repeated.

"Of course" she said. "Wouldn't you be?"

"No."

"Bullshit" she said, "you're full of crap."

"Am I?"

"Questions, questions" she said. "So who is the kid?"

"His name is Gerald Mayfield. He is very intelligent. Good athlete, a good musician, and very mature."

"So what's his problem?"

"His brother died last month" said Alexander. "He won't acknowledge that he's dead."

"That's too bad."

Alex nodded.

"No I'm sorry."

"I know you are." Alexander's voice was tender and his eyes turned momentarily to the floor. When he looked back at Cindy she was taking another drag. "So I guess he's got the same problem I do" she then said, blowing the smoke out into the air.

"What's that?"

"Sits in a bed of tulips trying not to smell the shit."

"What are the tulips?"

"I don't know."

Alexander looked into her eyes. Cindy lifted her cigarette and pursed her lips to the side. "What is the shit?"

"I don't know "she said. "I'm horny."

"How so?"

"I don't know" she said, "maybe it's you."

"In what way?"

"Because" she said, (without finishing). "I don't know" she said again. "I think maybe it has something to do with greed."

"Do you think maybe there is some relationship, in your mind between material possessions and possessing people sexually?"

"It's both power" she said. "Two forms of power. And, if you play it right, one leads to the next."

"How so?"

"You know how so" she said. "This is boring. I'm tired. And hungry. You know what I want right now?"

"What?"

"Some ice cream" she said. "Pistachio. Doesn't that word sound sexy? Pistachio."

"How is Alvin?"

"Don't say that!" she snapped. "I can't even stand the word, anymore. Alvin. It sounds like somebody that has died. Or a chipmunk. Or a fag. I mean who lets themselves be called Alvin his whole life. You would have to be a real Alvin to let somebody call you Alvin, you know what I mean?"

Alex gestured, (not quite a smile).

"I wish he would go out and have an affair" she said. "But he's too pathetic for that. That's all he is. Pathetic. I used to think he was the end all be all. I thought he was so handsome. Suave. I even thought he was intelligent. Christ, I thought I was too intelligent for that. But I guess I'm not. After all, intelligence is for the most part recognition."

"Sometimes" said Alexander, "that is true."

"Sometimes" she said. "But anyway, he's just pathetic. That's all I think when I look at him, pathetic. I used to pity him, feel sorry for him. But now all I feel is contempt. That's the way it always happens, you know. You start out with empathy, and then the empathy turns to sympathy, and then the sympathy turns to pity, and finally the pity turns to contempt. And that's all I have left for him, nothing, but contempt."

"Why do you think that is?"

"Because he's pathetic! Dammit! Don't I pay you to listen to me? Listen. Pathetic. Impotent. Hollow. Stupid. Ugly. Baron. Barren. Goofy. Blundered. Misplaced. Gutless, heartless and sexless little pathetic twerp of a man. He probably doesn't even have the gumption to masturbate.

"I do, you know" she continued. "I even think about you sometimes. Alexander." Cindy dropped her white fingers, and the scarlet tips gingerly danced across the fabric of her pants. "I think about you quite frequently, Alex." And as her lithe hand began to form circles, her nipples had blossomed underneath her blouse. "I imagine" she said, "that we were on the ocean." And the faint sounds were humble and red. "The waters would gush up over the gunwales and soak your wet body. And I would crawl on the deck across to you. And I would grab your naked thighs in my claws. And you're wearing a cute yellow slicker - I love that word, slicker, it's so fifties - and I would unfasten... the locks..."

"Why is it do you think you would have those feelings?"

"Do you ever think about me?" she whispered, "Alex."

"This is not what we are here for."

"Oh, I'm sorry, mister high and mighty doctor, I thought we were here for me!"

"We are."

"Yes" she said sternly, "we are." And then: "But I'll take that as a yes," and she smiled, snubbing her cigarette in the deep crystal ashtray before him. "You have put out my fires."

"So" said Alexander, "where are you?"

"Nowhere. I guess."

"Nowhere?"

"Nowhere good."

"What would be good?"

Cindy did not answer. The two then were silent for a time. Cindy removed a hairbrush from her leather handbag, and treated the brown-golden waves of her hair. Alexander checked his watch and reclined back deep into the chair. Cindy spoke again first.

"You know what I was thinking, Alexander?"

"No, what's that?"

"I saw this... thing, a sculpture. It was really beautiful. But there was this one finger that had broken off. And I was just so bothered, so consumed, and overwhelmed, by that imperfection. It's like having a pimple on your nose. And I just thought, when something stands in near perfection, how great its flaws appear.

"Where in lesser things" she continued, "we wouldn't even notice them. But in greater things, they are intolerable."

"How did that make you feel?"

"I wanted to rip it down and break it with a sledgehammer. Because it's like, if it can't be perfect, then it just shouldn't be." She took a sip from her cigarette and blew her smoke out into the air. "Do you know what I mean?"

"Yes" he said, "I do."

"It's like they have given us these things to look at, you know? To look to. And when - we just can't stand the sight of it anymore. Because... failed perfection is just so much more worse than just plain failure."

"Worse how?"

"Dangerous" she said. "Because it's a trap."

The two then were again silent for a time. Cindy took sips from her cigarette, and blew the smoke from her lips out into the air. Alexander checked his watch and brushed his fingers through the dark locks of his hair. Cindy spoke again.

"Did you know that they have Napoleon's penis on reserve in some museum in France somewhere?"

"No, I didn't know that."

"It's true" she said.

"I believe it."

"What are they gonna do with yours?"

"I don't know" he said.

"I can sew it onto Alvin. Give him some balls while we are at it. Nah," she then said, "why waste them on him. Give them to somebody else. Someone younger."

"Maintaining the youth of your lover" said Alexander, "won't necessarily preserve your own." Cindy Skinner lit another cigarette. "What the hell was that?" she asked him. "I thought you were just supposed to ask questions."

"Not give answers?"

"No."

"I'm asking you what you think about that."

"What do I think about that?"

"Yes."

Cindy lifted the cigarette and looked at him. Her lips were softly quivering. "Did you know that the average person makes love an average of two thousand, four hundred, and twenty three times in their lifetime?"

"Nope" he said. "I didn't know that."

"It's true."

"I'm sure."

"I bet you're about two thousand, four hundred, and twenty two behind." Alexander shook his head from side to side. "You want to get one out of the way?"

"No thanks" he said.

"The psychiatrist community would be up in arms, huh?"

"Does that concern you?"

"You know not, Al" she said. "What about you, darling? Do you care?" Alexander said nothing. "Come on, Alex, lets go. I have a house I'm showing on Melville Place; we can go there."

"I don't think so."

"Please," as she touched his shin and brushed it with the back of her hand. "No" he said, and "you know that the answer will always be no."

"Well fuck you" she said and recoiled.

Then Cindy lifted the phone. "Hi" she said, "is Michael there? ... Hi honey, it's Cindy.... Are you - excitable? ... Enticeable? ... Good. Well look, I'm showing this house on twenty-five sixty-two Melville

Place. Do you want to meet me there? It has a glorious bedroom.... Okay luv, ten minutes.

"Goodbye Alexander" she said, and was gone.

CHAPTER TEN

It was three days later when Alexander went to see the Judge. The gate was unlocked and the driveway empty, when Alexander crept slowly up the path to his home. The building rose out of the earth on doric columns. It was large, and square, imposing. The drive was bordered by rows of pine and white camellia bushes rising into rows of red hibiscus trees in bloom. Behind the flowers, to the right, was a tennis court, and to the left a thick green block of trees. A clearing opened where the home was flanked by a two-car/carpenter's garage; on the right, to the back of the house, a walking/jogging path meandered off behind the property, and into the forest beyond. A robin was singing. The sun was breaking down over the gutter and down through the columns, as Alexander opened the door to the Judge's home.

Once inside the bedroom, Alexander sorted through the photographs that he displayed. Other than the wedding picture, and another of he and Jessica together, there was a photograph of all his family with theirs. A photo album sat beneath the bedlamp by his bed. The first page was a photograph of Jessica. But much of the rest were many pictures of Carol when she was young, in bathing suits, in nightgowns, underwear; then also one of the Judge and Helen at the lake. On the last page, finally, was a photograph of Carol and Susan together, on Nantucket, seventeen.

Alex looked through all the drawers but found no diaries nor any dirty pictures hidden, nor any adult magazines.   In the bathroom he found one Playboy turned down over the bathtowels that were stacked in a rack next to the toilet, and in the den he found videotapes next to the big screen tv. The tapes to the left were recordings of Excalibur, Arthur, Lancelot, The Fisher King; Robin Hood, Three Musketeers, Ivanhoe; 12 Angry Men, To Kill A Mockingbird, Trial at Nuremberg, A Man for All Seasons, and Inherit the Wind. There was a series of cabinets and drawers, and Alexander opened one of three drawers beneath the video-tape machine.   There was an assortment of scissors, pens, files, and envelopes, pencils, papers, stickers, paper-clips, and tape. Alexander closed the drawer, and opened the drawer just below.   In that drawer were two tapes marked in red. One was marked Young Red Hood Riding, the other, Marry Had A Little Lamb But Her Fleece Was Blond As Snow.

Alex placed the two boxes beside the vcr, and put one of the tapes into the machine. He turned on the television, and a picture slowly formed, anticipated by the sounds of heavy breathings. First were a blurred smear of flesh-coloured images. Then the fat curve of a naked man.   He was inside a small girl, crying, moaning - her face appeared in quick glances among his ribs and arm. The girl had youthful eyes that were dark and confused. Her breasts were undeveloped, and her hair was a wet tangled ball of threads and brambled frays. She sucked on her fingers. She was whimpering.

Alexander took the tape out of the machine and turned it off. He also turned off the tv. The house was silent, though outside the robins were singing. And Alexander wiped his eyes.

Four hours later, Alexander was steering his old blue Fuji ten-speed bicycle up the road again to the Judge's home. He passed the rows of sugar houses stacked like gingerbreads across the hill. The homes had picket fences, that were nailed, untreated, broken by the limbs of myrtles, maple, spruce, and also gum. In front the white porch-swings were creaking gently in the breeze. The crickets had started singing, and the smell of honeysuckle filled the air. Alexander skated past a broken manhole, and rose up to the wall of bougainvillaea lined like royal gowns on the horizon - the setted sun off to the west in whiter skies. The homes stopped for a time, and all that lined the empty road were trees. The trees were bound by iron gates with rusted hinges that had been painted-over recently.

Alexander came to a gate, with a doorbell and a mailbox marked C Walsh. This was all dimly lit by a streetlamp, and Alexander leaned to the ground. He was wearing a pair of bright red sweatpants and a thick blue longsleeve on top. He removed his pair of running/biking shoes, and pulled from his sock a rusty nail. Then he drove the nail into the tire. He listened to the hiss, and pressed his face against the cold grey air that smelled like a freshly opened tennis can. Then Alexander took his shoe and with his great arms ripped the plastic sole. He turned the shoe into the dirt and pavement where he scuffed the nylon and the suede. Alexander rang the doorbell, and the Judge said "it's unlocked, come on in."

Alexander walked the bike on torn soles down the fresh brick drive that led to Cleveland's home. The path was bordered by two rows of trees with white camellia bushes grown amongst them. The tennis court off to the right, the road curved up to the white column mansion. The pale gray-purple colours of the night were turning with the many shadows, and the Judge was standing at the doorway to his home.

"What happened?" asked the Judge, and Alexander said "just a spill." The Judge was as a grizzly in the doorway, his black mass leaning on two paws against the door. "Come on in" he said, and Alexander brought the bike up to the steps that rose before him. The Judge was cleaning his teeth with a wooden toothpick. His left hand dangled at his waist, where a warm pair of dark cotton pants was tied about his hips and thigh.

"What happened?"

"I was coming up the hill, and it just popped. I put my foot down to keep from falling and my shoe got a little torn." The two men were entering a large room where the ceiling rose to fourteen feet, and a thick L couch enclosed a fireplace, a rocking chair, and a deep red persian rug. "Sit down" said the Judge, "can I offer you something to drink?"

"Nah."

The Judge left the room, and Alexander stood, and stepped towards the kitchen where a dining table was supporting a ceramic bowl with five ceramic fruit - a banana, an apple, some grapes, a pear, and orange. Alexander lifted the apple and tested it with his hands. "Do you appreciate my orchard, Alexander?"

"I do."

"Here you are," and the Judge handed Alexander an identical pair of shoes. "I've got three or four pair."

"It's a good thing we wear the same kind" noted Alex.

"Hell, you turned me on to them" the Judge said. Alexander placed the shoes on the edge of the table beside the couch. "And how was your run?"

"Excellent" said the Judge. "I just got in about five minutes ago. Then I took a shower, and you arrived." Alexander moved his eyes to view the narrow path that crawled and climbed, meandering up through the grass and trees that rose behind the home. "That path grows small" said the Judge. "Smaller every day." Alex nodded. "Yet larger at the same time." And Alexander almost smiled. His dark locks fell about his ear and brow, and the two men sat down on the couch where Alex placed the pair of good shoes on the carpet at his toes. "Just came by to visit with you."

"Thank you, Alex" he said, "I appreciate it."

"My pleasure" said Alexander.

"No no no no."

The Judge was fixing his toothpick between two top right teeth. Alexander stared into the fire. "How is Carol doing?" he asked him. "Okay" the Judge said. "You know how she is and always was."

"She still involved with the bulls?"

"Yes" said the Judge. "But I think she is happy. Or at least happier."

"She should come back for a visit soon. Susan would love to see her."

"I believe that they do keep in touch" the Judge said. He placed his toothpick down beside him on the coffee table, and motioned with his fingers to the television screen. "I was going to enjoy a movie" he said. "Choose one."

Alexander rose up to the shelf of tapes marked with a thin black sharpy marker. He lifted the right two marked in red. "Young Red Hood Riding?" he inquired. "Marry Had A Little Lamb, But Her Fleece Was Blond As Snow?"

"Can you believe it?" answered the Judge. "I hate these damn First Amendment cases."

"So this is evidence?"

"Sadly" said the Judge. "Calypso Productions v MacIntyre."

"How about The Fisher King?"

"Place it in."

Alexander placed the dark cassette into the silver ghost of a machine and turned the television on to static bunching up in a confused mix of blacks and blues. Then the picture evened, and the chameleon warning from the FBI was changing colors. The Judge said "this film is so refreshing."

"I agree" said Alexander, who was standing beside the tv. The left side of his face was warmed in fire, the right side frozen in those cold beams emanating from the television screen. "So how is Susan?" asked the Judge.

"Has a new boyfriend" he answered sitting.

"Really?"

"Yeah" said Alex. "He is taking her out of town for a few days next week."

"Oh, well well."

"Short guy" said Alex. "I don't like him."

"Where are they going?"

"Yeah, he's flying her out for the opera, and then some two night... something or other of elegance."

"You seem bothered" the Judge teased.

"I am, Judge" he said. "I'm very protective of my sisters."

"As it should be" said the Judge. "Anyway" he said after a time, "I really enjoyed your friend, Trevor."

"Yeah."

The Judge turned. His eyes were on the television, and he said "so Susan's leaving you next weekend?"

"No, she is coming back on Thursday."

"Oh, because I was going to see if you guys wanted to come up to the lake house. Your dad asked me to take Helen."

"Maybe" said Alexander. "Will see."

"Query" said the Judge. "It involves a story, which involves a soldier, who was marching home from a great and lengthy war. The soldier was very tired and hungry, and so he stopped in this town, where an old woman was cooking dinner over a fire. He said, 'hello, I am Roger,' and she said 'sit down here, Roger, my name is Elizabeth, and I will feed you.' So the soldier sat at the table while the woman stirred and basted over the fire. 'Tell me of your adventures,' she asks him. And so he starts to tell her about himself, and as it happens, this soldier was a medic, who had taken the oath of Hippocrates, and therefore could not, nor would he, take battle in the war. Rather this noble man had gone from front line to front line, dragging people from the grips of death and healing them. Once he had even crawled among a minefield, just to comfort a dying soldier whom he knew would die, but went to him and held him in his arms anyway. The soldier had an iron cross, and a purple heart, and a congressional medal of honor, and not only that, but the woman could sense and feel that he was knightly and noble, and full of grace. But waiting there a butterfly came down and it hovered about his face. The soldier brushed at it, but it came back, and he brushed at it, but it came back, and each time the butterfly came back and hovered about him. The soldier was annoyed, and he grabbed the butterfly, and crushed it in his hand. Now the woman knew that the soldier was a noble man, that he had been truthful in telling all of the stories of his life, and that he was all these things which he claimed and which he appeared to be. But nevertheless, because of what he had done, she refused to feed him, and spoiled all the food. And the soldier moves on, and dies of starvation. Now, was that just remedy?"

Alexander thought for a time. "Remedy is a consequence of law" he finally said. "You, for example, deal solely in remedy. You can look at a matter, and you can look at the law, and it is generally easy to determine an appropriate remedy. But justice" said Alexander, "justice lies beyond the law. Justice is not left to the scrutiny of judges. Because justice has no consequence."

"But what itself is remedy if not justice?"

"Order" said Alexander. "Social contract."

"And so the answer to my query?"

"Starving a soldier to death because he killed a butterfly was not an appropriate remedy" concluded Alex. "But it was just."

"Excellent" said the Judge, (he was pleased). "You grow old, indeed."

Alexander was staring deep into the face of Cleveland Walsh. The Judge smiled nodding, and turned his eyes to the tv. "What do you think about those films in question there?" he asked. "Art?"

"I don't think it matters" said Alexander turning, "as to art, has nothing to do with it. Just because something is art doesn't mean that it's worth anything. And just because something has value, that doesn't make it art. The question is whether it's good. And when it's not good, like this, when it's crap, the real question is: what do you do with the crap? Do you hoe it into the fields and watch it grow? Or do you flush it down the toilet and watch it float away."

"I love you, Alexander" bellowed the Judge. "You are an honest man."

"I love you too" said Alexander. "I always will."

By then the motion picture was well into its many surface images. Alexander's eyes moved briefly to the path outside. The light was dim, and the trees were black against the sky. Turning back he caught the eyes of Cleveland Walsh. They were noble eyes: ashen, neutral, pelican. They shone like silver in the platinum light - and in the fire light like gold. Alexander's own eyes burned, confused among the passing images; and the red-orange warmth of fire which gave no sanctuary.

It was two hours later when Alexander left the Judge's home. He was wearing a new pair of shoes and carrying the torn (and good) shoe in his hand. The two went out to the Judge's garage where two old blue Fuji ten-speeds - one for ladies, one for men - were propped up in the corner of the room. "Same bikes, same shoes" said the Judge. "What hearts have we so forged forever now in union bound."

Alexander smiled, and the Judge handed him the man's bike, and took the other old blue Fuji ten-speed bike with the flat tire as his own.

Alex peddled swiftly down the hill. He stopped beside a bed of plastic garbage cans that were in the driveway of someone's home. The house was small and brown, rectangular, and the driveway rose up to a shanty carport made of aluminum. A white ford was parked there beside two more empty cans. Alexander lifted the top of the can before him, and untied the plastic bag. He threw his shoes into the bag and wrapped it tight again. Then he sat back squarely on the seat, and peddled off coasting down the road.

CHAPTER ELEVEN

The next day Alexander was waiting in his office. He wore a khaki suit and yellow tie. His feet were dressed in leather shoes and were propped onto the swell of his desk. His eyes were catching light, and his locks fell down about his ears and brow. It was raining outside. The drops were tapping out a measured cadence on the sill as Alexander lifted a Newsweek from his desk, turning to the page of cartoons and overheards.

No, I wasn't offended, you no-platform-having, flip-flopping, stump-standing, gay-bashing, 'Dukes of Hazard'-sounding, inch-high private eye, got-a-million-dollars-in-the-bank-but-go-to-Supercuts-to-show-off-them-big-stupid-Dumbo-ears-of-corn, no I wasn't offended at all.

ARSENIO HALL, responding to
statements made by billionaire and MIA
activist, Ross Perot, addressing members
of the NAACP as "you people".

No, I really do, believe in, some of these... uh... uh... things, that I am - that we are... talking about.

GEORGE BUSH, during a speech
on the environment in Colorado last week.

The poor 7-year-old is probed, badgered, made to recite, led, photographed naked and coached by the off-camera voice of her mother who herself gives a performance that is not exactly of Academy Award caliber.

WOODY ALLEN, reacting to a videotape made
by Mia Farrow to support her claims that he abused
their daughter Dylan. Allen denies it.

Isn't that gross? I've tried to shield myself from it, but I know it does go on.

ABC News spokeswoman DAPHNE
MAGNUSON, on correspondent Sam Donaldson's
habit of tearing off and devouring the
chocolate frosting from his breakfast doughnuts,
leaving four or five "carcasses" to be cleared away.

2:30 open window, 3:15 dispose of body, 3:45 be home on the couch
   making out.

From instructions allegedly written by
ALLEN GOUL, 16, charged in the brutal murder of
his girlfriend's mother in Gulfport, Miss.

The phone rang. Alexander lifted the receiver, dropping the magazine. "Hi, it's Kim." Her voice was rough like gravel, but warm. "Hi Kim" he said, "how is Bob's mother doing?"
Alexander rubbed his contemplative eyebrows, and she was saying "doing pretty well."

"That's good."

"So" she said. "How is Helen?"

"I think she's doing okay" he said.   There was a brief pause, and then: "I pried it out of her. It happened about a year ago. Somebody offered her an ice cream - one of those things. I'm sorry, Kim, I know--but I feel ambiguous about discussing this with you, I mean-"

"no, I completely understand." "I just-" he said. "But thank you. For everything."

"So she seems... (?)"

"I guess she is doing pretty good considering. You know it feels good to get it off of your chest. But then when you do, it's very shameful, and you feel very naked and dirty, even though it's somewhat liberating."

"Is she gonna go in for counseling?"

"I want her to go into therapy, but you know how my mother is. Therapy is for other kinds of people."

"Well I would like to string the guy up by his balls" she said, "I can tell you that."

"Yeah" said Alexander, "well, I'm just mostly worried about Helen."

"Well I'm glad to hear that it wasn't more... complicated-"

Alexander said nothing.

"Not that I'm saying anything about your family, Alex, but you know that most of these cases involve someone that's close to home - well you know."

"I know, Kim, I'm not offended. I, um, well you know I kinda went through Susan's things to see if anything similar had happened, and didn't find anything. So then I, you know, pried it out of Helen, and I have to say that I am pretty relieved - I mean as much as one can be relieved in such a case."

"Well that's good, I guess" she said. "Well take care of yourself Alex, and if you need anything, please give me a call."

"Thank you Kim, for everything."

"Goodbye Alexander."
"Goodbye Kim, thanks again."

CHAPTER TWELVE

A week later Alexander sat inside his bedroom on the floor. The light was broken by the shadows of the fan which spun above him and beneath a yellow bulb. The sound of opera was pouring in among the boards from Susan's room. Alexander placed before him the pistol forty-five with the iron checkmark scarred into its side. From beneath his bed he pulled a bass shoe shoebox, and opened the cardboard lid. Inside the box was an almost identical gun. There was also a pair of surgical gloves, a bottle of rubbing alcohol, two bicycle tubes, a pair of running shoes, a bottle of superglue, a knife, and a stone. Outside the sun was slanting over all the roofs and warming all the leaves and branches that collected in the gutters, and elsewhere on the slates and tiles. The music from the other room ceased suddenly, and Alexander stepped to, unlatched, and opened his door. He stood in the doorway, immobile, so that she could not quite see the insides of the room.

His sister appeared like the wings of some glorious eagle. She was robed in white silk, and wrapped in a dewlike perfume. Her longer curls fell about her naked shoulders, and on the tops of her breasts. Her eyes were as brown maple olives, and her cheeks, naturally dark, were dressed with soft blankets of rouge. Her lips were dark red painted waxy, and her white teeth sparkled and shined.

"You look beautiful" said Alexander.

"Thank you" she said.

"Do you want me to carry your bag?"

"No, I can get it," and Susan lifted the black garment onto her back. A carhorn sounded from outside. "Well have fun" he said, and Alexander kissed his sister on the cheek. "Thanks, you too."

"I'll see you on Thursday."

"Bye" she said, "be good."

"I will."

"I'll call you tomorrow morning."

"Okay."

Susan stepped out through the den and to the front door, where she met a short blond man and kissed him on the mouth. The man was wearing a black tuxedo, and a red tie garnished his neck. He kissed Susan again, and took her bag in the curve of his small arm. Alexander returned to his room, and the shadows were getting longer on the wall beside his reprint Carravaggios. He took the unmarked gun, loaded in hand, and placed the scarred gun in the shoebox. Then he placed the shoebox in the drawer. He took a pair of surgical gloves and placed them on his fingers. Alex opened the plastic jar of rubbing alcohol, and that dry caustic odor was immersed throughout the room. He took a cotton swab and wetted it with the alcohol, rubbing thoroughly all grease and residue from the outside of the gun. Alex tossed the swab into the garbage can, and rose to his feet. He wore a pair of dark blue sweatpants with the round elastic bottoms bunched up to his knees. He took the cartridge from the gun and placed it in the elastic of one of his socks. To the other he taped the broad knife with a string. He placed the rubber tubes across his shoulder, and draped a thick dark sweatshirt over that. (It was for the most

part hidden; the bulge on his right shoulder negligible.)
He was wearing the Judge's shoes. He took an extra
pair of running shoes and tied the laces together,
flipping them over his neck. He placed the superglue
and the gun into the sweatshirt's empty pocket, and
took the stone in his hand. Alexander stepped and
turned against the window where he faced the sun now
creeping slowly through the golden branches and the
annatto roofs, the electric-line shadows forming longer
at his side. Gripping the stone in hand, Alexander
formed a sacred cross before his chest and eyes. He
placed the stone down gently on his nightstand, and he
was gone.

The roads were somewhat empty. It had rained the
night before, and the water had collected in the ditches
and the shells from the rain. The hood from his
sweatshirt was pulled up over his dark curls. The cloth
was flapping against his cheeks, and shielding his
brilliant eyes. Alexander's legs were driving fiercely
downward on the pedals of the Judge's bicycle, and the
children were playing football in the park as he changed
into the strongest, briskest gear. The spokes were
whizzing and the smell of honeysuckle melted in the air
against and with the sounds of croaking frogs and
crickets calling on till death, and on.
The sawed-off bushes capped with heathered crowns
of bougainvillaea crept up swiftly at his eyes and ears.
The almost-twilight was descending, as he coasted to
the Judge's gate and without sound unlatched the iron
folds. He peeled the gate back on its hinges, and crept
up with the bike inside the autumn grove to the right of
the home. Alexander crouched down, camouflaged,
and stared off to the house.
A mockingbird was singing on the edges of the
wood, and the sounds of distant crickets calling idled in

the mandarin air. The smell of bark and sap was at his nostrils, and he pinched them so he wouldn't sneeze.

Alexander's eyes began to water as he stood there pinching, and the Judge went streaking down the pathway from the home. The Judge was wearing white sweatpants paired with a red shirt, and a black bandanna wrapped around his arm. His silver waves of hair were briefly as a tinsel minnow in the sun. On his feet the Judge was wearing the same green-yellow jogging shoes, which disappeared among the weeds and shrub.

Alexander walked the bike up to the Judge's dark garage. Inside, beside the rusty mower and the tank of gasoline, were the two blue Fuji ten-speed bikes - one woman's and one man's. Alexander quickly moved to the other side of the garage where tools were spread out on a wooden table: hammers, wrenches, pliers, screws, and saws. Alexander, still in surgeon's gloves, picked up the pliers and a screwdriver, and returned to the bikes where they stood. Beneath the spokes, the gray sunlight was creeping from the dust-webbed window to the floor. He quickly removed the tires from the woman's bike and placed them on the table. Then he forced the tires, flat, from his own bike and fastened them to hers. He went to the table and emptied the hissing air from all the tires. He drove the screwdriver between the rubber and wheel, removing the hard semi-tube. Then he took his shirt off and crafted the fresh rubber he had carried with him onto the tire with his hands. He did the same again, and slung the two still black-snakes down across his shoulders, taking the air pump from the wall and filling the tires till hard.

When Alexander left the Judge's garage, he was carrying on his shoulders two dead tires. The fresh ones he had brought were sitting, on two wheels, upon the wooden table, the punctured tires still and flat beneath the woman's frame. Alexander carried the rake in his hand.

He made his way through the woods beside the out-path, propping and arranging some broken limbs and fallen leaves. The valley to the left revealed the deep expanse of all the city with her lights like fireflies that swimming hovered on the dumb terrene. The valley to the right was blooming marshes rich with absinthe trees.

Alexander reached a quiet brush beside the path. From a higher point a clearing formed, and he could see the breeze where it was playing on the jogging path-side leaves. Alexander crept into the cradle of the bush, and took the cold and heavy cartridge from his sock. He loaded the gun. And waited.

Somewhere, the labors of an industrious woodpecker proved neither foreign nor near. Alexander again covered his nostrils. With his pinky he then wiped his eye. The pecking ceased, and the sun was sinking lazily downward, so that all was August and gilded in the trees. Alexander held the gun in his palms. He inspected the cold machine there, as it formed a large L in his hands. The buzzsaw woodpecking resumed, and Alexander was standing and leaning to a thin branch that was blocking his view. He tugged at the bough, which was sturdy, and twisted the limb at its roots until it fell. He then took some mud in his hand and dirtied the cut where the bough had been broken, and he placed the dead branch by the rake at his thigh. And he waited.

The woodpecker's tapping continued. It sounded like a jigsaw, or an old typewriter tapping. The orange and the brass were slowly retreating, and the pecking was joined by a whisper of treeleaves that danced in the breeze, the crickets in a faroff chorus soaring, and the sound of Alexander's own breath when it came. And he waited.

The sound of his feet striking earth was escorting the Judge as his shape first appeared. His wet hair formed a thin serrate of harmless daggers. His aged yet fitted waist was bounding forward as he grew. The Judge lifted his hand to brush the sweat from his eyelids, and returned them to his side. And Alexander watched his figure grow.

The Judge's lips were dry and white, his eyes serious and gray. The sun like some great oxblood lion was down in the west, as the Judge drew last breath from the sky. The bullet entered at his temple, and the echo rode a formless carriage to the hills. Alexander emerged from the shrubs, and stood before the Judge. The Judge's hair was like a set of still woodcarvings, and his skin was like the pansy alabaster clouds above. His hands, still wet, were quivering at his side. Alexander looked into the hollow caverns of his eyes that breathed a silence absent threat or sanctuary, and he watched the dark blood spill out from beneath and mingle with the dust and mud.

Alexander turned to face the sun, and formed a fist which formed a sacred cross before his chest and eyes. Then he wiped his tears, and descended into the shrubs. He raked over all his steps and leafed over all of the rakes until the broken landscape signed no more. When he turned back lastly for his eyes to meet the Judge, a trinity of flies had gathered buzzing over the wound. The woodpecker was tapping a morse out with its beak into the hardwood, and the scent of honeysuckle yielded to the smell of blood.

Alexander returned to the house, raking and planting and replacing as he plodded along. When he returned to the garage, the sky was almost dark and he was forced to work in shadow, taking the tires from the table and placing them back onto his own bike. And not letting the rubber touch the ground. He re-placed the rake where he had found it; he carried the bike on his broad shoulder; and he left the Judge's land as he had come.

He walked on past the bougainvillaea through the darkness, and finally put the tires down onto a bed of shells. The shells were forming the base of a long white driveway where a small red house was lighted in four circles by four floodlights on the front two corners of the home. The lights were sphered by clouds of bollixed gnats and flies.

Alexander sped away. He peddled up to the heights of the long mountain, gliding down into the motionless wet earth. The mossy smell of mold was pungent, and the moon was but a sliver of a crescent in the sky, as Alexander drove down into the swampy marsh.

Alexander stopped in almost pitch dark blackness, propping the bike behind a row of bushes, and crawling for rocks in the shoulder beside the road.

Having discovered seven or eight half-pound stones, he took the superglue and fixed them to the sides of the gun. Soon the mass was indistinguishable, but for a cluster of heterogeneous stones.

He crept into the woods about a mile, where the broad water ebbed at the shore. The scents of mustards and molds was settled on the waters like some grey ghost of dark impenetrable fog. Alexander waited, with the scarce and scattered tears of his own eyes and his own sucking from the air, acquitted from him in due time. Soon the glue had cemented, and Alexander tossed the mineral collage into the black and glassy sea.

Alexander edged out of the woods, and rode his bike down further on the road. An old abandoned shack was sitting in the center of a clearing. Alex waded through stillweed grasses, parting the sea of insects with his hands. He reached the cabin in almost darkness, and jolted open the door. The cabin was empty save a cot and large wood stove. The matches had been placed beside the iron legs, and Alexander lit the pyramid of twigs and coals. The fire grew and Alex added cut logs from the pile at his side. He left the cabin briefly, solidly closing the door while he examined the absence of light escaping and the invisibility of the black smoke above.

Alexander reentered the cabin, and flung the Judge's shoes into the fire. A plastic stench of tar was burning, and Alex added the latex surgeon's gloves and the bottle of superglue to the flames. He untied the laces of the shoes he wore about his neck, and put them on. He again waded the grasses and weed. Then he mounted the bicycle and started back into town.

Alexander's legs like driving pistons drove the spokes and churned the tar across the cement of the road. The spokes were whizzing. The leaves were whistling by. Suddenly, he caught a snag with his untied laces in the chain and flipped onto his side. His thigh had landed on a jagged rock that pierced the skin. He tested the fresh blood on his fingers. They were salty and wet. He started to get up, when down the road he noticed two faint headlights widening, approaching.

Alex, clutching the ground, attempted to move the bike off of the shoulder and into the ditch below. The headlights were growing stronger. The metal would not give.

The sound of a car engine tested the air with ever increasing multitude. The headlights were swiftly approaching, and Alexander could not move the bicycle while prone.

Finally, the bike slipped into the ditch, and Alexander pulled the hood of his sweatshirt tightly across his brow. His cheeks were flush against the earth. He could feel the moisture on his eyelids, and the ground was shaking as the eighteen-wheeler rumbled with its headlights and its engines overhead.

Alexander was utterly still for several moments. His cheeks were cold and damp against the ground. The darkness was impenetrable, and only the sounds of crickets could be heard.

When Alex finally lifted his head, the faint red taillights were just then disappearing. He lifted his bike from the ditch, and inspected the tires. Alexander had to re-fix the chain, and when he had re-tied his shoestrings securely, he started off again down the road.

The toil of his brute legs battling gravity was badged by effortless and ease. With a quiet rhythm Alexander thus proceeded up through winding mountain road. The passing leaves formed walls of brier patched with bulb and thorn, and the sound of insects rose against the reeling of his spokes in some dismembered symphony. "Oh God, Father in Heaven" he started, but the words did not come.

The blood had begun to harden and dry on Alex's leg and on his clothes. Soon again the streetlamps lighted his way, one unto the next, until those circles formed a winding pathway to his home. Along the way he stopped and threw the rubber black-snakes from his neck into a junkyard. He reached his street and it was empty, and he coasted to his driveway.

Throwing the clothes into his washer with a cup of New Tide, improved, he placed the bike evenly on the floor. Alexander walked naked into the kitchen of his

home. The light on the answering machine was steady.
The clock inside the VHS machine read 12:18.
Alexander placed the knife and the string in his desk
drawer, and climbed naked into bed. He reached down
to his thigh where the blood had dried. Then he formed
a sacred cross before his chest and eyes, and looked out
to the sky where diamond asters were both blurred and
brillianced by the trace of his own tears. "Fated boy" he
said, "what have you done."

Book II

It is but law that when the red drops have been spilled
upon the ground they cry aloud for fresh
blood. For the death act calls out on Fury
to bring out of those who were slain before
new ruin on ruin accomplished.

The Libation Bearers

CHAPTER THIRTEEN

Carol Walsh was tall and graceful, beautiful yet aged by time. The shadow of her veil fell down on soft grey eyes and cheeks that were naturally rouge. Her black dress fell like cardboard on her thin and slender frame, and her arms were quivering almost imperceptibly at her side. Victor Thealah was standing beside a wooden casket filled with flowers. He was wearing a black suit and a pair of black leather shoes; his eyes avoided Carol's when they could. Susan was standing beside her friend with a soiled handkerchief she used to wipe her cheeks and eyes. Catherine held Theresa's hand, while Alexander was standing over Helen.

The rows of women and men descended for miles, it seemed, into the cemetery where the sun was beating down on ruddy faces, black attire, soiled eyes. And as Victor Thealah spoke, the many people looked down at their hands or at their shoes to keep from crying.

"I first met Cleveland forty three years ago. My family had emigrated from Greece, and we were living in New York City. I was running around with a group of hoodlums at the time. We stole cracker jack prizes and played stickball and monkeyed around. And every day, I came home, and in the building next to mine, there was a boy there, and he would sit there on the steps, trying to – he had one of those little wooden toys

that you buy with a stick, and then a ball on a string and
you would try to flip the ball up onto the stick, you
know, where it could fit – one of those little hand
games. And every day this boy would be there on the
steps with this game, except that early on I noticed that
there was a snag in the string, so that it was very short,
which made the game quite a bit more difficult. So I
would come home from my carousing, and I would
watch him there for a while. He had brown hair and
these grey grey eyes, that caught the sun when he
turned. He was always well-dressed, never dirty, never
muddy, never scraped.

"So one day I come home from my rugged travels,
and I watch him for a while, and for the first time, he
gestures to me. I accepted the game, and I immediately
proceeded to unfix the snag, returning the string to its
normal length. I flipped the ball up a few times, about
twenty or thirty times I believe, before the ball finally
landed securely in the frame, and I handed it back to
him quite accomplished.

"Well this boy, this odd boy with magic grey eyes,
he looked at me, and he looked at the hand game, and
he looked at me, and he looked at the hand game, and
he looked at me, and then he proceeded to tie the string
so that it was like it had been before.

"He looked at me again as he flipped the ball, and he
said, 'Everyone has to begin somewhere.'

"Now one would say that this boy was a little queer,
so it seemed. I mean he didn't play stickball or steal
things or try to secure a job. But you could tell,
everyone could tell. In an instant. Everyone just
knew... that Cleveland Walsh was no freak. That
Cleveland Walsh was something... that he was someone
marked for greatness and destiny. Cleveland Walsh
was an honorable man.

"I have met many men in my life. And I have met many men of honor in my life. But I have never met another like Cleveland Walsh.

"As a father, as a husband, as a godfather, Cleveland was always loving, always honest, always generous, fair, intelligent, and kind.

"One time, I remember, I was at the Judge's house and we and a group of men, many of them here today, they may remember, were discussing the election, the first election, and Jessica was outside with Carol - we could see her through the window - where they had this jungle-gym that had a bar which formed like a gymnastics highbar, and they had placed all of these bean-bag chairs beneath the jungle-gym, and Jessica was trying to instruct Carol how to get above the bar, but Jessica's arm was in a sling because she had fallen off of her horse the week before. And we were in a very hotly contested debate about something or other that seemed very important at the time, and all of the sudden, Cleveland got up, saying nothing, and stepped out into the yard; he just left us all, bickering at each other and wondering what the hell he was up to, and Cleveland went outside, and he climbed up onto the jungle-gym, and showed Carol how to flip herself up over the bar.

"I'll never forget it" he said, and wiped his eye. "It's just one story" he continued. "I could tell many. But it was beautiful and I'll never forget it." And Victor again wiped his eyes. "As a Judge" he said, "Cleveland Walsh was always a gentleman. He lived, and ruled, in that rare place where conflict trails beneath a field of truths that know no sides but for their own. He reached into the depths of justice, a place beyond the edges of his sympathies - though he had many - beyond vendetta and vindictiveness. The Judge gave every man his due.

"Yet all this being said, I loved the Judge not most for these, but for all the things that can't be said. I cannot say, nor to you describe, the way that Cleveland carried himself, the way he walked, the way he talked, the way he smiled. I cannot describe his eyes, his hands, the way he said finis when he was through. I cannot describe his love for Jessica, his love for Carol, for his mother, for his mother-in-law, for his father-in-law, who was like a father to him that he never had, his love for Catherine and Alexander and Susan, and Helen, and Theresa, and for me. And for many others. For every living thing, for every man, for every child, for every woman, person, every living breathing thing that walks or crawls or swims or flies or just plain lies down and does not move.

"But the Judge had something also deeper and more than love, something more important than love. Which was respect. Judge Cleveland Walsh was an honorable man, because Judge Cleveland Walsh was a man of great and profound respect.

"An artist who loves not his subject, he once said to me. A doctor who loves not his patient. A lawyer who loves not his client. This is the saddest of all knighthoods feigned.   This breed of men, without respect. What greater catastrophe? he asked me. What greater tragedy is there in man than this?"

And Victor was silent for a time. "I feel at a loss" he finally said, and wiped his eye. "I feel as if I am doing you a great injustice, Cleveland, here. Because I cannot here describe... All I know is that I loved you, and you are gone. And how are we to live with that?"

Tears were shed and eyes were wiped damp with soiled handkerchiefs. Victor Thealah reached into his pocket and drew a book of poems. He unfolded the book, and took from it a loose and single page. "I am now going to read" he started again, "something that the Judge always liked. It's called The Bear.

"There is some beauty on the autumn plain" he read, "where rolling tumbles like a bumbled ball, and lighted blades are beaded from the rain. A splashing through the crystal waters drain down through the charcoal rocks that slowly crawl, there is some wonder on the autumn plain.

"A clutching clawing through the black barked vein of trees, whose teeming height does form a mall of lighted blades yet beaded from the rain. With tickled stomach, eyes up to the crane who swims down to the grasses with a call, there is some beauty on the autumn plain."

Victor's hands were shaking, as he paused, wiping his eye.

"The wet and bubbled berry juices stain dark and furry whiskers combed, and fall among the lighted blades yet beaded from the rain. The night preserves a whisper; a far-off train is echoed to the rocky den, a slumbering hall. There is some holy on the autumn plain, and in the shaded blades still beaded from the rain."

Victor was sobbing as he folded the paper and returned it to the middle of the book. "Oh my god" he said as Catherine rose to embrace him. The two took Carol and the rest of the Thealah family, and stepped down among the red and watered faces about them. The sun was pouring through the trees and cutting over all of the tombstones and the flowers planted in their wake. Alexander turned briefly to the casket, and beside it where the granite tombstone lay fixed into the ground.

THE HONORABLE
CLEVELAND ELENOR WALSH
1935-1990
"I HAVE EATEN THE KING'S BREAD,
AND I AM TRUE TO THE KING"

The mass of people slowly crept back out of the cemetery, revealing the well-kept grasses to the sun.

Carol and Susan were stepping up out of the graveyard, when Carol turned back slowly to the casket dressed with flowers. She wiped her eyes beneath the veil, and whispered "goodbye daddy".

That night the families were gathered about a great and roaring bonfire at the Judge's former cabin in the woods. Their faces were teased and broken by the trembling branches of light, as Victor was telling a story from behind the fire. Carol sat between Susan and her uncle, who looked much like a mandarin shadow of the Judge. His wife sat beside him, and their daughter was fumbling with sticks in the mud. Her blond hair was gentle in the firelight, and at times emerged the soft blue tint from her eyes. Three old women sat with cups of coffee at the picnic table behind them. "Go then, said Arthur to his Knight" continued Victor, "take Excalibur to the water, and throw her to the gentle waves that lap at Heaven's brow.

"So faithful Bedivere mounted his ancient horse, and rode with Excalibur to the edges of the sea. He lifted the sword as to hurl it, but stopped in his motion, saying to the Heavens 'what good can come of this?' So the Knight took the sword, and he buried Excalibur in the marsh and reeds beside the sea. He mounted his horse, and turned back for the dying King."

Susan and Helen were listening attentively to the crickets and the frogs among his voice which fell like measured footprints on the rocky soil. "What has thou seen? What has thou heard?" continued Victor, their father. "And Bedivere told him that he saw the water lapping at the crag, and heard the waves washing in the reeds."

Victor was gentle as he spoke, and the old women behind him were sipping from their coffee mugs - one reaching for the kettle, another searching for a pack of cigarettes. From the doorway young Theresa stepped into the firelight and tip-toed to the other side of the fire. She crouched beside her mother, and asked "what's going on?"

"Your father is telling the story of King Arthur" whispered Catherine, (as Victor was still speaking), and Theresa asked why. "Because life goes on" she said. "As hard as that may seem right now to believe, life goes on. And tomorrow you will go back to college, and you will finish your freshman year. And your father will move ships, and try cases.

"And," she said, "we tell stories, because the legends and the mountains and everything that lived and has lived for a thousand years will go on. Through death, and sadness, and pain, these will live on. And that's why we tell stories, when someone close to us dies. And because Cleveland loved them. And because it helps us to remember him." Theresa hardly smiled, and sunk deeply into her mother's arms. "But the Knight would not do it" Victor was saying, "again he failed. And he returned once more to the King."

The fire was growing weaker as Victor spoke on, and Alexander threw a few more logs onto the pile. The firelight painted gracefully the faces of Helen and Susan, who sat beside Carol clutched in each others' arms. Carol and Catherine were sobbing softly, while the older ones wore mixed and almost happy gazes, sipping from their mugs. The younger children were tired, wiping their eyes, as Victor spoke: "The sun was melting with the water, and Arthur dying floated on to Avalon." With that Victor had concluded his story, scratching his moustache and lighting a fresh white cigarette. The sky overhead was filled with stars, and all the constellations seemed to circle on Orion, while the moon was cut in twos as it was rising just above the trees. One half was dark in shadow, the other terra cotta, almost red. The frogs were croaking in the distance. And the crickets called. Alexander's eyes were brilliant as the flames were rising to them, and standing, he told finally the story of noble Orestes.

"Orestes was the son of Agamemnon, King of Greece. He had two sisters, Iphigenia, and Electra. Iphigenia was young and beautiful, at the onset of the Trojan War. And Agamemnon and all of the troops of all of the armies of Greece were waiting at the cold Aegean shores. But the winds did not come. The sails were folded over, empty, lulling in the absence of any sign of ocean breeze. The prophets and the wise men looked to the heavens, and the gods called for the sacrifice of a virgin, of young Iphigenia, the daughter of the King. And the crew demanded the sacrifice of young Iphigenia, the daughter of the King. Agamemnon offered a kid, or a calf, or a young boar in her stead. But the gods demanded poor Iphigenia, the daughter of the King. Agamemnon reluctantly submitted, and his daughter was sacrificed on the altar of the gods.

"But his wife, Clytemnestra, the Queen, did not forget, nor forgive. And when Agamemnon sailed off to war, she took young Aegisthus to her bed. For ten years the two lived as adulterers, as infidels. And when the war was over, and Agamemnon returned, Clytemnestra took the King to her bed, and soon emerged, saying, 'I have killed him, this man who sacrificed his daughter for an ocean breeze.'

"For years, young Orestes wandered in exile. And his sister Electra waited for him, to return and to avenge his father's death, while faithless Clytemnestra lay with young Aegisthus on the throne. But Electra never lost hope. She waited for many months and many years, and one day faithful Orestes did return. The young warrior went to his sister Electra, and with his lifelong companion, Pylades, plotted vengeance on his mother the Queen. The two ventured into the palace, posing as messengers, and carried with them false news of Orestes' death. The custodians opened the gates, and led the Prince and his companion to the Queen.

"Orestes drew his sword and looked into the heavens, striking his mother down and cursing his own fate. From that point on, Orestes was haunted by the Furies, who demanded a trial. Soon they were appeased. Great Apollo served as counsel for Orestes at the trial, and he defended him with eloquence and godly majesty. The Furies, sometimes called Erinyes or Eumenides, acquitted Orestes of all of his crimes. But some of the Furies were not satisfied with the verdict, and drove Orestes again into exile, where he eventually climbed into the land of mighty Thaos, the Crimean King.

"There, in Tauris, waited poor Iphigenia, roaming beneath the altar of kind Artemis, the virgin goddess of the hunt, and protectress of the young. For Artemis had swept up the young girl there before the ships those years before, and carried her to safety, leaving only a phantom to be sacrificed in her stead.

"For all those years Iphigenia had waited in Tauris, a companion of Thaos the King. But when Orestes came to this land, the two were reunited, even though poor Iphigenia was still under the powers of the King.

"Orestes climbed the Tauric altar, where on a sacred tree he found a sacred bough, a golden bough. And from the tree he plucked the bough, (like great Aeneas to the Underworld), and drew his sword to kill the King.

"The bloody deed was done. And the two then fled to Italy, where they journeyed across the base of Mount Alba, and deep into the Arician Grove. Where there Orestes found another sacred bough upon a sacred tree, and built there altar to Diana in the woods. (For Diana was to Italy as Artemis to Greece.)

"And still, today, at the Altar of Diana, in that deeply wooded sanctuary, the priest and king of the wood, Rex Nemorensis, waits, with drawn sword for next to challenge him for title of Priest and King, the only ascension through the death of the one before him.

"Such passes then, from generation to generation, and poor Orestes watches from the heavens, watching over all of us, that we may be so happy, noble, blessed, as he could be or could not be."

CHAPTER FOURTEEN

The next day, Simmons and Kenner were stirring sugar into cups of coffee with two sticks of plastic straw. The keys of typing writers tapped and buzzed as fans were swirling and steam was rising off of styrofoam about the room. The tv droned in the background. A fat man in the corner was slumped on a footstool with a jelly doughnut and a copy of The Stand. "Hello Howley" Simmons said, and the fat man nodded to him with the jelly doughnut in his hand. Kenner was sifting through some papers with his left hand as he sipped the coffee with his right. "You hear about Jimmy Tasson?"

"Yeah" Kenner said. "I heard they got him doped up over on Julia."

"Cathy said that he wouldn't let them feed him nothin but cabbage or corned beef."

"No doubt" he said, "no doubt" and took another sip from his mug. "I once sat with him and watched him eat an entire honey baked ham."

"Is that right?"

"They, you know that place sells them, were having some contest, before Christmas. Jimmy sat down with a lawyer, a fireman, - you know Tommy Hebert over from the fire department?"

"Sure I know Tommy" he said. "I knew Tommy, his mamma called me up one time and said some punks beat Tommy up, back in high school or something; she wanted me and Joe go over and teach them a lesson."

"You learned em?"

"They learned."

"Anyway, Tommy, and this lawyer, and a lumberjack, sat down, and Jimmy ate an entire ham."

"He eat the bone?"

"No, he didn't eat the bone."

"I thought he ate the bone."

Simmons was wearing a polyester button-down and a pair of chocolate pants. His black hair cooled about his forehead. His eyes were white and brown. Kenner was wearing a hunter green sweater. His hands were stern and large, and his tall legs crept up from the ground. He flipped one more page with his left hand; he was sipping again from his mug. "So Maxine went out to check about the call?"

"Yeah" Simmons said, "the arrest."

"They arrested him?" asked Kenner, and he cracked his neck from side to side.

"Yeah, someone" he said, "but let him go." Simmons scratched his nose, and a thin man wearing a brown suit came into the room. "Kenner, Simmons" he said, and they turned. The man took his hands from his pockets. He was fixing a cigarette. "We got the match up" he said. "Clean bullet. Forty five." The two nodded. "Now we had a report about some guy snooping around in the Judge's yard two days before the shooting; Maxine and Bob went to check it out." The captain fixed his cigarette again, then fixing his moustache. "Now" he continued, "I want you guys to go over to all the shooting clubs, find out who has been around with a forty five. Then I want you to go to the courthouse, and I want you to help out Wanda and John. I want you to check out what was coming up on

Walsh's docket. And I want everything that's been up in front of the Judge in the past ten years. Good?"

"Yeah, we got Manny Toblerone and Spence looking through the binders-" "good, good" "-but I really don't think this is your business as usual, you know?"

"No, no I don't."

The captain continued through the room among the desks, "Howley", and Howley nodded, wiping some jelly from his lips. "Oh" the captain said turning, "thought you might like to know. They got a couple good prints from the house. Got a good print of a bicycle tire, couple good footprints. Experts are going over them right now." The two nodded. Kenner turned the last page over. Simmons finished his cup. "Lets go."

Two hours later, Kenner and Simmons were driving past Ol' Mary's Good Times & Ribs. The line of people waiting at the walk-in window drank from cans of Bud, Bud Lite, or Miller beer. One gang of cops and two of big construction workers sat out front about the tables and beneath umbrellas with their onion rings and ribs and sandwiches - the police officers drinking Pepsi, the construction workers beer.

The two men pulled into the gravel lot. They stepped from the car and nodded to their friends. A black bird formed a shadow at their feet. "I got you" Kenner called to Simmons as he waved to the officers and stepped inside. Simmons nodded, and walked up to the table where the sun was slanting down across the red umbrellas and officer Michael Kahn lifted some rings. "You want some?"

"Thanks."

"What's up, Simms?"

"Not much."

"How you makin out?"

"You guys workin on Walsh?"

"Yeah."

"Man, people don't like it when you kill a judge."

Simmons grabbed another onion ring and took a sip from Jason's Pepsi can. Tommy was swatting at a fly that buzzed about the table. Jason Brown was eating his sandwich, and wiped the barbeque sauce from his face. Tommy swatted at the fly. "Get the hell outta here."

"So you guys find anything?"

"Nah, we were down at some of the ranges, Stevie's and Security." Simmons took another onion ring and was tapping against the table with his thumbs. "Got a few forty-fives, but nothin to write home about."

"Forty five?"

"Yeah."

"I heard it was a three-fifty-seven."

"No" Michael said, "forty five."

"Get outta here you damn fly." Tommy was gritting his teeth, and then he lifted and sipped from the small Pepsi can. Jason wiped his mouth. "You guys think most people use the first urinal or the farthest away?"

"First."

"I think most probably use the farthest, huh?"

"You think?"

"One time, I went into the bathroom, and fuckin Bobby Coltrane was leaned down over the urinal, takin a dump - swear to god."

"Bullshit."

"Swear to god."

"Which one?"

"First."

"See."

"Bobby C busted ten kilos last night."

"Really?"

"Yeah, with Jesse and them."

"What urinal do you use, Tommy?"

"The first" he said, and Michael said "second".

"Second?!" they said. "Nobody pisses in the second."

"The third" Kenner said, setting a tray down between Jason and Tom. "You gonna use these?" he asked and took two chairs for he and Simmons, "first" said Jason. He, and the other three, were dressed in black to navy button-downs with black to navy pants and well-clipped ties. Jason was old and grey with curly hair and dark dark eyes. His skin was copper, his lashes deeply brown. Tommy was short with a crew cut; Michael was tall and blond. About each waist were two handcuffs. And a club. And a forty-four. "I mean the first one, it's just right there."

"Pass the ketchup... thanks."

"I mean why would you walk to the second urinal when the first urinal is just right there. It makes no sense."

"I like it" Kenner said.

"I mean I'm sorry, but only a serious kinda mental defective would catch himself taking a leak in the faraway pisser."

"It's got ambiance" Kenner said.

"Ambiance?"

"He doesn't know what that means."

"Sure" he said. "The window's there. You got your little sunlight. You got your paper towel machine. You got your who's who in good times on the wall."

"Hey, you been seein that chick in records?" then asked Simmons of Jason.

"Naw" Jason said.

"It's got ambiance" continued Kenner. "It's comfortable."

"That little Gabby chick-" "naw" "-with the buck teeth."

"No, I'm not seein her."

"Very comfortable."

"You're too old for her."

"Who's too old?"

"A sweet little thing like that" Tommy said. "A sweet little buck-toothed thing. You'd probably drop dead in the sheets with that girl."

"I'll drop you, man" he said.

Tommy was shaking his head, smiling, and Jason was propped back onto his chair, picking with a toothpick at his gums. And again he said "naw". The air smelled of barbeque sauce, and the sun splashed over the plates of white cardboard - the round licks of sauce and small pieces of cole slaw and onion ring. "I bet on the first" started Tommy, "five to one over the second, two to one over the third."

"I'll take a piece of that" said Kenner, taking a bite from his sandwich and cracking his neck from side to side. Michael scratched at his ear. "You wanna bet on it?" he asked them.

"Sure."

"Nah."

"How can you?"

"Yeah, how we gonna know?"

"Surveillance camera."

"No, the pink things" Jason said. "Whichever is the first to go."

"What pink things?"

"You know, those pink little chlorine circle things they put in there. Whichever is the first to go."

Each threw a five dollar bill on the table, and the officers (Michael, Jason, Tom) stood to leave. "Catch you guys later" they said. "Good luck."

"Take care."

The sun was higher now, and the two men sat well-shadowed by the red umbrella. Kenner was eating his last rib and Simmons was finishing his Pepsi from the can. The fly, and another, were landing about the red sauce and the greasy two or three onion rings. Kenner swept his great hands across the table, but the flies returned. "You wanna go over to Jackson's?"

"Guess we better."

When the two men pulled into the lot of Jackson's Mid-City Range, Kenner was cleaning the insides of his gun. The sun reflected from the black revolver and into the windshield of the car. His right leg was folded across the other's knee. Simmons put the car into park, and opened the door. "You comin?" he asked, and Kenner said that he wanted to take a couple rounds. He unfolded his legs, and the two men climbed out of the car. It was a dark brown Oldsmobile with four doors, green wall tires, and a Pay Cops Like Your Life Depended On It bumper sticker.

A line of buses roared by on the 4-12 Service Road, and through the tarry black exhaust emerged the distant smell of gunpowder, which was mixed with the stronger smells of cedar, pine, and gum. The two men opened the large wood door, and were greeted at the desk by two young women who said "hello" and "hi" in almost unison. One of the women was wearing a blazer and a bra. She whizzed her stringy hair with painted fingernails, and the other pursed her lips. "Hello officers" she purred. "What can I do for you, today?"

"Not today" Kenner said. He was scratching his grey curly head. There was some barbeque sauce on his collar: the red and the green of his sweater had formed a black stain. "We need to know" his partner started, "if you have anyone who comes in regularly or who has been in recently with a forty five."

"We better call Henry" the girl said. She lifted the phone and said "Henry, we have two very sexy police officers here. They would like to speak to you about something."

"So you guys eat already?" the other girl asked them.

"Yeah, we were over at Ol' Mary's on Jack Watson Avenue."

"Ribs?"

"Yeah."

As Simmons was saying "yeah" a large man with a shiny bald head stepped in through the doorway. He was wearing a Gold's Gym t-shirt and a faded pair of jeans. The sounds of bullets rifled in the background. The burnt smell of gunpowder blended with his employees' perfumes. "Can I help you, gentlemen?"

"Yeah, how you makin out? I'm James Kenner and this is my partner, Russell Simmons."

"Please, Simms."

The man nodded shaking Simmons' hand, and said "I'm Henry Madison. How can I help you?"

"We need to know if you have any customers who might have been here recently with a forty five."

"Who's got a forty five?" he said turning to the ladies. "Charlie Brazil?" (And he turned back to face Kenner and Simmons.) "Charlie Brazil" he said again. "Farrell Mathison. Alex Thealah. Meyer-" "Alex Thealah?"

"Yeah, he has a beautiful forty five."

"She's got a crush on him" the one girl said. The other blushed, closing her blazer by the lapel. "It's got this mark on it" the owner continued.

"A mark?"

"This scratch, you know, like a burn. Like this v, or a checkmark, like burned into the side."

"Thank you" the officers said.

"Is Alex in trouble?" asked the girl.

"I don't know."

Eloise McFadden was standing next to officers Wanda Menken and John Doufall. They were sorting through a series of multi-coloured files, as a small man with a leather belt and a pair of thick thick glasses carried a typewriter down through the hall. Eloise was an elderly lady with bushy eyebrows and matted brown-grey hair. Her glasses fell down on green eyes, (they were still a bit teary), and her lips were painted with light pink waxy lipstick. They were standing in the chambers of Cleveland Elenor Walsh.

Wanda Menken was tall and pear-like, with large breasts. The light from the ultraviolet ceiling fixtures formed a halo on her outer curls, and the blue reflection from the monitor was dancing in her eyes. John Doufall, on the other hand, was sitting on a stool so that his feet could not reach the floor. His belly fell about his belt, his elbows propped on his knees. "... malpractice ... malpractice ... p i ..." he was saying, "... burglary ... rape ... divorce ..." and he was flipping the files one by one.

It was then when Kenner and Simmons entered the room. "Wanda" "Kenner" "Doufall" "Hey Simms" said the four to each other, and Wanda introduced the two to Eloise.

"Nice to meet you."

"My pleasure."

"Nice to meet you maam."

"Find anything?" asked Kenner, as he stepped to the coffee table and took a cup. Simmons was looking at Wanda. "Not too much" Doufall said. "Got a big murder comin up. But it's not gang related and the guys got no bail. Got a few p-i cases. Porno case. Theft. Big rape. You think anything to that Wanda?"

"Don't know. Could be."

"Does the name, Eloise, it was Victor Thealah who delivered the Judge's eulogy, is that right?"

"Um-hmn" she said, "they were very close."

"But why kill a Judge before he hears your case?"

"Does the name" Simmons continued, "Eloise, does the name Alexander Thealah mean anything to you?"

"Of course" she said. "That's Victor - I mean Mister Thealah's - oldest son."

"Doesn't make sense" continued Doufall.

"Unless you know in advance how he is going to rule" Wanda offered.

"Was he close to the Judge?" asked Kenner.

"Alexander, oh yes" said Eloise. "Very close."

"Or" offered Wanda, "if you think he knows something. Afraid it might be uncovered."

"Blackmail?"

"Walsh?"

"The Judge was not involved in any improprieties of that nature, I assure you" assured Eloise, "or of any kind."

"What about Alexander Thealah?" asked Kenner, as he cracked his neck from side to side.

"Is a prince" said Mrs. McFadden. "Bite your tongue."

"What about revenge?" asked Doufall. He set the stack of files on the desk beside the monitor and formed a fist with his left hand. Simmons was looking at Wanda, where the light formed a curve on her breast. She was wearing a black cotton blouse. It clung to her tightly, and a cloth skirt fell from her wide hips. Doufall ungripped his fingers, and then formed a fist again. "You okay John?" Kenner asked, and John said "it's just this damn arthritis. It gets bad when it rains."

"It's blue as an ocean outside" Wanda said.

"It gets bad when it's sunny too."

"You know what?" she then offered. "I don't think it was revenge."

"How come?"

"Gut."

"It's a thin one" Simmons said. He was wearing his chocolate pants cuffed about the rims of his brown leather shoes. His hands were cupped at his side. And Wanda offered a quizzical smile.

Kenner and John exchanged glances. Eloise was boxing her pictures and her frames. The short man with the typewriter was standing off in a corner down the hallway. He was alone. He had removed his glasses and he was wiping his eyes.

Kenner looked to Simmons. He was watching as Detective Menken sifted through the folders almost cautiously. Her partner was propped like a cabbage on the rim of the high stool. He rubbed his forehead and wiped his eye. Kenner exhaled impatiently. "Simms, man, lets go."

"You're not gonna help us?" asked Wanda.

"We have to check something out."

"What?"

"Will catch you later" Simms said.

"Wait a minute" she said. "Come back here."

"Bye."

"Nice meeting you" Simms said to Eloise. "Take care."

"This is James Kenner; let me talk to the captain." Kenner was speaking into the police radio. He was riding in the passenger seat, where the sunlight was falling down to his lap through the trees outside. Simmons was tapping his thumbs and pinkies against the steering wheel. The wheel was lined with a roam-colored leather. There were some dice hanging down from the rearview mirror, which was cracked in the very left hand corner so that Simmons' eye appeared shattered in the glass.

"Hello?" came a voice over the police radio.

"I think we got somethin captain" Kenner said.

"Go ahead."

"Yeah, this guy, Alex Thealah, you heard of him? His daddy is Victor Thealah; some hot shot big guy friend of the Judge."

"So?"

"Been working out at Jackson's Range every week with a forty five."

"Talk to him" the captain said after a brief pause. "Maxine is in there right now with the guy they caught snoopin around in the Judge's back yard."

"Say anything?"

"Not yet" he said. "We got him cooling out for a while. But question this Thealah guy. We still need a gun. What the hell."

"Yes captain" Kenner said. "On our way."

"We got the prints back, by the way" the captain added. "Didn't pan out. All the tire tracks were from the Judge's bicycle, all the footprints from the Judge's own shoes."

"Shit" Simmons said, "that's too bad."

"No boys" the captain said, "he didn't leave nothing but the bullet."

They looked at each other, and Kenner shrugged. "Out captain" he said.

"Ten four guys. Be careful."

Simmons was still drumming his thumbs and pinkies against the leather of the steering wheel. Kenner was tying his shoelaces, and cracking his neck from side to side. Then he looked out the window. There were a few birds dancing in the sky above. The cars outside were loud and heavy, and the thick clouds were forming in the eastern part of the sky.

"Why you always gotta be tapping?" asked Kenner.

"I like to tap" Simmons said.

"It's annoying."

"It's a habit."

"I don't like it."

"It's better than pickin my nose."

"Yeah" he said. "So?"

"You want me to pick my nose?"

"No, I don't want you to do neither."

"I gotta do somethin."

"How come?"

"I don't know."

"You think this guy Thealah killed this guy."

"Yeah, probably so."

"I don't know" Kenner said.

"I can smell it." Simms was still tapping his fingers on the steering wheel. "I don't know" he then said. "I gotta do somethin."

Maxine Thompson was seated at the edge of a large wooden table. The fluorescent lighting danced on their outer edges, creating a transparent gentian glaze. Her skin was warm and musical, noble and antique. She was wearing an alesan blouse and a silver barrette in her hair. She had a yellow mug of coffee in her hand. Her eyes were dark and opaque. She took a sip from her coffee, and scratched at her hose, behind the knee.

The table was in the center of a concrete room. In the corner of the room was a window. It was near the ceiling, very high. There was an ashtray on the table, with three and a half burning cigarettes. The smoke gathered in the upper parts of the room, forming a haze with the lamplight and the light from outside. The air was warm, and damp. It reeked of body odor, and the faint smell of coffee, and the fresh burning smell of tarry nicotine.

Across the table was a large man, for the most part jelly-like. His skin was bony and silver, his short red hair tangerine. His fingernails were black; they were cupped before him calmly on the table. His shirt was a tank-top, white, so that the tattoo on his shoulder was exposed. Before him sat a stack of note paper on the desk, and a pen. Beside the pen was another sheet of paper with EXPLANATION OF RIGHTS written across the top of the page.

"Do you see that first paragraph there?"

"Yeah."

"Read it" she said. "Do you understand that you have a right to remain silent."

"Yeah."

"Place your initials there."

"Here?"

"There" she said, and took a sip of coffee from her mug. "You see the next paragraph?"

"Yeah."

"You understand that if you do say anything it can and will be used against you in a court of law?"

"Yeah."

"Initial it. Read the third paragraph. Do you understand-" "yeah" "-that you have the right to an attorney?"

"Yeah, yeah" he said. "I want an attorney."

"Initial it. Read paragraph four. Do you understand that you have the right to appointed counsel if none can be afforded?"

"Yeah" he said, "I want an attorney."

"Initial it" she said. "Do you wish to waive you rights at this time."

"No" he said, "I want my attorney."

"Okay" she said, "we will wait for him."

The cigarettes burned on in the ash-tray. The accused cracked his knuckles and brushed with his fingernails at the beads of sweat that had formed on the side of his face. "We can wait here all day" said Maxine, "for your lawyer; but you better realize that once you call for a lawyer, we can't do anything for you. No sir, all bets are off. Cuz when you get your lawyer, we get our lawyer, and then you're in the big time, cuz those boys don't fool around. They have been trained in a shark tank more deadly than any jail cell, with more eye-clawing low-life and blood, and scum. And when they get out they don't look back for no one, no deals, no exchanges, that's it, murder one. No, honey, this isn't some drunk and disorderly like last time. This isn't some little aggravated assault, this is murder one. And once you get the lawyers in here, we can't do anything for you. You understand? There isn't gonna be any murder two when you get your lawyer in here, much less don't even think about manslaughter, no, not when you get some prosecutor born and bred with nothing else on his mind but to put you in the chair. That's what they ask them at the interview. Sit there, right in that chair, before the d-a and the mayor and God, and there is only one question. If you get them where you want them, do you put them in the chair? Yes. Fucking A. So I just want you to understand, there won't be any murder two involved, once you get your lawyer in here."

"I don't care what you tell me" he said. "I'm not saying anything without my lawyer."

"Yeah, okay, that's your right. Sixth Amendment. It's in the Constitution. Number Six. I'm just saying that once you walk out of here, that's it. End of story. The end. Once that little pin-head pip-squeak of a beady-eyed little four-eyed attorney steps into this room, you are history." She took a sip from her mug, and wiped her lips with her hand. "Now is the time to speak up" she said as she swallowed. "Because once you leave this room, you are never gonna get a chance to tell your side of the story. Your side of things; is gone. No deals. That's it. Murder one."

The man again cracked his knuckles and wiped the sweat from his forehead and from the side of his face.

"Yeah we can wait here all day" Maxine continued. "I don't even need you. I got three other witnesses in three other rooms ready to spill their guts all over the place. We got fingerprints. We got blood stains. We got the gun. I don't even need you at all. I'm just giving you a chance, you understand, giving you a chance to come clean right now and spare yourself a lot of pain. Because once your lawyer gets here, that's it, the gas chamber. The electric chair.

"Did you ever see a gas chamber" she continued. "They are a big ugly son of a bitch. Cuz you got to have enough room so that everyone can watch. Your family. While you are dying like some filthy farm animal in there. With your mamma watching. Or the chair. You ever see One Flew Over The Cuckoo's Nest, what they did to Jack Nicholson. But a hundred times worse. Because when you go into the chair, if you're lucky, you die. But sometimes, just between you and me, and you might have heard this somewhere else, but sometimes it takes two or three times. And in the middle you're just frying up there, half burnt up, writhing and wriggling in pain, with your mamma there watching. And you've soiled yourself all over your pants and your shoes. But it's your feet. Cuz they don't give you shoes because they want the shock to move better. So one time, they got someone really that they didn't like, killed someone important maybe, like a judge, like you, maybe they leave your shoes on accidentally, on purpose, so you don't die the first time. Maybe it takes two or three tries with you lyin there all burnt up with your mamma watchin and soil all over your pants and your shoes."

The man looked at her blankly with his dulled beryl eyes.

"You ever seen a hanging?" she asked him. "If you're lucky, your neck breaks the minute they pull the plug. But if it doesn't, you just hang there. Drowning in the air, and hanging there on the gallows for all to see, with your face all red and your pants all soiled, like a fish out of water, before you just turn white and die.

It's really a relief I imagine, to be dead, by that time. So it's really in your best interest just to tell me. Because if you don't, we can't do anything for you. So really, for your own good, what were you doing snoopin around there in the Judge's yard?"

"You're not gonna get me" the man said. "I'm waiting right here for my lawyer."

"Okay" she told him, taking a sip of coffee from the mug. She swallowed, wiping her cheek with her fingers. "We can wait here all day."

The man laughed. "Little mama" he said, "you aint got nothin."

"We got you snoopin around in the Judge's back yard two days before his death. We got two priors, one for drunk and disorderly, one for aggravated assault. We got a sack of shit with an attitude and a nazi tattoo that the jury is just gonna love. And we got a dead Judge. A loved, respected, honored, powerful, big time Judge. And somebody shot him. And somebody is gonna pay."

The prisoner sat at the edge of the table. He was cracking his pale white knuckles and rubbing the side of his face. The light was breaking through the high corner window, exposing the stark cement wall and a spider's artful web. Maxine sipped again from her coffee, her lips leaving prints on the edges, and she rolled the mug gently in the palm of her hand.

"Yeah, well, maybe your lawyer won't show up" said Maxine. "That's really the best thing that could happen as far as you're concerned. Maybe you'll wise up and tell us what you were doing in the Judge's yard two days before he got slaughtered. Maybe you'll tell us how you went back, two days later, and killed him with your piece of crap gun. Because once you get your lawyer, we can't do anything for you, no sir. Once you get that slimy little helpless nerd down here - and I know who they are sending, a little four-eyed flat-faced pip-squeak of a piece-of-shit lawyer nerd - and once that happens, then all bets are off. We can't do nothing for you. That's it. We can't help you. Murder one."

"I didn't kill him" the man said. "I didn't kill no one. Give me my lawyer. Let me go home."

"He's on his way, I told you" said Maxine. She placed the cup down on the chair beside her. It was empty save a few grains. She scratched at her temple, and yawned. "We can wait here all day."

Alexander was working at his desk with a series of journals. The grandfather clock was ticking-tocking and the sun was sprinkling in over the green wet spider plants at the edge of the room and the corner of the persian rug. Alex was dressed in a charcoal suit. He wore a white shirt, black leather shoes, dark socks, and a paisley blue tie. He was writing with a thick black fountain pen. The journals were thin books, black bound.

Kenner and Simmons were knocking on the door, and Alexander looked up from the desk where he was writing. "One minute" he called.

When he opened the door, Kenner and Simmons stood shoulder to shoulder and Kenner was cracking his neck from side to side. "Hello" Simmons said. "This is detective Kenner and I am detective Simmons. Are you Alexander Thealah?"

"Yeah" and Alexander extended his hand.

"We would like to ask you a few questions" said Kenner, (ignoring his hand), and Alexander said "okay, go ahead."

"Would you mind coming down to the station house sir?"

"Well I would mind" said Alexander, "of course. But I would certainly be willing to do so."

"Good."

"Let me just call my answering service real quick."

"Sure."

"This isn't gonna take long."

Alex left the door open. The two detectives stood on the porch. Kenner scratched his chest through his sweater. His fingers were lost in the wool hunter green. "By the way" he said, "we are gonna need your gun."

"Which one?" said Alexander. "The Winchester, or the forty five?"

"I think we will need to see them both."

"No" said Kenner, "that won't be necessary. Just the forty five."

"Well they are locked in my apartment" he said. "I don't keep them here."

"Of course" said Kenner. "We can stop on the way to the station house."

"All right" said Alexander, now closing and locking the door behind himself, "I will be happy to assist in your investigation in any way that I can."

Four hours later, Alexander was sitting in a concrete room. He was seated at a large wooden table with three empty chairs. In the corner of the room was a window. It was near the ceiling, very high. One wall was a mirror. Alexander could see his reflection: his own white shirt collar, his muscular neck, curly hair, rounded nose, noble ears, piercing eyes, and paisley blue tie. There was an ashtray on the table, with three or four burning cigarettes. The smoke gathered in the upper parts of the room, forming a haze with the lamplight and the light from outside. There was a stack of note paper on the desk, and a pen. Beside the pen was another sheet of paper with EXPLANATION OF RIGHTS written across the top of the page. Beside each paragraph were the initials AT, and at the bottom appeared Alexander's signature on a line.

The air was warm, and damp. It reeked of body odor, and the fresh burning smell of tarry nicotine. Beads of sweat had formed on Alexander's brow. His eyes were bright and shiny, nonetheless, and his lips were thirsty and dry.

Detectives Kenner and Simmons, with an officer, entered the room. Kenner and Simmons sat at the table across from Alexander. There was a chair beneath the window, and Howley, the officer, was sitting in that chair. He was eating a sandwich, and reading The Stand. Simmons was tapping his thumbs against the table and Kenner was cracking his neck from side to side.

"How long had you known the Judge?" Kenner asked him.

"All of my life."

"When was the last time you saw him?"

"At his home" Alexander responded. "It was about a week before he died."

"What were you doing there?"

"Just visiting."

"Did you visit him often?"

"I saw him often" Alexander said. "Not necessarily because I went to his house, but I would go to his office and visit with him, or we would have him to dinner. I also did some things for him, through the court."

"What kinds of things?"

"Evaluated witnesses. Defendants."

"Aren't you kinda young to be a shrink?" asked Kenner.

"I finished school a bit early."

"Yeah?"

"Well I finished undergrad in only three years - I had a lot of a-p credits going in, took a few extra courses. And I finished med school in only three years."

"Instead of five?"

"Instead of four."

"We got a superkid here Simms" said Kenner to Simmons.

"I know" he said. "Big shot."

"So you saw the judge a week before he died."

"Correct."

"What did you talk about?"

"Uh," Alexander paused briefly, "I think we talked about justice."

"What do you mean?"

"The Judge liked to talk about justice. What was justice. What was just. You know."

"No, I don't know" Simmons said. "Enlighten me."

"He would tell me a story. Hypotheticals. Ask me if the result was just. And why. Like a law school professor, I suppose. He also liked to play games. Logic games. Other types of esoteric games. Inquiries into the nature of justice, and politics, and law. He was a brilliant man."

"Yeah, well, not any more."

Alexander was staring then into Kenner's eyes. The ashes were building in the tray, and the smoke continued to gather at the upper part of the room. Simmons asked Alex what else they talked about. Kenner looked away.

"We talked about movies" he said. "Um, Excalibur, I believe, or The Fisher King. Something medieval. The Judge liked that age. Of knights, and kings, and..."

"What else?"

"I don't know" he said. "Although, you know I think he was watching, not that he was watching, he wasn't watching, but he had on his shelves these pornographic films, which he was keeping, or was going to watch, or had watched, because of a case."

"What kind of a case?"

"A pornography case I imagine" said Alexander. "We were talking about whether those kind of films are art."

"Art?"

"Yeah."

"Then what?"

"Then I left."

"That was the last time you saw him?"

"I think so, yes."

"So you had been to his house?"

"Yes."

"How many times?"

"Many."

"You knew the grounds well."

"Pretty well."

"Do you know of any enemies that Judge Walsh may have had, or anyone that would want to harm him?"

"No."

"Some family thing?"

"No."

"Something personal?"

"No."

"Something professional, maybe?"

"No."

"You have no idea, absolutely no idea, why anyone would want to kill Cleveland Walsh?"

"No."

"Well how do you think that he died?"

"It is my understanding that someone shot him" said Alexander.

"Who?"

"I don't know" he said.

"Well do you want to know what I think?" asked Simmons. "I think you killed him. I think you knew he was gonna be jogging, you went to the house, you took your forty five, you hid in the bushes, and you shot him. That's what I think. The only thing I don't know is why. But I am gonna find out. One way or another. You can tell me, or we can sit here; we can sit here all day. But when they come back with the results from ballistics, then we are going to book you my friend, and when that happens....

"You ever been in a cell, Alex?" Simmons continued. "Excuse me, Doctor Thealah. Superkid, I should say. Well, Superkid, a jail cell is a very unpredictable place. A lot can happen in a jail cell. Pretty much anything."

Alexander was still looking at Kenner.

"It's not like it used to be, you know" Simms said. "You're lucky about that."

Alex said nothing.

"Yeah, we used to take people in here. Blindfold them. Tie their hands behind their back. Then we would take a rope. Wet it. Tell them it was a snake, and if they didn't tell us what happened, we would put it down their pants.

"Or sometimes" he continued, "we would put a rope around their neck. Tie the other end to the doorknob. Prop his chair up on two legs. Say the sergeant should be coming in in about five minutes. And you know what would happen if someone were to open up that door. So you just better start talking buddy.

"Or put a bag over their head" he continued, laughing, "hit them with a telephone book six or seven hundred times."

There was a haze which lingered in the corner of the room beside the window. And Howley turned the pages to his hardback copy signed by Stephen King. Kenner rubbed his hands on the thigh of his pants legs. Simmons' eyes were as a machine.

"But you know what worked the best?" he asked him. "We used to bring in this big old van battery, used to be in Henry Kavanagh's van. All big and rusted, nasty looking. Tie up a few cables to it. Throw a wet rag on your chest. It didn't take long in those days" he said. "It didn't take long."

"It was different in those days" Howley said from the corner, (still reading). "People didn't think about shooting at a cop. People saw a cop coming, and they were afraid." He paused to turn the next page. "Now people shoot a cop just like anybody else. People even writing songs about killing cops. No respect for cops at all. No respect for the law. No respect for any human life."

"Yeah" Simms said to Alexander, "so now we just pretty much leave it to the guys inside."

Alexander was still staring into Kenner's eyes. Kenner looked at him, and cracked his neck from side to side. Simmons was tapping his thumbs on the table. Howley rubbed his nose with his hand. "Yeah" he said, "there were days when a cop would step into a bar and everything would go dead. People were afraid of us. Now cops won't even go into some of the bars around, cuz they're afraid. It's not like it used to be" he said. "It's a damn shame."

"The party is over here boys" said the captain as he opened the door. His left hand was fumbling in his brown suit pocket while his right fingers fixed his moustache. "We just got the results from the ballistics test. No match." There was a uniformed police officer beside him. He handed Alex his forty five. "Let me see that" asked Simmons, taking the gun. "What's that?" he said. "What's that mark?"

"I am sorry to inconvenience you sir" the captain then said to Alexander. "You are free to go."

"Thank you captain."

Alexander took the gun from Simmons. He then shook Simmons' hand. He went to the captain, and shook his hand as well. "I am sorry that I could not give you any more information. If there is anything else I can help you with, please let me know." And he was gone.

"That bastard is guilty" said Simmons to the captain. "It's as plain as the nose on my face."

"I don't like the guy either" Kenner said. "I don't know if he's guilty, but he's guilty of somethin."

"I think it's Maxine's guy" the captain said, "but still, we got no gun."

"Nah it's him" Simmons said. "That son of a bitch." The captain was lighting a cigarette and Kenner cracked his neck from side to side . "What's he say, captain, anything?"

"Didn't break" the captain said. "Lawyered up."

"He's got no soul" Simms was saying, tapping Kenner on the shoulder. "You know what I mean. It's like you look at him, and there is no conscience there. Like he is above everybody else or something. Untouchable. You know?"

"Yeah" Kenner said. "I didn't like him either."

"I'm gonna touch that asshole" Simmons promised. "We will see how untoucha-fuckin-touchable he is."

When Alexander got home, Susan was seated at the dinner table with someone. He was short, and blond, and was pouring red wine out into their glasses, saying "when crows come out to perch on those straw figures and then the eagles come down and eat the crows, then it will be time."

"Time for what?" asked Susan.

"Time for a new scarecrow."

The two laughed.

The table was set with plates and linen napkins, silver forks and spoons and knives. There were two white candles burning at the center of the table, and beside them a vase, with one red rose. Alexander said hello and Susan's friend stood to greet him and to shake his hand.

"I'm Michael" he said.

"Pleased to meet you" said Alexander. "I think I saw you last week actually, when you came to pick up Susan."

"Yes I think so."

"How are you doing, brother?" And Susan gave Alexander a big hug. "I'm okay" he said. "How are you?"

"I'm doing all right" she said. "Michael came to cheer me up, wasn't that nice?"

"Very nice."

"It was nothing" Michael said, and Alex said "please, sit down."

"Did you get any work done?"

"Not much" Alex said.

"It's late" she said. "Where have you been?"

"I spent about the last five hours at the police station."

"Five hours?" she asked him. "They were asking you questions about the Judge?"

"Not just questions."

"What do you mean?"

"It's nothing" said Alexander. "I don't want to disturb your dinner. I'll talk to you later."

"What?" (Susan was impatient.)

"It's nothing" Alex said, opening his bedroom door. Susan was standing behind him. She was wearing a white t-shirt and a pair of jeans. Her red curls fell down about her shoulders, and she grabbed Alexander by the arm. "Would you tell me what happened?!"

"I think that they thought I killed the Judge-" "Oh my god, why didn't you call me?" "-but then they did a ballistics test, and realized that this wasn't the same gun, so they let me go."

"They asked you questions?"

"Yeah, some."

"Why didn't you call me?"

"I don't know."

"So what happened?"

"They knew I knew him, and they found out I had a forty five, so they brought me in. They let me sit, in a room, a hot room, with four burning cigarettes, for about three hours, and then these two cops came in with their fat friend and asked me to initial a form, so I did, and asked me to sign it, so I did; and then they asked me how long I knew him, when was the last time I saw him, what did we talk about and all that. I told them the truth. They didn't believe me. Then the captain came in and told them that the ballistics didn't match up, and that I was free to go. So I did. And then I came home."

"My god" she said, "I can't believe it." And she shook her head from side to side. "Why didn't you call a lawyer? I can't believe you let them question you without a lawyer. And you signed a waiver?! What were you thinking?"

Alexander looked plainly into his sister's warm eyes.

"Well, goodnight, I guess" she said. "Sleep tight. I'm glad it's all over." She kissed him on the forehead. He kissed her on the cheek, and went to bed.

CHAPTER FIFTEEN

It was a few hours later when Alexander came out into the kitchen and opened the cold refrigerator door. Susan and Michael were sitting on the couch, watching an almost silent television screen. Alexander was pouring a glass of milk. Michael was folding Susan's fingers in his own. "There is a change" she was saying, "which takes place in a defendant over the course of a trial. Even if he is found not guilty. There is something about putting all of the evidence together, and people pointing their fingers, that says to the defendant that he is doing something which is not acceptable. A sense of justice, which takes place in the trial itself. Whereas with a plea bargain, the defendant's sense of justice is just whether he got a good deal."

"What do you think about the death penalty?" he asked her.

"Well, you know, philosophically, I am not really sure that the government should be engaged in the business of killing people. But, at the same time, if you have done something so terrible that twelve strangers can come together, and decide that you have done something so terrible that you deserve to be killed for it, then I don't really have any problem with it."

"Why not?" he said. "I don't understand the distinction."

"Well, you have to separate your opinion as a juror from that of a judge. As a juror, I would probably vote no in most cases, but as a judge, I am willing to let people vote yes."

"Well-" "there are really two questions. One is what is your vote, as an individual juror, or a voter. The other is whether there is going to be a vote at all."

"Well what about all the studies that show that people are not executed proportionately across racial and gender lines."

"Well that's really a different issue. I mean you have to tailor the solution to the actual problem at hand. If there are more blacks or hispanics being executed in proportion to whites, that really doesn't speak to whether you should allow capital punishment to exist. That is merely a problem with the application. And so that is really what has to be changed. So you could, for example, have a law that would mandate that in any capital case, at least three of the jury members, say, would have to be the same race and gender as the accused."

Alexander was tearing slowly a paper towel from the round dispenser. There was some milk he had spilled out onto the counter, and he was sopping it up with the paper towel. The moonlight was swimming down like a delicate sandfall, on and against the wood wind-chimes outside the window behind the door.

Alex placed the damp towel into the wastepaper basket, and wiped his wet mouth. Susan was scratching the hem of her jean beside her knee; Michael was still folding her white fingers in his own. "You know what I think?" she said, (somewhat rhetorically). "Public hangings."

"Oh my god" he said, rising in his seat. "That's barbaric."

"I think it's almost barbaric to do otherwise."

Alexander took a sip from the edge of the glass. He was looking to the window.

"How so?"

"Because ultimately vengeance, and anger, and punishment have no place in the legal system" she said. "If we are going to be engaged in the business of execution, then it must be for the purpose of protecting and preserving and maintaining the sanctity, and the value, of life. And if that is our aim, we should do so as effectively as possible. With the greatest deterrent effect."

"You don't believe that" he said. "What about the Judge? When they find his killer, you will not say that vengeance and punishment and anger have no place. You will cry for his blood. You won't even want a trial."

"You're right" she said, "I won't."

"I mean that's the bottom line" he continued. "Noble thoughts and purpose are all well and good when it's someone else's child, someone else's brother, someone else's friend. But...."

"That's true" she said, "and maybe if I were on the jury in that case I would vote yes, he should be hanged. But, again, you have to step back and separate yourself as a juror, or a voter, from your opinion as a legislator, or a judge. You can't sacrifice the integrity of the law, or the integrity of society, or the integrity of one human life, as disfigured and ugly and hideous as it may be, to the irrational outrage of the affected few."

"Oh Jesus" said Michael, as Alexander was turning the glass in his fingers. "Hey Alex" Michael then called to him. "Hey Alex, what do you think?"

Alexander placed the milk on the counter. The glass was cold and icy, a thin ceramic; and there were tiny white ripples that lingered inside. Alexander's fingers were blue in the moonlight. He was looking at the tree leaves outside. "Time brings all things to pass" he said finally. "It can carry on its shoulders the burning and the stench from any broken household, with ceremonies that cast out all of the demons, and wash out all of the ill feeling, and the blood."

CHAPTER SIXTEEN

"Hi" the voice said. The room was cold and dark, and Alexander was wiping his half-awakened eyes. He looked at the clock, where the red light seemed folded, back on itself, and then he said "hello?"

"I heard about the Judge" the voice said. "I'm sorry."

"Thank you" said Alex. "I know." Alexander was scratching the razor burn on the left side of his face. He was speaking into the phone.

"How are you guys?"

"Pretty good" he said. "You know. Okay."

"How is Susan?"

"She's okay, I guess."

"Yeah" the voice said. "Give her my love."

"It's... hard" said Alexander. "But she has a new boyfriend, who came over to cheer her up last night; and so we are just trying to get along, as best as we can."

"I, uh," the voice stuttered - "how are you, Alexander?"

Alexander did not reply for a long time. He was again picking at the razor burn that was dry on his cheek. Outside the clouds were breaking in front of the moon, half-lit and broken by the shadow of the earth before the sun. The thin rays curved into the room, and

Alexander's blue shadow was softened on the floor below.

"Is Helen safe?" hesitated the voice finally through the silence. And another silence came. Alex wiped his eye with his fingers. He drew his thumb against his index finger, and then tested the cold nighttime air.

"Yes" Alex said. "She is safe."

There was another silence. In the distance the crickets were chanting softly through the grasses, and the wind was tumbling gently through the leaves. Cars passed in the far-off hum of their engines. Then the voice again spoke through the phone.

"Take care of yourself, Alex."

"Thanks for calling" he replied. "Give Julie and the baby my love."

"Goodbye Alexander."

"Take care, Trevor."

"Goodbye."

CHAPTER SEVENTEEN

"We just got a call from someone" the captain was saying, "who claims that he was with the Judge two days before he died, and knows something. But he won't come in."

"He won't come in?"

"No, I want you guys to follow Maxine. She is going to meet this guy in a bar. I want you guys to follow along. Take care of her. Make sure the guy's not some psycho nut or something."

"Where are we going?"

"Some bar down on Jazz Marine. I thinks it's called Betsy's. Some kind of lunch place and bar."

"Yeah I been there."

"They got a great macaroni and cheese."

"You know what this guy looks like?"

"Said he will be wearing a red shirt and yellow tie."

"Is he retarded?"

"I don't know."

"You ever had the macaroni and cheese there, Simms?"

"Could be."

"It's good macaroni and cheese."

"Will get some."

"Yeah, lets go" Kenner said. "I think I'm gonna get a milkshake too. Vanilla. Goes good with mac and cheese."

"Hey! Fellas." The captain fixed the wiry edge of his moustache. Then he lit a cigarette, saying "and remember, as far as you're concerned, right now this guy is suspect number one."

Betsy's was red. The carpet was carnelian. The tables were cardinal. The walls were ruby and wine. And the yellow lighting imposed a Paris dimness that fell down over and across the room. There was a man with a rattle in one hand, (tempting his child), and eating with his left hand scrambled eggs. He wore a leather jacket with black leather tassels; his baby dressed in an alice blue nightie with legs.

In the corner of the bar, two women were smoking. The bartender passed them a box of matches and poured the larger one a swallow of gin. Kenner and Simmons were seated to the left of them. Simmons was tapping with his thumbs on the red table. He was wearing a navy blue sweatshirt and a pair of tan cotton pants. Kenner was eating his plate of cheese and macaroni, sipping from his vanilla milkshake and cracking his neck from side to side. He withdrew from the table slightly. Then he scratched at his temple with his left hand, and with the right wiped some cheese from his lips with the back of his palm.

Across the bar, Maxine was seated with a man who wore a red shirt and a wide canary tie. The man was sipping lemonade. He picked at some french fries, and then put his lips again to the straw. Then he returned his hands beneath the table to his thigh. The man was a small man, balding. His hands were shaking beneath the table; his lips were nervous, and he had a tic on the left side of his face, next to the eye.

"Look I'm really busy" Maxine said. "It has been a pleasure meeting you, really, but I can't sit here all day with you wasting my time."

"Okay, okay" the man said. "Um, um, um..." he then stuttered, as he looked around the restaurant, studying for a moment the thick red embellishing air. His agitated fingers were restless beneath the table. His anxious eye again fluttered. "Um, um, well I went to the Judge" he continued. "I went to see, um, Judge Walsh."

"What about?"

"Well, well," and he sipped again nervously. "Good lemonade" he said. "You sure you don't want any?"

"Why did you go to see the Judge?"

"You see he has this case, um, um."

"Which case?"

"It's got to do with pornography" the man said. "I don't, um, um, know, um, the name."

"So?"

"So they guys, who, um, um, who made this stuff, who sell this stuff, it's just one on trial. Just one of them."

"Okay." Maxine was making notes in a small leather booklet. "What kinds of stuff?"

"Um, um, well, all, um kinds."

"Okay."

The man wiped the front of his tie with his fingers. Then he placed his lips briefly again to the straw. "But there is, um, a lot, more, to, to to to to it."

"That's okay" she said. "Slow down. Take your time."

"See I was scared to go to the, the, um, cops, or the d-a, so..."

"Why?"

"Because, um, because I thought they might be following me."

"Who?"

"Well see there are these, um, um, guys. And what they do see, is um, they get all of their money from, um, well this pornography. That's how they, um, fund everything. And they didn't want everyone, to, you know, to know."

"Okay" she said. "To know what?"

"The, um, um," the man stuttered. "The k-k-k."

"The k-k-k?"

"That's who it is" he said. "Who does it. That's where they get all their money. From the, from the pornography; and they don't want anybody to know, how big it is."

"How big is it?"

"See, you don't, the Judge didn't, and the d-a or the cops, don't, really know what all goes on. They think it's just a couple of skin flicks, but it's not. It's, um, all kinds of stuff."

"Like what?"

"Like um, um, um, kids" he said. "Children. Um, um, um, boys."

"Who has them?"

"They do" he said. "See you guys just caught the, um, the tip of the iceberg. They got so much going on. And they need it, well they think they need it, cuz that's how they back the whole thing."

"The k-k-k."

"All over the country" he said. "That's how they pay for it."

"The Ku Klux Klan."

"Um, yeah," he said, taking one last sip from the lemonade. "The k-k-k."

The next morning Alexander was in his bathroom soaking his face with a damp washcloth. He stood over the sink, while the sun flattened down across the rooftops and lighted the steam. He drew a foamy snowcone from the shaving cream can, and coated the noble lines of his face. Then he wetted the platinum razor and began to shave.

Outside the wind brushed gently at the face of his window. Sparse and high wispy clouds were moving cautiously through the sky. They climbed to where the taller trees rose gracefully in the west, and then disappeared. The vines that crawled about on the outer wall were wrapping through and about the gutter, up towards the roof of their home. A robin was singing, her red breast and tyrian feathers brushing outward from the cotton-green tree.

Inside Alexander said "god dammit" as Susan stepped into the shadow of light behind the bathroom door.

"What's up?"

"I cut myself shaving" he said.

"I'm sorry."

"It's okay."

"You got some blood on your collar" she told him.

"Damn" he said, inspecting the collar and beginning to loosen the buttons of his shirt. "That's what I get for putting my shirt on before I shave."

"If you do it right away" she said, "before it dries, you can get the red out with some cold water."

"Yeah."

"But if you let it set, it's almost impossible to get it out again."

Alexander was scrubbing at the collar of his shirt. The water rushed furiously, and splashed down where his thumb drove over the raisin stain. "They caught someone in the Judge's murder case" she told him. "I just heard it on the news."

"How do you feel about it?" he asked her. Susan was brushing the lass tendrils of her hair. "I don't know" she said. "I thought I would feel... vindicated. But I don't."

"Vindication has no place" he said blankly, pressing his fingernail against the wet cloth below the stain.

"I know" she said. "But I want to feel, I think that I should feel, very angry. But I really just feel tired."

"Maybe the anger will come."

"How do you feel?" she then asked him.

"I don't know."

"I miss him" she said. "But I don't miss him really, but just more miss the fact that I don't think about the fact that he is not there. You know?"

"No."

"It's hard to explain."

"Yeah" he said warmly. "I miss him too, a great deal."

"I know," and Susan touched his shoulder. Alexander rolled his wet shirt into a ball and threw it onto the floor in the corner of the room. He took a hand-towel from beside the mirror, and dried his chest and his hands.

"The guy they caught is a klan member" she told him. "He was apparently involved in this pornography cover up, which the Judge discovered, so he had him killed."

"He did not kill the Judge himself?"

Susan did not reply.

Alexander lifted his head to find her staring blankly at the wall, a tear dripping reluctantly from her eye. Alexander clothed her beneath his great arms. He brushed her hair back with his fingers, saying "it's going to be okay", "it's going to be all right".

"What were you doing there?"

A large man was sitting at the center of a large wood table in the center of a concrete room. There was an ashtray on the table, with four or five burning cigarettes. The air smelled of body odor, oil, and the

stale smell of nicotine. The man was for the most part
jelly-like. His skin was bony and silver, his short red
hair tangerine. His fingernails were black, and he had a
nazi tattoo on his shoulder which was exposed. Before
him sat a stack of note paper on the desk, and a pen. "I
told you" he said. "I was just there to spy on him."

"He's told you everything" the attorney said.

"I want to hear it again."

"What's his name?" Kenner asked him.

"Barry."

"Barry Richards?"

"Barry Richards."

"Sounds jewish" Kenner said. "You been letting
jews in the klan these days? No wonder you got
problems."

"He aint jewish" the man said. "He's American."

"Why were you following him?"

"I told you" the man pleaded, "like I told you a
hundred times already, we didn't trust him. We wanted
to make sure he didn't go to the cops, or the d-a."

"Or the Judge" added Maxine.

"I didn't know he was a judge."

"Who did you think he was?"

"I didn't know."

"What were you scared he was gonna tell them?"
asked Simmons.

"I don't know" he said, "stuff about the movies."

"Like what?"

"I already told you guys."

"We want to hear it again" they said. "What was in
the movies?"

"Everything."

"Like what?" Kenner said.

"Everything."

"Like what?" he said again. "I want you to say it
right here in front of this pretty woman officer; I want
you to admit it, what you went and did. Tell her."

"Nothin" he said to Kenner. "I didn't do nothin."

"What was in those films?" Maxine asked impatiently.

"Everything" he said. "Like I told you. Everything."

"Wait a second" interrupted the attorney. "I am just making it clear for the record, out of an abundance of caution, that this is full immunity for everything involving the tapes. Possession, distribution, or any underlying crimes."

"Yes, we've already established that, Mister Davis."

"Go ahead."

"What's everything?"

"Kids?"

"Yeah."

"Boys?"

"Yeah" he said. "Everything; boys, girls, men, women; gays; chips, dips, chains, whips; wax, leather, blood."

"What do you mean, blood?"

"I don't know" he said. "Blood."

"Torture?"

"Sometimes. Sometimes torture. Sometimes rape."

"Christ."

"What else?"

"Nothin."

"What else were you afraid of this guy, what's his name, Barry? What else was he gonna tell the judge."

"I don't know what he was gonna tell him" he said.

"Well what were you afraid he was going to tell him?"

"I don't know" he said. "Stuff."

"Well what could be worse than torture and rape?"

"Who made these tapes?"

"I don't know."

"What stuff?"

"You don't know who made the tapes?"

"No."

"What stuff?"

"Stuff about the organization."

"What organization?"

"I don't know."

"The klan?"

"Yeah."

"So he told all this to the Judge?"

"I don't know" he said. "I don't know what he told him. I didn't know it was a judge."

"Who did you think it was?"

"I don't know" he said. "I told you already. I don't know. I was just watching. From the bushes."

"Did you write down the address, or make any notes?"

"No" he said, "I just remembered."

"And then you found out it was the Judge's house."

"No, I never found out nothin" he said. "One of the other guys was gonna do it."

"What's his name?"

"I don't know."

"Listen asshole, I'm getting sick and tired of your bullshit, and I'm getting sick and tired of you. I know you know his fuckin name, and I want you tell me his goddamn fuckin name."

The man did not reply. He reached into the ash tray and took one of the cigarettes. He put it to his lips and inhaled. "Tommy" he said. "The guy's name is Tommy." And the smoke poured out of his nose.

"Tommy what?"

"Tommy Kramer."

"So then you found out who he was, you got scared, you went back, and you whacked him."

"No."

"Where's the gun?"

"I didn't kill no one."

"I want that gun."

"How did you kill him?" asked Maxine.

"I want that gun."

"Could you see his eyes?"

"I didn't kill him, you fuckheads! Why would I kill him, and we wouldn't kill Barry? That is the son of bitch I want dead, if anyone."

"You gonna kill him too?"

"No, I aint killed no one. And I'm not gonna kill no one. I'm just saying-"

"God dammit."

"I'm just saying why would I be so stupid to kill him just two days after I'm found in his yard. Why would I be so stupid?"

"Ah, that's what you want them to think," and Maxine said "you look pretty stupid to me."

"But what good will it do me?" he said. "Why would I kill the Judge? Why would I be so stupid, and why?"

"I am really getting sick of this guy, Howley" Kenner started. "He takes these girls, these little girls, like our own daughters, right out of the crib, innocent babes, and he FUCKS them and SUCKS them and abuses them up on his dirty filthy disgusting god-forsaken screen; and he is abusing little boys too, with his little FAG DICK, crawling around with all of his filthy trash, and scum, klan nazi kraut cross-burning david duke bastard sons of a bitch, and THEN! Then he finally goes and whacks a judge. And now he's got the BALLS to come in here, and ask me, to say to me, to ask me to my face, how could he be so stupid? CUZ YOU'RE A FILTHY GOD-FORSAKEN IDIOT, you ass hole."

CHAPTER EIGHTEEN

"Got a riddle for you."

"What's that?"

"If you took the smartest kid in the world, and the strongest kid in the world, and the fastest kid in the world, and the bravest kid in the world, what would you get?"

"You?"

"No" Gerald said, "not you" he was smiling, "me."

It was two months later. The three of them, Alexander, Gerald, and Mrs. Mayfield, were all in the room and smiling, amused. Gerald blushed beneath his curls, rubbing his hand against his jeans. His cheeks formed not quite dimples as he was smiling, still blushing, and Alexander placed his hand on the back of the boy's small neck. Shelly Mayfield rose like some majestic figure from the floor. Her eyes like deep mahogany were looking down at Gerald; an emerald blouse lapping at the edges of her warm alesan skin. "Gerald" Alexander said kindly, "would you step into the other room for a moment. I would like to speak to your mother alone."

Gerald skipped into the next room, and Mrs. Mayfield sat down on the edge of the couch. Alex sat opposite her in one of the chairs. He adjusted his tie. "I think we are progressing well."

"He hasn't mentioned anything about him yet, has he?"

"No" he said, "but that's not unusual. I want him to feel comfortable here, comfortable with me, and then hopefully he will feel comfortable enough that..."

"That he will talk about it."

"Yes" Alexander smiled, and then more seriously: "I wanted to ask you. Has Gerald ben having any nightmares?"

"No" she said, "not that I have noticed."

Alex nodded.

"Is that bad?"

"No" Alexander said, "but it would not be unusual. Somewhere deep inside, Gerald is dying to live through everything that happened to his brother. But he is so mature, at this age, and his mental faculties are so advanced, that he has a very good defense system. And his defenses keep him from thinking about what has happened while he is awake. But when he sleeps, his defenses rest, and he is allowed to experience all of these thoughts and feelings and fears. So what we want to do is create an environment so that when his defenses slip, and there is a, a kind of breakthrough, through kind of a freudian slip, so to speak, or de ja vu, where he will be comfortable, and will talk, instead of shoving everything back inside."

Gerald's mother nodded. Her legs were crossed beneath a linen skirt, and her arms were folded on the tip of her knee. The skirt fell where the calf met her ankle, and taunted her rich, honest skin. "Should my husband and I try to elicit anything?"

"I don't think so. Under some schools of thought, Gerald shouldn't be forced to deal with something until he is ready. If you force him prematurely, he won't - it's kind of like the way in which we tell children that they shouldn't have sex until they reach a certain age.

They can do it, physically, but they are not ready for it. And so there is the possibility for some trouble."

"Right" she nodded. "That makes sense."

"In Gerald's case, if he is forced to deal with it before he is ready, then he might not be able to work out, or work through, his emotions, I cannot say correctly, but for lack of a better term, correctly. On the other hand, if he waits too long, then there might be so many mounting thoughts and tensions and emotions, and fears, in the sub-conscious, building up, then one day they will just kind of explode."

"What do you think?"

"I think right now everything is still in his sub-conscious. But soon, through dreams, nightmares, freudian slips, de ja vu, it will start to enter his conscious mind. And then, as I said, he will really want to talk about what has happened. And that is when I want him to begin the kind of catharsis that he needs."

"When you say catharsis, do you mean just a good cry?" she asked him. "Or..."

"Well, that's the way it happens in movies" Alexander explained. "But the idea of a catharsis as a one-time event, a good cry, so to speak, was dismissed a long time ago. And now we see catharsis as something that happens over a number of years.

"There is a phenomenon, nevertheless, which is quite common" Alexander continued. "When someone close to you dies, there is sometimes this fear of saying it out loud. Because, for some reason, while it is just going around in someone's mind, it is still very surreal. But there is this fear, that if I say it out loud, then it'll be true. And once you say it out loud, once you admit it to the outside world, that this person has died, you can never go back. And sometimes that is very hard, especially for one as young as Gerald is right now. But when the time is right, that is what Gerald needs. He needs to admit that his brother has died, not just to himself, but he needs to say it out loud. And then the catharsis, or washing out, can begin."

Mrs. Mayfield smiled.

"And that is when he will need all of our support."

Gerald's mother stood, brushing her hand across the lap of her blouse. Alexander stood and took her hand. "Thank you, doctor."

"How is your husband?" Alexander asked as she was turning. "Is he handling everything okay?"

"He is very sad" she said. "We are both still recovering. It's very hard. But he is okay."

"And you?"

"I'm okay" she said. "Devastated, but all things considered, okay."

"Good. It's important for Gerald. If the three of you need anything" Alexander said, "anything at all, you can call me, night or day."

"Thank you" she said, nodding. "For everything." Mrs. Mayfield opened the door where Gerald was sitting in the depths of a waiting chair and reading one of three Discover magazines. He looked up through his curls, and placed the magazine down with the others on the table beside him. "You can take it with you if you want."

"No, that's okay."

"Go ahead" Alexander said. "I would just throw them away."

"Thanks" the boy said, rolling the magazine into the back pocket of his jeans.

"Thank you" his mother repeated. "We will see you next week." Alexander nodded, closing the door, and the two were gone.

An hour later Alexander was getting his hair cut in the Silver Shears. There were three chairs, with three mirrors, and a counter that ran across the back of the shop, with sinks, and razors, and scissors, and blow-dryers and brushes and combs. On the other side, beneath the three mirrors, was a line of smaller chairs. An old man was reading a Playboy. There were two more on a stool in the corner; they were placed upside down. Beside the stool was a set of shelves, which were filled with hair products and with comic books, Sports Illustrated, People, and Newsweek magazines. Alexander was in the center chair. There were clumps of hair around him on the floor.

"They should write the story about Rudy the jelly doughnut killer" the barber working behind the left chair was saying. "They find all his victims with five jelly doughnuts stuffed down their throat. They caught you by the red stain in your car."

Alexander's barber was wetting his head with a mist gun. He was reading the perspectives section of a Newsweek magazine.

I admire Ted Kennedy. How many 59-year-olds do you know who still go to Florida for spring break?

PATRICK BUCHANAN, on the Democratic Senator.

The Jews at work! Damn their fathers! Dogs! Filthy! Dirt!

PLO leader YASIR ARAFAT.

If it makes Tina's nipples firm, then she goes with it.

Vanity Fair writer KEVIN SESSUMS, on how Vanity Fair
editor Tina Brown determines what a good story is.

We pulled [the baby pictures] out of the envelope and [said]: "Whoa, who does she look like?" And we both had the same feeling - she looked a lot like Dr. Jacobson.

An unidentified woman testifying in the trial
of Cecil Jacobson, a fertility doctor in Farifax County, Va.,
who allegedly impregnated women with his own sperm.

Doctor Kevorkian doesn't support the death penalty.

GEOFFREY FIEGER, attorney for Jack (Dr. Death) Kevorkian, on why his client wouldn't assist a convicted drug felon - serving a life sentence - who wanted to use a suicide machine.

I'd like to thank my family for loving me and taking care of me. And the rest of the world can kiss my ass.

The last words of convicted killer JOHNNY FRANK GARRETT, who was executed last week in Texas for killing a Catholic nun in 1981.

The barber was starting to cut his hair as Alex put down the magazine. "You can keep reading while I cut" the barber said, but Alex said "nah, I only like to read the overheards."
The barber was short. He had a warm face, and wore glasses. His hair was dark, and combed back over the top of his head. He was wearing a calico shirt and a pair of pressed jeans, with a crease that ran the length of his legs. "Yeah" he was saying to Alexander, "I go dancing with these teachers, see, and they kinda, I think they kinda like me. They teach, you know, they know a foreign language, and they teach adults, when they

come here, you know, english. And what I found out they do is, they tell all of these Rudy stories, that I have told to them over the years. So when the students know the stories well enough, they can translate them, you know, into english. So last night they brought this sample over, from like years. So I'm like how many people have you been telling these Rudy stories to, and they are like thousands."

"So do they know that Rudy exists?" the other barber was asking.

"I don't know Paulie" he said.

"You should go to one of the classes, and just walk in, and say here I am, I'm Rudy. That would blow them."

"No" Rudy said, "I think, from what I can gather, my impression is that now they are kinda starting to believe that I exist."

"Yeah?"

"I don't think they thought I existed before" Rudy said. "But now, from reading the papers, from what my understanding is, they are starting to believe that I exist."

"Well those orientals believe in dragons and all kinds of things."

The two barbers were laughing, and Rudy said to Alexander "yeah, you can tell what ethnicity they are by what S.J. buys at the market. Like if they are buying rice and chickens and stuff then you know they are oriental. And if S.J. is buying all of these fruits and vegetables, then you know they are hispanic. The germans buy sauerkraut. Irish cabbage."

"You ever go out dancing at Neon Beach?" Paul then asked Rudy.

"I been there one or two times" he said. "I don't like the d-j there."

"No you don't?" Paul said. "I like him."

"And we are teasing Tom" Rudy was saying into Alexander's ear, "cuz he likes jelly doughnuts. That's why they was calling me like the jelly doughnut killer."

Alex grinned. "I got a Rudy story" he said. "Tell them about that time, one time you were telling me about some time when you went to that hotel-" "yeah" "-and you went into the wrong room."

"What happened?"

"Yeah" Rudy said laughing. "I went out and I came back, and the girl I was dating and went with was in there, and I said thanks for that pie, honey, that was really good - cuz I had come back and eaten this big apple pie - and so I went out and came back, and I said thanks for the pie honey, and she says what pie? I didn't bake you any pie."

"So you went in the wrong room?"

"Yeah, and I ate their pie."

"Yeah doc" Paul said, "that's a good one."

"What are you getting you hair cut for doc?" asked Rudy. "You goin out?"

"Yeah, I gotta go to this party tonight" he said.

"They got dancing?" Paul asked him.

"Yeah, I guess."

"Could be fun."

"Hey you hear about the trial for that guy shot the Judge?" asked the barber on the right. He was getting paid and saying "thank you" as the old man put down the Playboy magazine and moved to the empty chair. The barber was wiping the stray hairs from his shirt, (it was a black short-sleeve button-down), and then helped the old man into the chair. "Yeah" he continued, "they are gonna start selecting the jury next week."

"Doc was close to the Judge, huh doc?"

Alexander nodded.

"That's terrible" they said, "just terrible."

"I heard he is involved with the nazis" the old man told them.

"The klan" Rudy said. "The klan and all that porno stuff."

"You ever seen any of those porno films?" Paul was saying. "I saw some once a few years back. They are somethin."

"I can't believe what people will do these days."

"Yeah, well, they got all those people goin out on all of those talk shows every day" said Rudy. "That's just like stripping on tv."

"At least the pornography is only physical."

"I know" Rudy said. "I don't know what's worse."

"Those talk shows are on there bearing their souls."

"What do you think, doc?" Rudy asked him. "You're a shrink. You think any of that stuff that goes on on tv is therapeutic?"

"I don't know" he said.

"They must be stealing your business, huh?" the two were laughing. "Why go pay doc a hundred bucks to talk about what's bothering you when Oprah will pay you a thousand."

"That guy is gonna hang" the barber on the right continued. "The guy that killed that judge."

"It'll depend on the jury, I guess" said the old man.

"How much Oprah pays do you think for going on one of them shows?" asked Rudy. "Do you think she pays a thousand?"

"Yeah."

"Nah" the barber said, "any twelve men you get is going to hang that guy."

"A thousand bucks?"

"I bet he only gets a life sentence."

"They probably pay stars more. But like you and me, just normal people, they probably pay like a thousand."

"Nah, he is gonna fry."

"I bet they pay less than that."

"You think?"

"They probably pay like a couple hundred, plus plane tickets and hotel rooms."

"Oh yeah, I forgot about plane tickets and hotel rooms."

"Well she can't be paying them too much cuz she is like the richest woman in America."

"Who?"

"Oprah."

"No she's not."

"Who is?"

"Jackie O."

"Mary Tyler Moore."

"Mary Tyler Moore?"

"I'm tellin ya, Oprah is the richest woman in America."

The barber removed the white tissue from Alexander's neck, and he examined his newly cut hair. Some of his curls were gone, but he still had some locks which were thick, and some waves. "It looks good" he said, handing the barber a ten and two ones. "Thank you, doc, I appreciate it."

"Thank you" he said.

"Have a good one" Paul was saying, "and hey" said Rudy, "have a good time at that party tonight."

"Bye now" the older barber on the right waved and smiled, and Alexander said "take care." As he was leaving, the barber resumed on the old man's thin hair. "Yeah, well" he continued, "I still think that the guy who killed the Judge is gonna fry."

CHAPTER NINETEEN

Around the room the chimes of glasses and silver cooperated with the less important music from the stage in the other room. The two rooms formed an L, with the tables in one part, and the dance floor in the other. Around the tables people sat in groups of two, mostly women, with white wine glasses or hot hors d'oeuvres. On each table stood a centerpiece with white azaleas and green and blue confetti ribbons and strings. The dance floor was constructed of black and brown wood squares, with red and yellow lights that fell from the ceiling above the stage. The stage itself was a raised black platform, upon which played a seven piece band. The singer was dressed in a black tuxedo. He had a microphone in his left hand and a glass of water behind him on a stand. There were trumpets also, and guitars, a piano, and drums. The dance floor below was empty. In the center of the L was a bar.

Alexander was wearing a charcoal grey suit with a tie of rare italian artistry. He was sipping a gin and tonic, and talking to a slender young man with blond curly hair. "When you travel" he explained, "it's always better looking back. Because you take all of the good things with you."

"Excuse me" said Alexander, and turned to the large man who had made his way to the bar behind him. "Jimmy, do you know Bruce Haflin?"

"No."

"Nice to meet you Jim," and the two shook hands. Alexander settled back into his seat, as Mr. Haflin took a scotch and soda with a cocktail napkin from the counter. He placed his arm on Alexander's shoulder and then threw a dollar onto the bar. "Thank you, sir" the bartender said. Mr. Haflin said "take care Alex" and stumbled off among the tables where his wife was sitting alone.

"Who is that?" asked Jimmy.

"A friend of my father" Alex said. "He makes ships."

"Oh."

"So what were you saying? I'm sorry."

"Everything" Jim said, "that was interesting or beautiful or wonderful that you saw or did, you take with you. But everything that is bad is all transient. Your impatience, your temper, your mood. The smell. The waiting. The not understanding the language. The plane rides. The bad food. All of that is gone when it passes. But you never lose the sight of San Marco. You never lose sight of the Duomo. You never lose sight of the way that the sun cuts down across the vineyards, the grape leaves. All of that, you take with you."

"Right, right."

"I have never been on a trip that wasn't more fun when I got home than while I was there."

"Well we loved your postcards" Alexander said. "I saved them all for you in case you wanted to have them, as mementos."

"Thanks, I might do that."

Alexander took another sip from his glass. His eyes were brilliant, even in the heavy indoor light. Jim finished his beer, and asked the bartender for another. He was wearing a navy blazer with a pair of khaki pants and a yellow tie. Across the bar a man was tapping his pinky ring against the counter. There was a blond woman beside him. She wore a blue sequins dress, with errant cleavage that supported her mischievous curls. Her lips were painted red, and she had thick blush and powder which did not quite blend to her nose. The man was still tapping his ring while she laughed intemperately.

"Bourbon" the man finally said. "And white wine, or do you want champagne?"

The girl shrugged.

"Champagne" he said. "Have champagne."

"But when we were coming back on the plane" Jimmy said, paying for another draft beer, "they said that someone's luggage was on the plane and they were going back to take it off."

"Bomb scare, huh?"

"I'm sure" he said. "I didn't say anything to Karen, but I was thinking there is definitely a bomb."

"So what happened?"

"We waited about two hours, and then we just left."

"I don't care, see" the man across the bar was saying as he circled the ice and the bourbon in his glass. "If God is vengeful, then I have no cause to appease him. If God is benevolent, then he will love me regardless. If God is indifferent, then he doesn't care what I do."

And the girl laughed, spitting her champagne up into the cup as the man took his napkin and was wiping her chin. "So, I don't care."

"But when we got back" Jim continued, "we talked to our friends that were leaving a few hours after us, and they said that there was a bomb scare in the airport, and that they had to wait for four hours before they could get on the plane."

"Wow" Alex said, "they must have gotten the call just as you were taxiing out onto the runway."

"That's why I don't care" the man continued. "And you shouldn't care. You know?" The man was older and balding. He wore a pair of blue slacks, and a bright peachy tie. His shirt was pink, and his jacket was a thin madras weaving of peaches and whites and blues. "Who cares?" he said again, and she was laughing. "Come on. Lets dance."

"Wait" she said. "I have to finish my champagne."

"He is robbing the cradle" Jim said, and Alexander took a sip from the top of his glass. "That's one person I have no respect for at all. Older guy, forty to fifty; sunglasses, in his expensive convertible; balding on top with longer than it should be hair in the back; leaves his first wife for some twenty year old bimbo; has a new kid with her now that he really has quality time to give for the family." Alexander nodded. "That's just someone that misses the whole point, you know? Just doesn't get it."

The bartender was serving a glass of white wine to an older lady wearing a white evening gown. She tested the first sip, and winked approvingly. There were two young boys at the other end of the bar with a hand-held electronic computer video game. They were drinking coca-colas, and sneaking maraschino cherries from the plastic container behind the bar. Alexander was watching this and asking the bartender for another gin and tonic when Cindy and Alvin Skinner stepped together through the door. (Cindy first, with Alvin following behind.) "Get me a drink" she said immediately, "I'm going to powder my nose."

Alvin moved toward the bar placing his car keys in the pocket of his dark Armani jacket and adjusting a Nicole Miller tie. "Hello Alexander" he said, shaking his hand, and then Jim's, "good evening James."

"How ya doin Alvin?"

"Pretty good" he said. "How was your trip - I need a Beefeater and soda, and an Absolut on the rocks."

"It was good" Jim said. "Very good."

"Good to hear" said Alvin, taking a toothpick. "How is your family, Alex, holding up okay?"

"Pretty good" he said, "thank you for asking."

"Thank you" Alvin said to the bartender, and threw a couple dollar bills onto the bar. "Yeah, well, I hope they hang that son of a bitch."

Jim sipped from the top of his beer.

"Are you going to watch the trial."

"Yes" said Alexander, "for opening and closing arguments at least. And I want to be there with Carol when the verdict comes in."

"Is she coming in for the trial?"

"I think so."

"Do you think that is a good idea?"

"I don't know" he said. "Will see."

Cindy Skinner was standing beside the restrooms. She was talking to a young boy who was holding a glass of something with both hands before his chest. He was a tall boy, not quite awkward, with athletic arms and a pimple to the right of his nose. Cindy was laughing, and when she did so the bleached curls of her hair danced eloquently about her. Alexander could see the absence of color in her eyes from across the room. She had lit a cigarette, and propped it carelessly to the right of her ear. She wore a dark blazer, and a thin white sweater which was cut to reveal the inner curve of her breast. She put the cigarette to her lips, and then laughing she touched the boy's face.

Alvin's eyes turned away as he was finishing his first gin and soda, and saying "another Beefeater please."

"And tonic?" asked the bartender.

"Soda" he said, "please."

Cindy rubbed the edges of her button nose, and then took the boy's hand briefly in her own. The boy was blushing, his eyes cast downward, as he followed her shapely hips to the black leather stitching of her cowboy boots that were pulled up over the ankles of her jeans. She let go of his hand, and made her way to the bar. "Hello Alexander" she said, kissing him on the cheek and leaning to lift her Absolut on the rocks from the bar. "Hi James" she said, and left a red wax impression of her lips on the side of his face, and then on the glass. "The ice is melted" she then said to her husband. She lifted the glass and swiftly drained the vodka out from among the cubes. "I'll have another" she said, and settled the glass down upon the bar. Then she moved her fingers again to the edges of her nose.

"How are you tonight?" Alexander asked her, while Jimmy was wiping the lipstick with a napkin from his cheek.

"Pretty good" she said. "Alvin has been out of town and I have been home masturbating all day."

"I don't understand, you're just filthy" Alvin said. "You have no respect."

"Sorry" she said, and "thanks" to the bartender.

"I don't care if you have no respect for me" Alvin continued, "but you can at least have a little respect for our friends. And yourself."

Cindy laughed. "Come on" she said, taking her husband by the wrist, "lets go eat."

"Bye guys" he said to James and Alexander, "we will be seeing you later I'm sure."

"Take care."

Jim shrugged his eyebrows, and then said "what does a girl from New Jersey say when she loses her virginity?"

"What?"

"Get off, dad, you're crushing my cigarettes."

Alex formed a grin briefly, and then more gravely turned his eyes into the center of the room. Jimmy asked if Susan's new boyfriend was coming to the party. "No" said Alexander, "he's got something to do, I don't remember what."

"Do you like him."

"Ahh" Alex said, "he seems nice enough."

"What's his name again, Michael?"

"Yeah, I don't remember his last name."

"That's good" Jim said. "I wonder where the heck Susan and Karen are (?) "

"I don't know" Alex said. "I think I saw them eating at one of the tables."

"Hey, did you and Cindy ever?"

"No."

"I figured you didn't" he said.

Alexander and Jim sat drinking for a time. The hand held electronic computer video game had run out of batteries, and the two boys were playing penny football with two quarters and a dime, the taller boy reaching for the last cherry. He bit it in two, and offered half to his shorter companion. He ate it willfully.

Susan and Karen were whispering to each other and laughing with a plate of chicken and two bloody mary's at a table in the corner. Cindy and Alvin were seated with several others in the center of the room. Cindy was chatting with a gaunt young lady and smoking cigarettes, while Alvin was speaking in a business-like manner to three financial planner / money managers. The older man was dipping the young blonde girl with errant cleavage. Bruce Haflin was dancing with his wife.

"I wish, sometimes" said Alexander, "that I could just wake up one morning, and everything would be the way that it should be. You know?"

"I don't know" Jimmy said. "If you want to see David, you cannot just open up a book of Michelangelo and look at a picture of him. You have to fly to Italy, and take the train to Florence, and walk to the Academia, and journey into the room."

"Why?"

"I don't know, you just have to. To appreciate it. You have to go to the mountain, so to speak. He cannot be brought to you."

Alexander finished his last gin and tonic and the gaunt woman behind Cindy reached to the ash tray in the center of the table and snubbed her cigarette. Then she stood and made her way to the vegetable table, as Cindy's lips parted from the edge of her cigarette and she threw the butt down into the tray. While Alvin was leaning to pick up the butt, still lit, and snub it properly, Cindy was making her way to another table where the boy with the pimple sat with his parents eating finger sandwiches of ham and roast beef. She tapped him on the shoulder, (he was chewing as he turned), and Cindy took his hand, saying "Mike is my date tonight." His parents smiled, and the two went off dancing on the brown and black checker floor.

It was an hour later. Alex was sitting at one of the tables with Susan and the gaunt young woman who was smoking. She wore an apricot dress, which fell about her limbs in the same way that her skin fell about the bones of her face. Karen and Jimmy were dancing at the edge of the dance floor. In the center of the floor, Cindy Skinner's lithe fingers formed a fixed impression on Michael Grayson's young back. Her chin was resting on his shoulder, and his arms were wrapped comfortably about her side. Drops of sweat formed on his brow and fell softly towards a pair of undaunted eyes.

Michael suddenly gripped his hands about her graceful back; she wore a devilish smile.

The trombone on the right was taking a solo, as the trumpet player had set his instrument into the stand and was trying to pry a young girl from the lap of her mother so that she could dance with him. Finally, with some prompting, the girl stumbled up to the floor. At first, she just shook her head, her dark pigtails wrapping from side to side. But then she began to imitate the trumpet player, who lifted his legs back and forth like an american wrestler. The small girl was wearing a blue and white checkered dress. She had great big dimples and large warm eyes. The older people formed a circle about them. They were clapping. The trumpet player took the small girl's delicate hands, and shook them gracefully from side to side.

"Are you watching this?" asked Susan. "That is darling. Just darling."

"There is a noble purpose" the man at the table behind them was saying to another.

"She is adorable" the gaunt woman said.

"The man who does right, free willed, without constraint," and he took a sip from his wine glass, "shall truly be happy." And, "he shall not be forgotten."

"Is that Russ and Barbara's little girl?"

"Yeah" Susan said. "She is their youngest."

"She is just adorable."

"To him" the man behind them said, "to him, it was not a drama, a conflict, among the soldiers. But the story of one man, facing his own destiny, wrestling with his soul."

The song ended and the whole room was clapping feverishly, and "how drunk is this guy behind us?" said the gaunt woman in Susan's right ear. Alexander was surveying the dance floor. Cindy Skinner and the boy with the pimple were gone.

There was a mirror and some white powder on a desk. Cindy was leaning over it, and rubbing the delicate edges of her nose. Michael was on his knees behind her. He loosened the button and then unfastened the zipper of her jeans. He took the waist in his hand, and slowly lowered them to her knee. Then he lifted the tail of her blazer and ran his fingers over the edge of her silky black underwear. She leaned again over the cocaine. As Michael started to lower her panties, she lifted her head and wiped her fingers again at her nose. Then she turned to face him, and grabbed his shoulders with her delicate but virtuous palms. She lifted him to his feet, and leaned back, with her jeans and panties resting at the top of her cowboy boots about the knee. She pulled him close to her. They kissed. And she began to unfasten the zipper to his pants.

His hand was inside of her by this time, and she was gripping his lyrical arms and running the back of her hand across the ribbed muscles of his stomach beneath his shirt. Her nipples had formed with the cloth of her sweater. She combed his short hair with her fingers, and moved her lips skillfully over his confident face.

And she touched him. He kissed her rouge cheeks, and touched her shoulder with his hand. And he was inside her. Her blazer was winged back so that only the sleeves covered her arms, and Michael watched her breasts move beneath her sweater as he moved upon her somewhat indelicately. His moist hands then moved to her hips, and she attempted to follow his warm but determined eyes.

It was then that Alexander opened the door. Cindy's groans loudened, with the young boys naked buttocks, and the eyes and the hair, and the waxed lips and painted fingernails, and athletic arms, and cowboy boots, and the confident young face with the pimple, and the hips and clothed nipples, and ankled jeans. Cindy's fingers were wandering in the spill of cocaine.

"Michael, get dressed." He did. And Alexander dressed Cindy, brushing the cocaine into the trashcan and breaking the mirror in his fist. Cindy stiffened suddenly, as the young boy disappeared into the hallway, and said "Alex, what are you doing, I despise you, don't touch me, don't see me, don't look at me ever again."

He grabbed her by the wrist. "Stop it" she whined, "you're hurting me."

"Stop, quit it," and he was dragging her out of the office and down the hall. "Stop it, quit it, I'm serious," she was crying, and attempted to grip the sheetrock with her nails. "Come on" said Alexander, and she dug into the carpet with her heels. The music was getting louder; and the sounds of men talking to women and women talking to children, and children talking among themselves.

"Where are we going?" "Stop!" "Alexander?"

"I am taking you to the hospital."

"NO! NO! NO!" she was screaming and kicking and fighting as they entered the room where the music continued but the party was coming to an end. "NO! STOP!" she was crying, and Alvin appeared. "Help me Alvin."

"What's going on?" "YOU GOOD FOR NOTHING-" "I'm taking her to the hospital." "IF THERE IS ONE THING YOU EVER DO, IN YOUR WHOLE GOD FORSAKEN LIFE-" and Alvin nodded, "-help me. Take me home."

"I'll follow y-" "TAKE ME HOME, ALVIN, PLEEEAASE!" "I'll follow you" Alvin said.

"Don't take me to the hospital." She was sobbing. "Please" she whispered, "please take me home. I'll do anything. I just wanna go home."

The night air was cool, and damp. Cindy was lying in the front seat of Alexander's car. Her legs were folded beneath her, and her hands were cupped delicately beneath her chin. Alexander was combing her hair with his soft fingers, and the tears were slowly drying about her eyes. "I'm sorry, Alex."

"It's okay, sweetheart" he said. "I'm gonna take you home."

"You promise?"

"I promise."

"I don't know how I got here," and the tears were again forthcoming. "I don't know what I did, what did I do?"

"Nothing, sweetheart."

"What did I do?"

"Shhhhhh...."

"Why did-" "Shhhhhhhh..." and Alexander was caressing the soft curls of her hair. "We will find the way home, honey, I promise."

"Promise?"

"Yes, sweetheart" he said. The streetlights formed a row of clouded figures at the road's edge, marking the curves and the straight-paths, and then descending slowly away. There was no moon, (or it was hidden beneath the clouds), and the frogs and crickets were too gullible and distant for them to hear. It was Alexander's voice which came gently, as from the heavens.

"Down in the valley" he sang, "the valley so low; hang your head over, hear the wind blow. Hear the wind blow, child, hear the wind blow; hang your head over, hear the wind blow..." Alexander touched her quiet forehead, and her locks were as some noble fabric in his hands, "...ever been lonely, have you ever been grey; did you ever need someone, who then went away. Roses love sunshine, violets love blue; angels in Heaven, know I love you."

The car rolled past a blue hospital sign, and Alexander followed Alvin's car towards the red brick building at the end of the drive. "Down in the valley" his song ended, "the valley so low; hang your head over, hear the wind blow. Hear the wind blow, child, hear the wind blow; hang your head over, hear the wind blow."

CHAPTER TWENTY

"The defendant shot Judge Cleveland Walsh. That man, sitting right there, at that table, in that chair, got a gun, and he went to the Judge's home, and he climbed over the fence, and he hid in the bushes, and he took out his gun, and he aimed it at the Judge's head, and he shot him.

"It was a beautiful afternoon" the prosecutor continued. "The sun was setting in the west. And Cleveland Walsh, a father, a philanthropist, a philosopher, a good man, an honorable man, a judge, was jogging on the little jogging path that ran through the wooded area behind his home. Where we all feel safe, in our own back yards. And he came out of the woods. And he was watching the sky, where the sun was setting softly behind the clouds, and the trees. And a moment later, he was dead. Because Mister Raintree, the defendant, shot him. And the world will never be the same.

"The evidence will show that the defendant was both a member of the American Nazi Party and a member of the Ku Klux Klan. The evidence will further show that the Ku Klux Klan was involved in an elaborate, intricate, nation-wide, underground, pornographic, criminal, pornography ring. And that Barry Richards, another member of the Ku Klux Klan, had some misgivings about these activities. But Mister Richards was afraid to go to the police with this information, so he went to see the Judge.

"The evidence will show that the defendant's chapter had some suspicions about Mister Richards, and the defendant himself agreed to follow Mister Richards, to keep an eye on him. And that's just what the defendant did.

"The evidence will show that Mister Raintree was at the Judge's home just two days before he died. What was he doing there? Well he was in the Judge's back yard, peering through the window, watching Barry Richards tell Judge Cleveland Walsh that he and other klansmen were involved in a lucrative, criminal, pornographic, obscene, underground, pornography ring. The defendant was spotted by a neighbor, who just happened to be passing by. The neighbor called the police, and the defendant was subsequently arrested for criminal trespass.

"The evidence will show that just two days later, Judge Cleveland Walsh was shot to death through the head in his own back yard. The evidence will show that he was shot once, in the temple, with a forty-five caliber handgun. The shot was fired by a man, who was crouching in a bush nearby. The evidence will show that, upon being struck by the bullet, Judge Cleveland Walsh soonafter died. The defendant shot Judge Cleveland Walsh. And the world will never be the same."

"Good morning. My name is Quentin Jamison, and I represent the defendant, Mister Raintree, who is accused of murder in the first degree.

"Now the rules of professional conduct say that I am not permitted, during my opening statement, or at any time during the trial, to tell you what I think, or what I believe. And the reason why we have this rule, is because we don't want the trial, or any trial, to be a popularity contest between the lawyers, or between the parties involved.

"You see it doesn't matter whether you like me, or don't like me. And it doesn't matter whether you like or don't like the prosecutor, or whether you like or don't like the defendant, Mister Raintree, sitting here beside me, or whether you liked or did not like the Judge. There is only one issue in this case. In this trial.

"Did the defendant kill the victim. And the answer is no.

"This is not a trial about whether the klan is good. This is not a trial about whether pornography is good. This is not a trial about whether Mister Raintree is a good person. And this is not a trial about whether you like him. There is one issue in this case. One issue only. Did the defendant shoot the victim. And the answer is no.

"During this trial, you will hear from a number of people. You will hear from several police officers, a coroner, a footprint expert, a gunshot expert, a crime reconstruction expert, a pornography expert, several neighbors, Mister Richards, and one or two members of the klan. But you will not hear from one person who saw Mister Raintree shoot the Judge. You will not hear from one person who heard Mister Raintree shoot the Judge. You will not hear from one person who saw Mister Raintree at, or near, the Judge's property at any time, the day he died. You will not hear one piece of evidence that in any way indicates that Mister Raintree committed this crime.

"You will see videotapes, photographs, magazines, diagrams, maps, a tattoo, and maybe even a robe. But you will not see fingerprints. You will not see footprints. You will not see powder burns. You will not see blood, or soiled clothes. And you will not see a gun. You will not see one piece of evidence which in any way indicates that Mister Raintree committed this crime.

"No witness, no evidence, no gun. No witness, no evidence, no gun. No witness, no evidence, no gun. Not one piece of evidence that indicates that Mister Raintree committed this terrible crime.

"There are three things I would like you to consider when you are listening to the facts and the evidence presented in this case. Why would Mister Raintree go back to the Judge's house and shoot him just two days after he was arrested on that same property for criminal trespass? Why would Mister Raintree, according to the prosecution's hypothesis, kill the Judge and not kill Barry Richards? And where is the gun?

"Why go back? Why not kill Richards? Where is the gun?

"You have the power. You twelve men and women have the power in this trial. You are more powerful than me. You are more powerful than the prosecutor. And you are more powerful than the judge. You are more powerful than the media. You are more powerful than public opinion, and public sentiment, and perhaps even public outrage. You are more powerful than the Supreme Court, and you are more powerful than the President of the United States. Because you, unlike the public, unlike the media, unlike the Mayor and the Governor and the President himself, will sit here, and you will see all of the evidence. You will hear all of the testimony. And you will know that my client, the defendant, Mister Raintree, is innocent."

CHAPTER TWENTY ONE

It was three days later, and Kenner and Simms were eating two sliced pork
sandwiches and a loaf of onion rings beneath the red umbrellas of Ol' Mary's Good Times & Ribs. There were some construction workers and a few other police officers in uniform at the tables around them. They were eating hamburgers and pork and roast beef sandwiches, with barbecue sauce and baked beans and cornbread and onion rings and ribs. The police officers were drinking Pepsi and the construction workers were drinking beer. There was a loud noise coming from across the street where some road workers were fixing some pot-holes. A series of orange signs forced the traffic into the left lane, and a large man with a blue flannel shirt and a bandanna on his head was working a jack-hammer near the curb.

"I don't understand the point of a sex change operation" Simms was saying. "Because you have a man, right? And then he becomes a woman, right? Now who wants to fuck that? Because no man wants to fuck a woman that's really a guy, unless he's a fag. And he doesn't want a girl anyway. He wants a guy. That's why he's a fag."

Kenner shrugged, finishing the last few bites of his sandwich. Still chewing, he dipped some onion rings into the catsup, and put the rings into his mouth. He wiped his large hands on a paper napkin and brushed his fingers through his grey curly hair. Then he cracked his neck from side to side. "So how is the Walsh trial going?"

"They are gonna convict for sure."

"You think?"

"You still think it's that doctor?"

"I really do" he said. "Because too many things don't make sense. Like for instance, why would the Judge ride his bike, and then go for a run?"

"What do you mean?"

"Well it rained the night before, right? But we had prints of both the Judge's bicycle and the Judge's jogging shoes. So you got this busy judge. He comes home, hard day's work, and so he goes for a bike ride. And then he puts his bike up, puts his running shoes on, and then goes for a run? Doesn't make sense."

"You're right" Kenner said, and again cracked his neck from side to side. "Plus the shot" Simms continued. "That shot was so accurate. So perfect. Right?"

"Yeah."

"Right smack dab in the middle of the temple, right?"

"Yeah, so?"

"So the only reason Thealah isn't on trial right now is cuz the bullet didn't match up. If that bullet had just been a half inch away, it would have cracked into the Judge's skull. The ballistics would have been inconclusive, and the shrink would have been our man."

"You think he could have made that shot?" asked Kenner. "At that distance, a moving target, in that light, with a handgun? No one in the world could have made that shot."

"All I'm saying is, if that bullet were just a half-inch over, that shrink would have been sitting on trial today."

"Maybe" Kenner admitted. "But you still got a guy who has a much better motive, at least so far as we know about, who's a nazi to boot, caught trespassing on the property just too days before. Thealah's lawyers would just point the finger at him, and that's reasonable doubt."

"Probably" he said. "But ninety percent of people are murdered by someone they know. If we had looked long enough, we would have come up with some kind of motive. I mean there musta been some reason. Go figure it out."

The sound of the jack-hammer was still ringing from across the highway and Simms was tapping his fingers on the table beside his empty plate. "Besides" he said, "the reason we didn't go after him was cuz we didn't have a gun. But we don't have a gun with Raintree. So why is it good enough to go after him?"

"I guess they figure with the klan and all the pornography, no one is going to miss him. Thealah is a big doctor and all."

"One time we stopped some rich guy for d-w-i" Simms said. "Rich guy, smart, good for the community, all that stuff. No point putting him in jail, right? Everyone was all set to let him go. Makes sense, right? Then the prosecutor all of the sudden, she gets up and she says that they are acting like rich guys have less of a responsibility to obey the law. But they have more. The people that can afford to be moral in this society, have all the more responsibility to do so, because if they don't, no one will. This rich guy could have easily afforded to call a cab, she says. That makes him all the more guilty for not doing so."

Alexander and Susan were sitting at their breakfast-room table with Karen and Jim. Jim was wearing a white oxford and a pair of faded jeans. There was a red stain on the collar of his oxford, which brushed against the edges of his yellow curls beside his ear. Karen was a younger girl. She wore a sleeveless light blue button-down shirt and long silk skirt which was gold and rose. She had bangs, which fell delicately about her sinewy eyebrows, and gentle mischievous green eyes.

There were a few pieces of chicken in the center of the table with a thick tomato sauce. There was also a bowl of salad, and broken loaf of bread. Each wine glass was filled with various amounts of water, and the napkins were placed, (or bunched), on the table beside each of their plates. "Have you ever noticed" Jim was saying, "that a five piece pack of gum is thirty-five cents, but a six piece pack of gum is fifty cents. Does that make sense? I mean all of the other pieces of gum are seven cent pieces of gum, and then, all of the sudden, along comes a fifteen cent piece."

"How do you know which piece is the fifteen cent piece?"

"You don't" Jim said. "You might give it away. Someone might come up to you and say can I have a piece? And you say sure, there you go. And that was your fifteen cent piece and you didn't even know."

"Did you see Kevin Mack at the trial yesterday?"

"Oh my god."

"I really don't like that guy" Jim said. "I mean you got all of these people, every day, on tv, who really don't know what they are talking about, or have anything interesting to say. It's just crap. It's really just unacceptable."

"It's not so bad" said Susan. "It's entertaining."

"It's crap" Jim continued, "wears an earring."

"You are so intolerant."

"I have a great tolerance" Jimmy said, "when you are talking about what can be, but I have a very limited tolerance when dealing with what should be."

"What kind of tolerance" asked Alexander, "do you have for those things which should not be?"

"I usually just cry and complain" Jim said.

"Speaking of crap on tv" said Karen, "did you guys see that show on the convent, in France, with that student that went crazy and chopped up the little girl?"

"Oh god, that was terrible."

"I hate nuns."

"There he goes again."

"Why do you hate nuns?"

"Because they are denying a part of themselves" he said. "Pretending that it's not there."

"I disagree."

"The nuns have all the forms of faith arrayed in order" he said, "but can they deal with the truth?"

"What?"

"Where did you get that?"

"I read it in Newsweek" he said.

"Oh, he read it in Newsweek."

"Or maybe it was Vanity Fair."

"You read Vanity Fair?"

"I just don't like them" Jim said.

"Well I don't think they are denying a part of themselves" said Alexander. "I think that they, and monks, and priests, for that matter, are doing something very noble. They are like nazarites. Separate unto God."

"You're telling me that you have respect for priests?"

"Sure."

"You're talking about an entire class of perverted, confused, socially inept child molesters that lock themselves away behind the cross while raping little boys."

"Not all priests are like that."

"I know, but-"

"A lot of them are."

"But even assuming that they are" said Alexander, "the fact remains that just because certain nuns, or monks, or priests themselves might be weak or fallible, that doesn't lessen the beauty or the power or the righteousness of the priesthood itself."

"I agree."

"I am sure there are thousands of priests that are good people who do good work" offered Karen, "but I still think it's kinda weird."

"You guys want anything else to eat?"

"No thanks."

"No, I'm fine. Thanks."

"So what do you guys think about the trial?"

"I don't know" Alex said. "They're giving closing arguments tomorrow afternoon."

"They're gonna convict."

"You think so?"

"Definitely."

"What do you think, Alex?"

"I don't know."

"They're gonna convict" Susan said again. "If they are out more than thirty minutes, I'll be surprised."

"How is Carol?"

"She's holding up okay, I think."

"We should have invited her."

"I called her" Susan said. "She said she wanted to be alone."

"I hope she's okay."

"She'll pull through."

"That was funny when the juror wandered into the witness stand."

"Yeah."

"What happened?"

"The bailiff filed the jury into the courtroom, and this one old juror - this adorable old lady - kept going straight, and before she knew it, she was standing on the witness stand."

"That's funny."

"So the sheriff comes up to this farmer in a small town. And he says 'Bill, I'm sorry, but I'm gonna have to arrest you. Someone saw you making it with one of your cows.'

"'So what do you think I should do?' asks the farmer.

"'Well, you got two choices' says the sheriff. 'You can go with Richard, who can really put together a case, or you can go with Bob, who really knows how to pick a jury.'

"So the farmer goes with the lawyer that can pick a jury, and the prosecution calls the first witness, and she explains how she was driving down the highway one evening when she sees the farmer off in the pasture having sex with a cow. And he finishes. And the cow turns around, and licks the farmer's privates, cleaning up the mess.

"So the first juror turns to the second juror, and he says 'a good cow will do that.'"

The four laughed together, as Jim filled the wine glasses, starting with his own. "One time" Karen said, "when I was first clerking for an assistant d-a, it was my first week, and we were in arraignment, and the defendant was hispanic. And the public defender said that he could not be arraigned today because he couldn't speak any english, which means that he would have been let go. So I made the mistake of mumbling that I could speak spanish, and the d-a stands up and says wait, judge, judge, we have a translator. So I translated for like ten minutes. And the judge would say something and he would look at me, to let me know that he knew the judge had spoken, and I would tell him in spanish what the judge had said. And then he would tell me whatever in spanish, and I would tell the judge. And this went on, back and forth, back and forth, for about ten minutes. So the judge says okay, we are finished, and he gives me a date, to tell the defendant, and the defendant and I turn around, and I say in spanish that you have to be here on such and such a date, and in perfect english, he says, 'Okay, thanks a lot.'"

The four of them laughed, and drank from their water glasses, wiping their mouths with their napkins and breaking off the last pieces of bread. "The evening has been wonderful" Jim said, "but I'm getting tired."

"You need any help cleaning up Sue?"

"No, I'll take care of it" Susan said, as the four of them were standing. "Thanks."

"You want to rent out a movie?" Karen asked Jimmy.

"I don't know" he said. "You want to?"

"It will probably take us forever to find what we want."

"Just think of something you want before you go in" Susan told them.

"If one person goes into a video store, it takes him thirty seconds to get what he wants. If two people go in, it takes them half an hour, to get something they kind of want. Three people it takes an hour to get something that no one wants. And four people, they just don't get anything at all."

"It's like Congress."

"I know."

"Well, goodbye" said Susan, hugging Karen, "thank you for coming."

"Thank you for having us."

The phone rang, and Alexander went to answer it as Jim was saying "goodbye Alex, take care." Alexander nodded and placed the cold receiver to his ear. "Hello" a voice said, "is this Doctor Thealah?"

"Yes it is."

"We found Jeffery Stiles in Saint Louis" the voice said. "He's dead."

CHAPTER TWENTY TWO

"When I was a young kid, I used to have to come to the courthouse sometimes after school to wait for my father. And so there was nothing better to do than sit in the back and watch some of the trials. I really didn't think very much of what was going on. The judge was like a crusty old teacher, or a boss, who looked down at everyone, and handed out orders, with grey hair. The jurors were like prisoners, rounded up by the sheriff and forced to listen to some trial. But one day I saw something which interested me. Because a kid was suing my school because they wouldn't let him play football because he was black, and I pretty much supported anyone that was suing my school. And my principal came in, well-dressed, and well-spoken, and I thought he was just about the most powerful man alive, unfortunately. But the jury, that day, showed my principal and me what power was. And I remember, sitting there shocked and amazed after the verdict, when this old man, an old court reporter, came up behind me, and swiped me on the back of the head, and said, 'Stand up, kid. The jury is passing by.'

"Along the way, through these many years, I have traveled through brief phases of doubt and concern about the legal system in America. Doubts and concerns which I'm sure you too have held. I have been among those students, those lawyers, those citizens, who have casted shadows over the marble of this noble courthouse.

"But I have also come to know that critics have their own various motives; that such critics, whether they be law students, or doctors, or even vice-Presidents of the United States, have failed to present a just, or fair, or reasonable alternative; and I have come to know that these reports we hear, from time to time, of unconscionable or unthinkable decisions, are not representative, but rather aberrations.

"I have come to know, in time, that twelve strangers, such as yourselves - you, Mister Johnson, and you, Misses Farrell, and all of you - you twelve strangers, coming together, and looking at the evidence brought before you, and casting your vote accordingly, is the most powerful system of dispensing justice we have ever come to know. It is the highest form of government, the richest form of assembly, and the purest form of democracy.

"Thomas Jefferson once said that the right to a trial by jury is more important than the right to vote.

"And I think Thomas Jefferson might have understood what that old court reporter understood: If we, as individuals, and as a society, can come together, when we have a dispute, and present our case before our peers, to render judgment; if we can keep government in the courthouse, instead of taking it out into the streets; we can build the most powerful, most beautiful, and most just society that the world has ever known.

"Judge Cleveland Walsh, like Thomas Jefferson, like that old court reporter, like my father, and like many of you, believed profoundly in our judicial system. And he dedicated his life to that legal system, and he dedicated his life to justice, and he dedicated his life to you.

"But as you know by now, Judge Cleveland Walsh is dead. He was shot to death, in his own back yard, by this defendant, who took the law out of the courtroom, and into his own hands. And neither the courtroom nor the law will ever be the same again.

"There are two questions to be answered today. How did he do it? And why. First, lets talk about why. The defendant, as you know by now, is a nazi. He pays tribute to Adolf Hitler, sends David Duke money, and marches with the Ku Klux Klan. These organizations, in order to survive, and to expand, and to spread their beliefs, like some infectious disease, produce, package, perform in, distribute, and sell pornography.

"And one of their shell corporations, one of these fronts, called Calypso Productions, was enjoined by the state, through the Attorney General, from selling a couple of their pornographic videos. This case came up, through the courts, before Judge Walsh. Calypso Productions v MacIntyre. Docket Number two-six-three-one-eight-five.

"Now Calypso v MacIntyre involved just one or two fairly innocuous, by their standards, films. And if they had lost that case, they might have lost a few bucks; but the klan and the nazis and the defendant would have come out of everything okay.

"But in the meantime, however, a man named Barry Richards, had a very uneasy feeling in his stomach, about what was going on, and he wanted to tell someone about it. And he was scared to go to the police. He was scared to go to the district attorney. He was scared, naturally, of the klan. And so he went to see the Judge.

"You heard his testimony. You heard Mister Richards say that just two days before Judge Cleveland Elenor Walsh was murdered, shot to death, in the head, in his own back yard, Barry Richards was at the Judge's home. And the defendant was there. The defendant was following Mister Richards. And he was there. In the bushes, watching, spying, on Mister Richards and the Judge.

"You heard Officer Caldwell's testimony, and Officer Doufall's testimony, that the defendant was found, and arrested, just two days before the murder of Cleveland Walsh, in his back yard. You read the statement of the defendant himself, where he admitted that he was in the Judge's back yard, the same back yard where the Judge was murdered, just two days before. Why? Why was the defendant following Mister Richards? Because he was scared. The defendant was scared of what Mister Richards might tell the Judge.

"And what did Mister Richards tell the Judge? You saw it. You heard it. You heard Mister Richards' testimony. He went to the Judge's home. And he told the Judge the truth about Calypso Productions. He told the Judge that the two films involved in the Calypso v MacIntyre case were just the tip of the iceberg. An iceberg which was essentially a mass of obscene, disgusting, and criminal activities. Bestiality, child pornography, pedophilia, incest, bondage, s-and-m, chains, whips, racial degradation, sexual degradation, excrement, urine, torture, rape, pain. An elaborate, intricate, nation-wide, underground, criminal, pornographic ring.

"This is the information that Mister Richards gave to the Judge. Information which, as you can well imagine, would make the defendant and the entire klan afraid, fearful, and scared out of their shirts that someone, anyone, everyone would discover what they had done. These are activities which are not only disgusting, immoral, and reprehensible, but also ones which pose a great threat to both the members of the organization, and the organization itself. Disclosure of these activities, this pornography, would not only threaten the lifeblood and the backbone of this organization, financially, but also subject the defendant, and many of its members, to criminal liability. To jail.

"So here was Mister Richards, telling everything to the Judge. Giving away all their dirty little secrets, spilling all the beans. And the defendant was there. Hiding in the bushes. Spying. And he looked at the Judge, that great, big, respected and powerful judge, and you know what he saw? He saw the law, he saw justice, he saw democracy, he saw anger, retribution, embarrassment, divorce, disgrace, jail. And that's why he killed the Judge.

"How did he do it? Very simply. He got a gun. And he went to the Judge's home. He knew the grounds. He had been there just two days before. He crept in the bushes. He waited. And he shot him.

"The defendant took the law into his own hands. He took something that belongs to all of us, and he stole it from the courthouse, and he killed it, and he buried it, and now it's gone. The defendant shot Judge Cleveland Walsh. And we will never be the same again."

"There has been a lot of talk, by the prosecution, about the wonderful Barry Richards, who testified and swore so eloquently before this court. But I would like to pass on something I heard from another Richards. Governor Ann Richards, of the Great State of Texas. It's been said, she said, that when the facts are on your side, argue the facts. When the law is on your side, argue the law. And when both the facts and the law are against you, holler. And all I see here is a lot of hollerin.

"There is no evidence, ladies and gentlemen of the jury, no evidence, which in any way indicates that Mister Raintree shot the victim; nor that he had anything whatsoever to do with the victim's death.

There is no witness, there are no fingerprints, there are no footprints, there are no powder burns, no soiled clothes, no blood, and no gun.

"No witness, no evidence, no gun.

"You have heard the testimony of four police officers, a coroner, a footprint expert, a gunshot expert, a crime reconstruction expert, a pornography expert, six neighbors, Mister Richards, the prosecutor, and two members of the ku klux klan. But no witness, no evidence, no gun.

"You have seen videotapes, photographs, magazines, diagrams, maps, a tattoo, and a robe. But no witness, no evidence, no gun. Not one piece of evidence that links Mister Raintree with this terrible crime.

"There is a very important rule of evidence, ladies and gentlemen. It is now known to us as code article four-o-four-b. But it goes back, all the way to the time of Magna Carta, and has been established and developed through the common law for hundreds of years. The rule reads like this: Evidence of other crimes, wrongs, or acts, is not admissible to prove the character of a person, in order to show action in conformity therewith.

"Now that's a lot of legal talk that some lawyers like to use to try to make people think that they are smarter than everybody else. But what it boils down to, is that we can't say that someone's guilty of one thing, just because we don't like him; and we can't say that someone is guilty of something, just because he or she did something else.

"What that rule says is that, just because we may not like Mister Raintree, that doesn't mean he killed the Judge. Just because Mister Raintree has a nasty tattoo, that doesn't mean he killed the Judge. Just because Mister Raintree has an unpopular political viewpoint, that doesn't mean he killed the Judge. Just because Mister Raintree is a nazi or a klansman, that doesn't mean he killed the Judge. Just because Mister Raintree may have been involved in pornography, that doesn't mean he killed the Judge. Just because Mister Raintree was found in a back yard, even just two days before his death, doesn't mean he killed the Judge. And just because you do not like Mister Raintree, that does not mean that he killed the Judge. There is one issue in this case. One issue only. Did the defendant shoot the victim. And the answer is no.

"No witness, no evidence, no gun. Not one piece of evidence, not one sliver, not one shred, that in any way connects Mister Raintree with the crime of which he is accused.

"The prosecutor spoke of the jury system. The power of the jury system. The beauty of the jury system. The justice of the jury system.

"Some people out there, in the public, reading the daily reports, or listening to the news, believe that there is an answer, to this case. And that they have the answer. And that it is your job to find that answer, which they have chosen to be appropriate. But we do not try cases in the media. We try cases in the courtroom. Before you, the jury, who see all of the evidence, who hear all of the testimony. And you have no duty, but to come to the truth.

"The truth is, whatever your personal feelings are about Mister Raintree, he had nothing, absolutely nothing to do with the death of Judge Walsh. All you have to do is ask yourself three questions. Why would Mister Raintree go back to the Judge's property and shoot him just two days after he was arrested on that same property for criminal trespass? Why would Mister Raintree, according to the prosecution's hypothesis, kill the Judge and not kill Barry Richards? And where is the gun?

"Why go back? Why not kill Richards? Where is the gun?

"You have the power, ladies and gentlemen. You are more powerful than me. You are more powerful than the prosecutor. And you are more powerful than the judge. You are more powerful than the media, and public opinion, and public sentiment, and public outrage, all put together. You are more powerful than Supreme Court, and you are more powerful than the President of the United States. Because you have sat here, and witnessed this trial. You have seen the evidence. You have heard the testimony. And you know that my client, the defendant, Mister Raintree, is innocent."

"Why go back? Why not kill Richards? Where is the gun?" the prosecution began in rebuttal. "Mister Jamison is absolutely correct. You must be thinking, you must be wondering, you must be asking yourselves: who would be so stupid? Who would be so stupid, that he would go back to the Judge's home, just two days after being arrested there, and kill the Judge. And you know something, ladies and gentlemen, that's exactly what the defendant is counting on. He is counting on the fact that you will refuse to accept that anyone could be that stupid. That dumb. But that, ladies and gentlemen, is where the defendant's mistaken. Because you and I are on to him. Aren't we? It was just plain stupid. The defendant was just plain stupid. And that is why he went back, just two days later, and murdered the Judge.

"Why not kill Richards?" he continued. "Why kill Richards? Richards was powerless. He was afraid. That's why he didn't go to the police in the first place. You heard him say it. I was afraid. I was afraid of the defendant. I was afraid of the klan. Which is something that the defendant was counting on. He was counting on the possibility that when they killed the

Judge, it would send a message to Mister Richards as well. That when Mister Richards saw that the Judge has been murdered, it would shut him up for good. But again, the defendant underestimated Mister Richards, the same way that he has underestimated you. Because Mister Richards was outraged. He was angry. He was betrayed, by the defendant, and the klan. And though he was fearful, though he was afraid, Mister Richards overcame his fear, and went to the police, and testified honestly, and courageously, and forthrightly, in these proceedings, in an effort to see that justice is done.

"And finally, where is the gun? I don't know. I have been up front with you throughout this trial. And I just plain don't know. I, we, could not produce the gun. We couldn't find it. But is that really so surprising? Consider the organization the defendant belongs to. Consider the networking. Think about all those computer systems, and underground newspapers, and other publications. Think about how easy it would be to obtain, and then later dispose of, a gun.

"'You've got to take this guy out,' someone might have said to the defendant. 'We'll get you what you need. We'll take care of everything. We'll take care of the gun.'

"No, the defendant did not do this alone. But he did it. And you know it.

"The defendant shot Judge Cleveland Walsh. That man, sitting right there, at that table, in that chair, got a gun, and he went to the Judge's home, and he climbed over the fence, and he hid in the bushes, and he took out the gun, and he aimed it at the Judge's head, and he shot him. And we will never be the same again."

CHAPTER TWENTY THREE

There was a large wooden table in the center of the room. Seated around the table were Alexander, Susan, Quentin Jamison, the prosecutor, Kenner, Simms, and the captain. Each person had a mug of coffee, and Alexander had a stack of journals, leather-bound.

"Jeffrey Stiles" he started, "was a patient of mine. He was a pyromaniac, he was possibly a thief, he was rich, and there was a dispute over his mother's will. The dispute was brought before Judge Walsh, who decided the case in a manner which, while just, was nevertheless unsatisfactory to Mister Stiles. The Judge, realizing that Mister Stiles needed some help, asked me to handle his case. These are my notes. They indicate that Mister Stiles was often irrational, sometimes violent, and that he held a deep resentment for Judge Walsh. He hated him. He wished violence upon him. And he also had a gun.

"One day, all of the sudden, Jeff Stiles disappeared. This was several months ago; a week or two before the Judge died. I looked for Mister Stiles, I could not find him, and two weeks later, the Judge, as you know, was shot in the head with a forty-five."

"This is a load of shit" Simms said. "He did it. He set the whole thing up."

"Wait a second" said the captain. "Now. Mister Thealah, why did you not come to us with this evidence before?"

"I   couldn't"   he   said.   "Doctor-patient confidentiality."

"Good christ. Can you believe this?"

"Wait a second, Simms. Just a minute. Now, Mister Thealah, you're saying that this information, which is evidenced by these journals here, I assume-" "that's correct" "-is protected by the doctor-patient privilege?"

"Yes, sir. I-"

"Then why are you here now?"

"I learned last night that Mister Stiles was killed in Saint Louis. It's my understanding that the privilege dies with the patient."

"This is such crap."

"This is the law, officer Simms" Susan replied. "Do you have some special problem with my brother obeying the law?"

"I have a problem with him breaking the law" said officer Simms. "I have a problem with him killing someone, and then trying to plant the blame on one of his own patients, probably some crazy nut who can't even defend himself. I have a pro-"

"That's enough" interrupted the prosecutor, "for now. I would like to ask Mister Thealah a few questions. Mister Thealah, you claim that this patient of yours wished violence upon the Judge?"

"Yes, sir."

"What do you mean by that?"

"He said that he hated him. He made derogatory comments about him. He said he hoped the Judge would burn in hell. He said he wished he could blow his whole house up. He said he had a dream in which he poured gasoline over the Judge's car, and watched him burn."

"Did you warn the Judge?"

"No."

"Or report it to the authorities?"

"No. I did not think that there was an imminent threat of harm. I just thought he was blowing off steam. I now see that maybe I should have taken it more seriously."

"If Stiles is so infatuated with fire and explosives, why did he shoot him?"

"I don't know if he did shoot him" Alexander said. "I don't know if he had anything to do with anything. All I know is that this is evidence which would seem to be relevant to Mister Raintree's trial."

"But is it really relevant?" asked the prosecutor. "I mean we have a pyromaniac, who you claim has fantasies about burning someone alive, and then, with pretty respectable accuracy, shoots him in the head with a forty-five? Someone who hadn't been seen in town for two weeks prior to the Judge's death. And when he was found, turned up in St. Louis? I am not sure if it's relevant at all."

"Well I'll take it" laughed Quentin Jamison, as Susan said "maybe that is a question for a jury to decide."

"Look, honey, I don't know where you got your legal education, but around here, juries don't hear anything until we press charges. So you can take your smug little ivy league attitude, and you can keep your mouth shut, until I get finished asking a few questions. Did-" "You listen to me, you ignorant, incompetent, piddly little neanderthal son of a bitch. I got my legal training on Mountain View Avenue, right down the street. I graduated magna cum laude from Johns Hopkins, and I graduated from law school, on law review, order of the coif, with an l-l-m. I also participated in the constitutional law clinic, where I tried several civil rights and discrimination cases, and if you ever so much as think about calling me honey again, I will slap a nineteen-eighty-three suit on your ass so fast, you won't be able to sit down for a week."

"Oooo, I'm really scared..."

"Would you two cut it out?" said the captain. "Fuckin lawyers. Good christ."

"Mister Thealah" asked Kenner, "How did Mister Stiles die?"

"He died in a fire, about a month ago, apparently."

"Where were you at that time?"

"Here."

"Do you have any proof of that fact?"

"Yes" he and Susan together said. "He has not been out of town since the Judge died."

"Did your patient, at any time, actually threaten Judge Walsh?"

"I wasn't there" he said, "but he apparently threatened Judge Walsh, with an unloaded gun."

"A forty-five?"

"No" he said. "Something smaller. Maybe a twenty-two. Or a twenty-five."

"You're quite a shot yourself, aren't you Mister Thealah?" pressed Simms.

"I'm okay."

"Did anyone-" "Good enough to hit a jogging man in the temple from fifty yards?"

"Possibly."

"Don't get arrogant, Alex" whispered Susan, as the captain asked if there were "any witnesses to this incident?"

"Yes" said Alexander, "I believe the Judge's bailiff, and the Judge's secretarial assistant, Eloise McFadden."

"They witnessed this incident with the gun?"

"I believe so, yes."

"And those are your office notes?"

"Right here."

"He did it." (Simms was standing now.) "Don't you see? He had two guns. He had one forty-five that everyone knew about, with the little doo-hickie, that everyone knew to be his gun. And he goes out, and he finds another gun, also a forty-five, which he uses to kill the Judge. Then he dumps it somewhere. He knows he might be a suspect, but that we won't have quite enough evidence to convict. But what he doesn't know is that there is some poor stupid nazi bastard hiding in the bushes. So along comes Mister Raintree, who he doesn't know nothin about, and when he realizes poor Mister Raintree is about to get the chair, he starts to feel guilty. His conscience gets to him. So he manufactures up all this crap to get him out."

"That" said Susan, "is the most preposterous story I have ever heard."

"Well I don't know if it's preposterous or not" said Mister Jamison, "but now that you were kind enough to bring up Nineteen Eighty-Three, it sounds like we might have a nice little case ourselves."

"He did it" Simms said. "It's plain as the nose on my face. And one day I'm gonna prove it."

"Well, well," said Mister Jamison to the prosecutor, "civil suits aside, I would think that all of this would be quite enough to warrant a mistrial."

"Why don't we see what happens" suggested the prosecutor. "If the jury acquits, you won't have to put your client through another trial."

"I can't risk that. If the jury does come back guilty, it will be all over the news. Even if I get the new trial, he won't have a chance."

"Well, lets go and talk to the judge. But then I'm gonna take a good look at all of this. And so help me god, someone is gonna hang for this. I don't care who. But when it's done, someone is gonna fry."

"Are we excused?" Susan then politely asked.

"Hell no" Simms said. "You're under arrest."

"Captain?"

"Well" said the captain, "while I do have my suspicions, Mister Thealah, we can't legally hold you in custody for the commission of a crime for which someone else is being prosecuted. So for the time being, sir, I guess you are free to go."

CHAPTER TWENTY FOUR

It was two years later. A blanket of dark thick clouds was roaming about in the west and shielding much of the valley from the afternoon sun. There was a W of birds that was migrating to the south, and the chipmunks and squirrels were darting over the sidewalks and the grasses among the oak trees where they searched for acorns. The darker leaves were falling from the trees.

Alexander drove past the concrete walls and benches scarred with brown graffiti, where the bus stops were strewn with half-torn motion picture posters, and the street lamps were stapled with ads. There was a black-robed woman on the street corner; the wind came down out of the north and swept the dark fabric across her face and arms. And Alexander drove on.

He came to a side road, where the plume of mosses formed a bridge across the narrow street below. The dark clouds loomed in the distance. The rush of birds swam behind him in the sky. His parents house rose gently from the soil where planted tulips grew out of the broken bark and shreds of wood that covered the dark damp earth. The walls were forged of brick and many windows, all around the first and only floor.

Alexander went to the great mahogany doors. He turned the bronze doorknob, and stepped into the atrium. "Hello?"

There was no answer. So he wandered into the kitchen and took some milk from the refrigerator door. He started to pour a glass for himself, but the carton slipped, and the cold milk spilled out onto the floor. Alexander took several napkins from the cabinet and sopped the liquid up with his hands. He threw the soiled napkins into the garbage can beneath the sink, and placed the carton of milk back into the third right shelf of the refrigerator door.

He stepped through the room where Catherine's pottery was exhibited along the shelves: the bowls, the hand-turned vases, urns, and trays, with blue and green and grey or earthen glazes, or wood-burned, or hand-painted with acrylics, hand-turned, wheel-turned, ridged. Alexander straightened some bar glasses and some plants, and stepped through the hallway to the back of the home. He heard a noise from the bedroom. He opened the door.

Two naked bodies moved beneath the blue-grey flannel sheets that lined a large brass bed where the small light slipped in through the almost darkness from a crack behind the shade. The figures formed a fluid motion, like one great writhing reed that washed beneath the cool waters of a desert stream. Alexander's fist tightened about the doorknob. One of the figures was Helen. The other was his father. And Alexander quietly closed the door. "Oh god" he whispered. "What have you done."

CHAPTER TWENTY FIVE

Catherine was working in the garden. It was one week later, and she was packing the dark soil into the ground.   The sun was slanting down across the silhouette of hanging plants that blossomed from the round clay pots, and sidled down like long elastic fingers flaunting small bright petals that seemed to harness all the warm red nectars from the air. Catherine scratched at her muddy fingers, and wiped with her forearm the delicate beads of sweat that had formed above her gentle brow.

The sun was also warming Catherine's high cheekbones, her soft black hair, and hickory eyes. She wore a white cotton dress, which fell gracefully about her tall and gentle frame. She kneeled back down beside the bag of soil and started to break the thick white plastic from its seam. Then the phone rang.

Catherine sprung to her feet and raced into the kitchen where there was another ring, and then she lifted the cold receiver to her ear. "Hello" she said, "Thealah residence."

"Mom?" the voice said, "this is Susan. Don't get alarmed, but it's dad. He's missing. No one has seen or heard from him since he left for Biloxi. He's gone."

Book III

It is the law that the man of the bloody hand must speak
no word until, by action of one who can cleanse,
blood from a young victim has washed his blood away.

The Eumenides

CHAPTER TWENTY-SIX

Lake Croce ebbed like a great majestic caldron with its dawn beryl waters creeping over the damp shoreline and into the marsh. There was a long dirt road which wound among the wall of pine that separated the lake, on one side, from the cold marsh below. Off in the distance, several white birds were playing over the reeds and the waters, while in the trees were pine-needled nests for all of the robins and the cardinals and the jays. The lake itself was clear, with a shamrock of clouds that formed a white grey mist to the left of the sun, and a woodpecker was tapping out a series of restless noises which fell from the cold bark like a strange foreboding. The wind swept over the waters of the marsh and through the arms and the fingers of all the branches, and against the side of the home.

The home rested, like a watchdog, over the large mysterious garden that was perched at the end of the tired dirt road. There was a porch with a red and white hammock. And beneath the house, where the robins bathed in a white porcelain bath and where swallows bathed in the soft arid dust below, sat the garden of grasses and tulips, of azaleas and poppies and roses, of honeysuckle, ivy and vine. A pair of blue-jays ate from the cottage feeder, and the wind-chimes danced gently in the breeze.

Men wandered the grounds, taking samples, as the birds would take flight - their wings near-wrapping the investigators jackets, beating effortlessly against the damp cold air.   Officer Simmons was standing on the porch beside Catherine.   "I'm sorry" he said, "that we have to be doing this right now, ma'am. I know it must be difficult, right now, in your time of grief."

"Thank you, officer" she said.   "I understand." Catherine touched her right eye with two fingers, and then swept some stray hair to the side. The gentle skin of her blouse was light against her shoulders.   It fell gracefully to her hips, where the tails of her shirt were tucked evenly beneath the waist of her jeans.

"I want someone crawling through every inch of this place" Simms called from the porch.   "And when we're done, we are gonna drag every inch of this lake, and every inch of that marsh."

"Do you really think that he could be out here?" she asked him.

"I don't know, ma'am.   But it's been two weeks. Something" and he paused, "must have happened."

"I know" she said, "but I don't really think that he would have come out here alone. Particularly without telling me."

"Well we have to check everything ma'am, for your own peace of mind.   It has generally been my experience, in these matters, that the not knowing, that is the hardest part."   Catherine nodded almost imperceptibly, to which Simms added: "We just want you to be able to put this all behind you."

"Thank you officer" she then said to him warmly. "I understand."

Inside, Officer Kenner was examining a hand-crafted vase. It had been molded and sculpted in the form of a cross, then finished with an emerald glaze. Alexander stood beside the potter's wheel, where there was a table with several tools and instruments, a bowl of dirty water, and clay. Beside the table was a kiln, and on the walls were shelves of various pots and bowls and vases, mugs and saucers and trays. There were also many brushes, burning chips, acrylic paints, and glaze. There was a short man taking fingerprints. He had a khaki army jacket and a limp in his lower left leg.

"You fool with this stuff at all?" asked Officer Kenner.

"No" said Alexander. "Not really."

"You got everything?" Kenner then asked the fingerprint man, who said "yeah I got em, lets go."

The three men ascended the wide wood staircase, and emerged in the kitchen, where Officer Simmons was standing with Catherine. Kenner examined the copper pots and pans that were hanging from an iron frame above the sink, as another man examined the stove. "What's that?" asked Simms, and gestured to the metal instrument that was fastened to the wooden countertop beside the cutting board.

"It's just an old meat grinder" Catherine said. "Alexander gave it to me." Simms ran his fingers over the cold metal. There was some blood which had dried at the base of the metal. Simms scraped at the blood with his fingernail, and brushed it into a clear ziplock bag.

"Excuse me, Misses Thealah, but do you think I could have a word or two with your son, alone?"

"Of course" she said, "I will wait outside."

"No, why don't we go outside. You can wait here."

Alexander followed Simms down off the porch and into the garden. They stepped across the dirt road and between a few trees to where the reeds and the waters of the marsh seeped quietly below. "It's a big fat ugly marsh, huh doc?" Alexander wiped at his chin. "It's a good place to hide a dead body, wouldn't you say?" But Alexander said nothing. He was watching the two white birds that were dancing above the weeds and the bushes in the grey southwestern part of the sky. "But, you know," Simms continued, "it takes a lot more than a few weeks for a body to decompose." Alexander again brushed his hand across his chin. "And we are gonna find it if it takes all day" Simms said. "If it takes all week, if it takes all month, if it takes all year."

"I hope you do find him" Alexander said. "He's my father. And I pray that he is alive. But if he is dead, then I hope you do find him, and I hope you find him soon. Because, as you said, we need to put this behind us. My mother, she needs to put this behind us. My sisters, they need to put this behind us. And so do I, Mister Simmons. I love my father. I love my father more than you could ever know. So I hope you do find my father. I hope you find him soon."

Simms laughed for a moment, to himself, and drew a breath-mint from his front pocket. He offered it to Alexander, who refused, and then placed the white candy on his tongue. "I know you killed him."

But Alexander said nothing.

"I don't know why yet" Simms continued. "And I don't know how. But I know. And one day, I'm gonna prove it." And with that, he lifted the clear ziplock bag and dangled it before Alexander's eyes. "I'm gonna prove that you killed your father, and then I'm gonna prove that you shot that judge.

"There's no statute of limitations for murder" he continued. "You want to remember that. You might think you're pretty smart, with your nice little house, and nice little family, and all of those nice little awards and diplomas and degrees. But they don't mean a shit to me. They don't matter in the real world, doc. All that matters is determination. Perseverance. Grit. The willingness to keep going. The courage to see it through to the end. And I don't think you've got what it takes, doc. I don't think you're strong enough. I think you're going to break. Maybe it'll be me. Or it may be a priest. It may be another shrink, it may be before God himself; but one day, you are going to confess. And when you do, I'm gonna be there. And then you will be sorry, my friend, because from that day forward, you will spend the rest of your life rotting in some jail cell. And then you'll die. Alone and afraid, and strapped to a chair. And then you will spend all eternity in hell."

CHAPTER TWENTY SEVEN

"We found your father's car" Officer Simmons was saying a few hours later, "as you may or may not know, about a mile from his home." Alexander nodded. He was standing in his bedroom, as a man in a jump-suit was taking fingerprints, and another was taking samples from his carpet and from his hair. Simms was holding a little notebook, and a pen. "And the last time you saw him was two days before he disappeared."

"Correct."

"I want you to go through his clothes" Simms then said to the man with the ziplock, "and if anything remotely looks like it might have ever been anything that even resembles blood, take it. Excuse me, Doctor Thealah" he then said, "you were saying?"

"That is correct. Susan and I went to their house for dinner two days before he left town."

"And he was going to Biloxi?"

"As far as I know."

"Do you have any reason to believe that he was going anywhere else?"

"No."

"An affair, perhaps?"

"No."

"Gambling debt?"

"No."

"Mob debts?"

"No."

"I hear the greeks have a pretty elaborate system of organized crime of their own. Your dad wasn't involved in that by any chance, was he?"

"No."

"Maybe that has something to do with why you killed the Judge."

"No."

"The Judge found out-" "no" "-was gonna turn him over."

"Officer Simmons" he said, "I have respect for your tenacity, and I appreciate your wild imagination, but you are truly barking up the wrong proverbial tree."

"Yeah?" he said. "I don't think so." He stepped to the wall and studied Alexander's wrestling trophies and six from the decathlon. Beside the stereo, in shelves, were hanging frames of Caravaggio reprints and the plaque and flag from his sixth and tenth grade science fairs. Simms studied the prints, saying: "The Sacrifice of Isaac" he said, and Alexander nodded. "In the Bible" Simms continued, "the Angel called Abraham from the Heavens. But Caravaggio actually placed him at Abraham's arm, to capture the drama, and the power of the scene." And Simms gestured, with his arm, to the angel in the corner of the print. His hair was curly and fair. He had a straight nose and grayish-blue wings. One hand gripped Abraham's beside the knife at his wrist, while the other hand's fingers were pointing Abraham to the ram. "See, you think I'm just some dumb fucking cop" Simms was saying. "And when it gets down to it, I probably am. Or else why the hell would I be a cop in the first place. But I know a few things myself. Believe me, doc. I know a few things too."

Alexander was looking at the knife that Abraham was holding. Isaac was young and fearful, with

deepened eyes and pale alabaster skin. His lips were
timid and red, as Abraham gripped the back of his
cheek and neck across his curls.

Officer Simmons moved to the dresser beside his
bed. He examined the clock and the model sailboat,
and the wooden cross of Jesus that was hanging from a
nail. He then opened the door to the closet, (where the
crime lab technician had left all of his clothes). There
were some running shoes and a toolbox, which Simms
opened, and examined the tools. There were some
screwdrivers, a hammer, some vice-grips, some
wrenches, and an electric drill. Simms ran his fingers
over the metal, and left the tools there on the floor.
"What's this?"

"It's a javelin" said Alexander, turning. "I used to
run the decathlon."

Officer Simms examined the tips of the javelin,
where there was a bit of dry dust and mud. There was
also a shot and a discus, and a large metal crucifix that
was crafted of silver or lead. Above were the suits and
white shirts, the belts and the jackets and the ties. "You
didn't find anything?" he called, and the other man said
"nah" who was now searching through the drawers.
Alexander was still standing at the Caravaggio reprint,
where Simms again joined him at his side.

"God said 'take now your son, your only son Isaac,
whom you love, and go to the land of Moriah, and offer
him there as a burnt offering.' And Abraham rose early
in the morning gathering the knife and the sticks for the
fire. And Isaac said 'Father, where is the lamb that we
are to offer?' And Abraham said 'God will provide the
lamb.' And Abraham built the altar there on the
mountain, and placed the wood in order, and bound
Isaac there on the wood. And he stretched out his hand
and took the knife to slay his son. But the Angel of the
Lord called to him from the Heaven, and said 'No,
Abraham, do not harm your son.' And when Abraham

looked, there was a ram caught in the thicket, and Abraham took the ram, and offered it up as a burnt offering instead of his son."

"But I will lie with my father" said Alexander, (when Simms was finished), "and thou shalt carry me out of Egypt, and bury me in their burying place. And he said, 'I will do as thou has said.'"

Simms drew a breath-mint from his front pocket. He offered it to Alexander, who refused, and then placed the white candy on his tongue. "He must have loved his son" he said, still looking at the painting. "It must have been very hard."

Late that afternoon, Alexander was sitting at home in his living room, listening to the television and taking a Smith & Kendon candy from its tin. He was holding a copy of Native Son, and flipping through the pages of a Psychology Today magazine. The man on the tv was talking about the new music generation, which was targeted at fusing the power of rap with the music of blues and pop and jazz. "Rap music has all of the great stories" he was saying, "which have been passed down orally, through toasts. For example, there is the toast about Smiley, the only black man - when they built the Titanic, it was going to be such a fine and grand and perfect creation, that not only were blacks not allowed to ride on the Titanic, but there were no blacks who were even allowed to work on the Titanic at all. And when the Titanic went down, white America mourned. But in Harlem, they were having parties. And this toast, this long rap-like poem was born, about this one black man, Smiley, who snuck on board. And after it hit the iceberg, he knew that it was going to sink. And he jumped overboard, and swam back to New York, and fought sharks with his bare hands, and by the time the ship hit the bottom, he was back in Harlem, shooting pool.

"And then of course" he continued, "you have Mack the Knife, and Frankie and Albert, and Stagger Lee. Which are really universal. Very powerful stuff.

"The problem with rap music" however, he went on to say, "is that, up until now, there is no music in rap music. There is just this artificial, monotonous, often stolen or sampled refrain, created on electric synthesizers, and a kind of dull, repetitious beat, which has been programmed into an electronic computer drum machine. So what we are doing, is taking the energy and the power of rap, and immersing it, and supporting it, and uplifting it, with the vitality of guitars and pianos and trumpets and trombones and drums."

Alexander changed the channel with the remote control device, as he turned the pages of the magazine. "They cover a story better than anyone" a man with long hair was saying on the television. "They go out and actually investigate, which is a lot better than most of what those lazy newspaper people do. Like Linda Smith, the so-called legitimate gossip columnist, just sits around and quotes from the National Enquirer. And then has the balls to say, 'I can't believe how disgusting the tabloids are. They say that such-and-such actress fucked a dog. That's disgusting. I don't agree with that.' And yet her entire column is about the tabloids. And so, the bottom line is, I think the tabloids write interesting material. It appeals to people. And nine times out of ten they get the story right."

"The Federal Reserve is printing an extra fifty billion dollars as the end of the century approaches, just in case the y-two-k glitch temporarily fouls up computer banking systems when the year changes from nineteen ninety-nine to the year two thousand, and people start stocking up on cash. The extra money would remain in the Federal Reserve's own storage vaults, and only go into circulation if the banks request it to fill consumer demands for cash."

"A sixteen year old boy in old town accused of raping his six year old cousin was already on probation for molesting a three year old girl, city officials say. The teenager, whose name is being withheld to protect the identity of the victim, is charged with aggravated rape, and faces a life sentence if convicted. He is being tried as an adult due to the nature of the crime."

Alexander changed the channel again, where the new station was promoting a set of knives that could be ordered through the mail, with a credit card, over the phone, or by fax, and as Alexander was starting to again change the television channel, there was a loud noise from outside beyond the door.

Alexander placed the magazine and the book on the table beside the Smith & Kendon candies, and, without great speed, stepped to the door. When he opened the door the street was empty, save an old abandoned car that was parked on the corner, (an old blue Cutlass with broken windows, no hubcaps, a dent, and three flat tires), and his own. There was a squirrel on the telephone wire, crossing between two poles.

The squirrel made it safely to the far pole, and in the distance the cars were passing with their carhorns and their engines and the sometimes screeching sounds of their brakes. The sun was setting in the west and all was crimson and gold, when Alexander turned on the porch-light, and quietly closed the door.

CHAPTER TWENTY EIGHT

"How are you?"

"I'm okay" she said. It was months later, and Cindy Skinner was tapping her fingers (it was habit now) on the gentle dark leather of Alexander's office couch. Her hair was tied behind her head, where a few strands had escaped the band and fell gracefully about her shoulder and upper arm. Her high cheekbones had dropped a bit, and were free of any makeup. There were faded yellow circles beneath her eyes.

"You look good" said Alexander. "You've been eating; I can tell."

"What? Do I look fat?"

"No, not all" he said. "You were too thin before. Now you've filled out a little. You look good."

"Thanks" she said. "You sure I don't look fat?"

"How's Alvin?"

"Good. I guess."

Alexander just looked at her for a time. He was wearing a charcoal suit and a prussian red tie. "There is nothing that you want to talk about?" he asked her. "What are you thinking?"

"Nothing."

"You have to be thinking something."

Cindy shook her head no.

And there was silence for a time.

"It's bad when other people are smoking" she said finally. "But people don't smoke as much anymore. You know? They go outside, and stuff. So it's really not that bad."

"What about alcohol?"

"Well, you know, I tell you every week that I want a drink every once in a while. But I'm okay. It's not that bad."

"And drugs?"

"No" she said, "never."

"That's good." Alexander scratched at the dry razor burn on his chin, and then scratched at the top of his head. Cindy sniffled, and smiled. She straightened her dress. "Do you think I'm..." she then suddenly asked, "mature?"

"I think you are more mature" he said. "Why?"

"Nothing."

"What?"

"I was just thinking."

"About what?"

"Nothing" she said. The grandfather clock was ticking-tocking, as Cindy drew a piece of gum from her leather purse, which was lying next to her on the floor. Alexander scratched his chin and leaned forward into the muse of sunlight that fell from the blue skies outside through the window, and at the hem of Cindy Skinner's dress. "When I was young" she said, "I remember, we used to have this summer home on Lake Griswald, and we had this old miniature golf course that my grandfather left us. And every summer my mom and I would live at the lake house while my father worked. And then on the weekends he would come up and stay with us. Anyway, I would go every day, and help my mom run the miniature golf course. There were always little things breaking, and I used to get to help my mom paint, and make all of the little repairs. And then, on the weekend, my dad would come, and he would make the really big repairs.

"When I was older of course, I would tease all of the boys who came in for the summer with their families. Tell them I would go skinny-dipping with them, and then when they took their shorts off, I would grab them, and call them perverts and run away.

"But when I was younger, we used, I remember, we used to sneak behind the - there was this, one of those houses, you know, with the little tunnel, through the front door. You know? So you couldn't see the other part of the hole, and you would have to walk around the house to putt your ball in."

"Right."

"So, the people would putt, and then we would run and grab the balls and jump back into the bushes behind the great big slot-machine. Everyone thought they had a hole-in-one, but when they looked in the hole, their ball wasn't there, and they would look and look and look. And we laughed and laughed.

"But one time, I was about ten, or twelve, and there was this little girl who was lost. I discovered later, which my mother knew at the time, that her parents had abandoned her. But my mom just told me that she was lost, and I should play with her until her mommy and daddy came back to take her home.

"I was so good with her. You know? And I think I was kind of aware, at the time, that I was good with her. I remember helping her arm into the sleeve of her little blouse. And I remember teaching her row row your boat, and when she slept with her head on my thigh as a pillow, I sang hush little baby, don't you cry.

"I took care of her for like six hours. And then the people from social services came, and she was gone." Cindy picked at her fingernails, and looked briefly out the window where some people were walking slowly by. "Can I ask you something, Alex?" she then said after pausing briefly. "When we were in school, one time, I don't know if you remember. We had to give these presentations in honors history. Everyone gave these presentations on Darwin and Jefferson and Queen Elizabeth and Plato and Freud. But I gave my presentation on Beth Richards, who was just this ordinary woman, that I interviewed, with a job and a husband and hopes and dreams and memories and family. Most people thought it was stupid. But you said that you thought it was the best presentation in the class. You said it was genius."

Alexander nodded, smiling. (He was behind her, at the desk, and she could not see him from the couch.)

"Do you remember that?"

"Yeah, I remember."

"Did you mean it?" she asked. "Or were you just trying to get into my pants."

"What do you think?"

"I think you meant it" she said. "But I think you wanted to get into my pants too."

"Why do you think that that sticks out, in your mind?"

"I don't know" she said. "I just wonder. If, do you think there was ever anyone that was ever completely honest with me?"

"What do you mean?"

"I mean, do you think that anyone is ever completely honest with anyone else?"

"I don't know" he said. "What do you think?"

"I think about what it must feel like. What it might feel like."

Alexander was scratching at his thigh beneath the desk. Cindy was still playing with her fingernails, and she paused again for a time, before saying: "Alvin mentioned something the other day about adoption."

"How do you feel about that?"

"I don't know" she said. "I don't know if I'm ready. I mean, I think maybe I should wait a little bit, to make sure I've got all my problems behind me."

"That might be a good idea."

"But you don't think I would be bad, do you? A bad mother?"

"Of course not, Cindy" he said. "I think you would be good."

"I'm scared."

"I know" he said. "But everyone is scared. That's not good enough."

"But what if something happens, though? What if I'm a bad mother?"

"Do you think you would be a good mother?"

"Yeah" she said with a hesitant smile. "I guess so."

"I agree."

"Don't you think it would be weird, though, to raise a child that's not your own."

"A parent does not become a mother simply because she gives birth to a child" he said. "A mother is the one who loves that child, and nurses that child, and helps it to grow."

"Yeah, that sounds good and everything" she said. "But..." and she paused, "I don't know. The thing I keep thinking is, I just keep imagining that I have a son, or a daughter, and she gets to be about twelve, when times are hard enough as they are, and I just keep imagining other children on the playground saying your mom is an alcoholic, or your mom is a slut, or your mom is a whore."

"You want others to call you virtuous" Alexander said, "but it is more important that you act with virtue."

"I don't care what people think" she said. "You know that. I'm only thinking of how it will affect the child."

"Yeah, sure. You don't believe that. Everyone cares what other people think about them. It's part of being human."

"Then why do people like me act the way I do?"

"Because you care what people think about you."

"People think I'm a tramp."

"Well isn't that what you wanted?" he asked. "Don't you think there is some part of you that secretly, or maybe not so secretly wanted people to think that you were a tramp?"

"Why?"

"I don't know" he said. "That's a good question. That's what we need to explore and listen to. But I will tell you one hypothesis. And this is only a hypothesis. We will have to listen further. But, just maybe, you resented all of the high, and maybe in your mind unattainable expectations. And you thought that if you could lower people's expectations, you wouldn't feel so guilty about feeling that you had disappointed them."

Cindy took the gum out of her mouth and folded it into a tissue.

"Don't worry" said Alexander. "You haven't lost any of that genius. It's still there inside. You're one in a million. And you know it."

"I'm like the color purple" she said. "It's royal because it's precious, because it's rare. But it is also dangerous. It comes from the poisonous myrex snail, and is an agreement between richness and death."

CHAPTER TWENTY NINE

"That Gloria Steinam is a hell of a penetrating social critic, isn't she?"

"You better not let Susan catch you making any remarks like that around this house."

"So is Susan getting married, or what?"

"I don't know" he said. "Probably."

Jim was nodding and breaking the shell of a pecan with a simple, two-piece, nutcracker, and placing the hard bits of shell into a ceramic bowl. Alexander was drinking water and tapping out a gentle rhythm with his shoe. It was dark outside, and some of the frogs and crickets began to moan and to call. There was classical music playing softly on the stereo, and the smell of baking tomato sauce and cheeses filled the air. Alexander went to the oven, and looked inside where a deep metal tray of moussaka was baking evenly. Jim cracked another pecan at the table. He was wearing a hawaiian shirt and a pair of shorts that fell comfortably about his knee. Alexander was dressed in a stone white oxford, whose sleeves were folded back so that they exposed his lithe and muscular forearms, and whose tails were tucked plainly into the waist of his olive slacks – a primitive blend of cotton and polyester, or wool.

"So how much money do you think they are spending?"

Alexander was sitting back down at the table. "Well I'm sure that Susan is spending a lot more than Karen is."

"Yeah" Jim said, "but that's not your money. Susan is your sister. Karen is my wife."

"That's what happens" he said, and raised his glass (as if toasting).

"Is that why you never married?"

"I don't know" Alexander confessed. "I don't think so."

"You're a snob" Jim said. "People are beautiful. Women are beautiful. You have this idea that there is this perfect woman, and that you have to marry her. But every woman is perfect, in her own way. Every person is perfect, in their own way" he said. "It's just the way it was meant to be."

"Well maybe for me" Alexander said, "it was not meant to be."

"Maybe" said Jim, popping another nut into his mouth. "So what is this stuff we're eating?"

"It's called moussaka."

"Isn't it just like lasagna?"

"Pretty much."

"Good" he said. "I like lasagna."

"Do you like this music?"

"Yeah, it's good" Jim said. "Is this Beethoven's Fourth?"

"Tchaikovsky's Fourth."

"That's right. I like it" he said. "You know, I was thinking the other day: I was at home alone the other day, with Topspin, Karen's dog. And I was listening to music, and thinking about how he could hear this whole other set of noises, all of these other sounds, that I couldn't hear. That I couldn't even imagine. You know? It's like, everything we do, in addition to all of these sights and sounds and noises that we see and hear, has all of these other effects, all of these other consequences, which we don't really intend, or even know anything about. Isn't that amazing?"

Alexander nodded, taking another sip of water from the glass.

"You know what amazes me the most, though?" Jim continued. "All of our knowledge is second-hand. Every year we know more and more and more and more and more, but we haven't learned or experienced any of this knowledge first-hand. Think of everything you know, everything you know and believe to be true, and see if you actually know it from personal experience. I don't know anything. There is almost nothing that I know. You know what I mean? We have a national conscience. We have this national, and even world-wide, set of facts and symbols and ideas, that everyone knows and shares, almost implicitly."

"And you think this is good?"

"I don't know if it's good" Jim said. "But it's incredible. It's something that no one, before the end of the nineteenth century could have conceived. And it's real. I mean, people love characters that are in movies and on tv. You know? Men are in love with Aleece Keaton, and Maggie Seaver, and Katie Couric, and Cokie Roberts, and Elizabeth Jones. My sister cannot have a relationship, because she compares every man to Paul Newman. And they all lose. That's why there is so much divorce. Women don't love their husbands, men don't love their wives, because they have already fallen in love with someone else. Someone on tv."

"Well, I assure you" said Alexander, "that's not my problem."

"I'm not saying it's your problem. I'm just saying in general. It's real."

"I despise people on tv" Alexander said. "They amuse me" he said, "but they do not endear me to them."

"Your problem is something different" Jim said. "I know. I don't know what it is" he said, "but it's something else."

"Well the moussaka should be ready" Alexander said moving into the kitchen. "Get up, and you can help yourself to a plate, and a fork, and whatever you want to drink."

Jim clapped the last pieces of shell from his hands into the bowl and straightened his shirt as he stood. Alexander was removing the tray from the oven, where the steam from the melted cheese and all the scents of mozzarella, lamb, and eggplant, tomato sauce and thyme, crept first into his nostrils, then onto his lips, and finally into his eyes.

"This stuff smells terrific" Jim said. "I can't wait to try it."

"I'm tellin you, it's just like lasagna."

"It smells great."

"Thanks."

"So did the police ever find any evidence, or any trace at all of your dad?"

"Nope."

"That's too bad" Jim said. "I guess it would be nice to have some sort of resolution, you know? Just to know."

"Yeah" he said. "I know."

"Is that cop still hassling you?"

"Nah."

"Yes he is."

"It's just–" Jim started, "I mean it's been years since the Judge died. Plus, to think that you had something to do with it. Or your father. It's ridiculous. Plus, doesn't this guy have something better to do? It's like out of a movie or a bad television show. I can't believe we're paying all these cops all this money for this kind of nonsense. Should be out in the projects, bustin up gangs, beatin up Rodney Kings. It's not your fault that your father died."

"Yeah, well, it's not his fault that he hates me" said Alexander. "I wish him no ill will or harm."

"Well that's very civilized" Jim said. "Lets eat."

CHAPTER THIRTY

Alexander was alone in his office, where the sun swam in through the open window and warmed the pastel prints and dark leather couch, as a cool breeze came in waves from the sidewalk and the grasses and the street outside. There were two nuns, who waited for the bus at the corner. One had a black leather purse, the other carried a brown paper supermarket bag. Inside, the grandfather clock was ticking and tocking, as Alexander watered his green wet spider plants at the edge of the room. A few drops of water spilled over the edge of the white ceramic, and Alexander dabbed at the water with the tail of his shirt. It was then that the phone rang.

"Hello."

"Hey buddy, it's Trevor" the voice said. "And I got roped into collecting for the alumni fund."

"Johns Hopkins or Alpha Chi?"

"Hopkins" Trevor said.

"Well I'll give whatever you want me to" Alex said, "you know that."

"Can I put you down for five hundred?"

"Sure" Alex said. "That's fine."

"Okay, great, thanks. I appreciate it."

"So how is everything?"

"Pretty good."

"How is Julie?"

"Fine."

"And Christie?"

"Fine" he said. "Keeps our hands full."

"She's what, three and a half?"

"Yeah."

"She must be adorable. Send me a picture."

" Okay."

"Did you hear that Susan might be getting engaged soon."

"I heard" he said. "That's great."

"So how is everything?"

"It's pretty good. Pretty well."

"What's wrong?" Alexander asked him. "How come you don't want to talk to me? I haven't heard from you in ages, and now you call, and you don't want to talk. What's up?"

There was a silence over the phone line. Outside the bus came, and the two women helped each other climb on board. There was another man, in a dark tan suit, who helped one of the sisters; he had a blue umbrella in his hand. Alexander scratched against his chin with his palm.

"Look" Trevor started, (with some difficulty), "I would never say anything. Because I love you too much. And because I love your sister, and I think your family has been through enough. But you betrayed everything that I hold sacred, Alex. You betrayed the one thing in this world other than my family that I love. I know you had your reasons, Alex, but that jury out there is the only thing that separates us from the cavemen. It's that jury, it's justice, it's respect, it's order, it is law, which makes us human. And you betrayed that, Alex. The world is bigger than you, Alexander. The law is bigger than you. I love you, Alexander, but I cannot respect you, any more. Because you betrayed me, Alex. You betrayed the

Judge. And you betrayed your family. You betrayed us all. And for what? For what, Alex? For nothing. For nothing more than your own sense of vengeance."

"Whatever I have done" said Alexander, "it was not an act of vengeance. It was an act of love."

CHAPTER THIRTY ONE

When Alexander opened the door to his mother's house, Helen was seated at the piano. Her dark curls flurried about her delicate ear-lobes, and her tender eyes shone brightly as they reflected the piano-lantern's sovereign flame. Her warm hands moved forcefully and eloquently over the raised bars of ebony and the ivory keys, as the richest, boldest, most majestic anthem of melodies came thundering into the air that Alexander was breathing, and over the walls and the floors and the paintings of that disquieted, astonished room.

"Isn't she just wonderful" her mother said with sincere elation as Helen finished, and Alexander kissed her, "hello gorgeous", on the forehead, before kissing, "hello gorgeous", his mom. "You are truly gifted" Alexander then said to Helen.

"Your father would be so proud."

Helen was blushing. She swept her hair back behind her shoulders, and the hem of her sun-dress fell gracefully about her ankles as she stood. "Hi Alex" she said.

"That was really wonderful" he again told her. "I'm really impressed."

"Thanks."

"So what did you bring us, Alexander?"

"Just some wine" he said. "An italian wine."

"Thank you" said Catherine, "that was very thoughtful." She was carrying spinach and salad and chicken and water and butter and bread to the table, and Alexander said "here let me help you mom" as Helen placed the three napkins beside the knives and forks and spoons.

"I remember when we used to have steak every night" Alexander said as the three of them sat around the table.   "Not every night" his mother said. "Sometimes we would have fish or chicken."

"No, we either had roast, or lamb, or hamburgers, or steak."

"Well, you can't eat like that, like we used to be able to."

"You know eighty percent of the girls in my school have an eating disorder" Helen asked rhetorically. "It's in."

"You should send them to Alexander."

"Yeah" he said joking, "where do they go?"

"I don't know" she said.   "But psychiatrists are definitely in. Every girl has one."

"You should advertise" suggested Catherine. "You can go around to all the high schools."

"You can advertise on tv" suggested Helen, "like all of the chiropractors, and the lawyers."

"Your father would turn over in his grave" their mother said, "if he could see all of these lawyers advertising on tv."

"Well maybe he can."

A silence fell over the table, as Catherine placed a piece of bread on her plate and began to cover it with butter. Alexander looked to Helen, who was trying to cut into the thigh of the chicken with her knife and her fork. Alexander said "this is delicious mom" as he was taking a spoonful of spinach out of the serving dish and placing it into the bowl.

"Mom sold some pottery."

"Really? That's terrific."

"She got five hundred dollars for five vases and a tray."

"That's wonderful" said Alex. "You must be happy and proud."

"Yeah" she said, "I am."

"Good. And what is going on with you?" he asked Helen. "How is soccer?"

"Pretty good" she said. "I am up to eighty-four goals, and I have two more games."

"Well tell me when they are, so I can come see them."

"That's okay" she said. "You guys have already been to two games this year. That's enough torture for anyone."

"I like to watch you" he said.

"Well I'm going to be there" said Catherine. "And I'm having a special sign made."

"Please don't, mom. It'll be so embarrassing."

"Please."

"Has anybody ever scored a hundred goals in a high school career?" Alexander wondered, as Helen said "mom, if you make a sign and embarrass me I'm going to quit school and never come back."

"Nope" her mom said. "Some girl named Jennifer Presley scored seventy-four goals at Saint Lutheran's, and some guy named Joey something scored eighty-one. That's the most."

"Besides Helen" said Alexander. "And you've got two more years."

"And she's got the Prom coming up, and Sweet Sixteen, and Easter Sunday. Can you believe? That school of hers schedules the Prom just one weekend before Easter, can you believe that? During Lent. I just swear they've got those kids sinning one weekend so they can go in on Easter and confess about it the next."

"Who are you going with?" Alexander asked her.

"Just girls" she said. "We are going stag. Only the seniors get dates, really."

"That's good" he said. And then: "I think Michael's gonna propose soon."

"Finally" Catherine said. "What do you think about that?"

"I don't know" he said.

"I don't like him" said Helen.

"I do" Alex said. "He is much more practical than Susan. They make a good pair."

"But does she love him?" asked his mother.

"I think she does" Alexander said.

"Well, that's really all you can ask for" said Catherine. "And really, she should be getting married soon, if she still wants to have kids."

"She has plenty of time" said Alexander. "She could wait another three or four years and still have three or four kids if she wanted to."

"Does she want to have kids?"

"I think so."

"She told me she did."

"When we're done with dinner" Helen then said to Alexander, "you have to come see my new garden."

"Oh yes, it's beautiful" their mother said.

"Okay."

"And I'm going to give you some cake, to take to your sister."

"Okay."

The three were eating their roasted chicken and creamed spinach, and Mrs. Thealah was also eating a lot of bread. The piano-lamp was still burning brightly, and there was a gentle flavor of honey and sunlight that drifted over the room. They stood to clear the table, and Helen started to explain that on her soap opera, the lead character was going to leave the show. "See she was married to Carl, from my other soap opera, in real

life, but they got a divorce. Then he got fired from that
soap opera and got hired again by San Francisco, and
she doesn't want to work with him, so she quit. And
they are having a fan write-in, to decide how her
character will leave the show."

"What are the choices?"

"She can get caught up in a love triangle and be
murdered, or die in a train accident, or get cancer, or
have an affair and run away to Europe, or she can just
mysteriously disappear."

"What are you voting for?"

"I sent in one vote for dying of breast cancer, to raise
people's awareness, and four votes for having an affair
and running off to Europe with the guy."

It was a half-hour later, and Alexander was in the
garden with his mother and Helen. The sun, by that
time, had descended, and there was a blue mist of
twilight that echoed throughout the northern and
western sides. "Look" Helen said, "there is Venus. You
can see her the best during twilight." And the three of
them were looking up at the small white-green fire-fly
light in the sky. In the yard below was a garden, and in
the garden was a stony pond. About the pond were
many lilies and water-plants and flowers, and beneath
the surface of the water swam a number of white and
red fish. Helen stepped to the pond's edge and dipped
her index finger into the water. All the fish came to
her, with open mouths kissing, along the surface of the
pond. "That's how I feed them" Helen explained.
"They think I'm going to feed them because I stuck my
finger in. But I already fed them today."

"It's beautiful" said Alexander. "You planted all of
this?"

"I planted everything from that tree, to the fence, to
the pond. Mom planted the rest."

"It looks really good" Alexander said.

"Well I'm tired" said Catherine.

"Okay."

"I'm sorry we didn't get to drink the wine" she said, as Alexander was giving her a great, encompassing hug. "Maybe some other time."

"Thanks mom, it was wonderful," and he kissed her on the cheek.

"I love you" she said, and squeezed him tightly.

"I know" he said. "I love you too." Then Helen kissed him on the cheek, saying "bye Alex, I love you, tell Susan hi for me."

"I will."

"And don't forget to bring her the cake."

"I won't."

"Goodbye" said Helen and Catherine. Alexander took the cake and wrapped it beneath his arm. He said goodbye, (his mother and Helen were still standing in the doorway), and he was gone.

CHAPTER THIRTY TWO

Gerald Mayfield was tall and lanky now. He had a bit of dark hair that was forming on his upper lip and at the base of his chin, and he also had a large adam's apple, which was a bit awkward as it moved about in his neck. He still had playful dark curls, and round cheeks, with not quite dimples, and curious, intelligent, boastful, dark eyes. He was wearing a red short-sleeve knit shirt and pair of cotton blue slacks, and he was sitting on top of his knees, in the center of Alexander's office floor.

The grandfather clock was ticking-tocking beside the soft warm pastel prints, and a bay of sunlight was breaking in from behind the clouds and splashing with kindness against the cool wet spider plants and over the persian colours quilted gracefully. Alexander also was on his knees, gripping the boys' hands in his own. There were tears on Gerald's cheek.

"Underneath the porch was cold" he said. (He was struggling.) "One of the boards was broken, and there was this piece of wood that was hanging by these very thin fibers. And I picked at it while I was listening. They were saying what did you call me, you should know better, threatening him, and all that. They hit him a few times. I heard that, and him saying please go. Please, just go.

"There was a spider web too, I remember, under the porch. But there was no spider in the web.

"I was thinking about that, and wondering where that spider was, when I heard the shots. I didn't know what they were at first. Because they surprised me. And then I told myself that they were just firecrackers, that it was just a car back-fired... But I knew.

"I heard their car speed away. And people were screaming and crying and yelling" Gerald was crying. "I didn't want to come out" he sobbed. "I knew not to come out..." he said, "because when I did... I knew it would be true.

"And so I stayed in there a long time. I heard my mom crying Gerald, Gerald, she was screaming for me." He stopped, and was crying. "But... but, I just couldn't..."

The boy stopped again.

Alexander was sitting beside him, squeezing his wet fingers, and staring into his eyes.

"So..." Gerald began again. "So, after a while, it seemed like forever, it started to get dark. And I could see the legs of all the police men... And then I saw my father's legs, and my mom's, and he hugged her..." (He had stopped crying.) "And I knew that I could come out now, cuz daddy was home.

"But when I started to crawl out from the porch, I stopped.... And my mom rushed me, and grabbed me, and lifted me, and held me in her arms. And my father was hugging us. He had his arms around us. And I saw tears coming from his eyes. And that was the only time I had ever seen my father cry..."

Gerald's tears started to well up again, and he was shaking, as if from the cold. Nervously, and timidly, he cuddled into a ball, and nestled into Alexander's lap, where he held the boy in his arms. "Shhhh..." he whispered. "It's okay."

"And I looked down..." the boy whimpered into his lap, "and that's when I saw all of the blood... And Angie was crying. And Tommy was crying. And Dexter and Manny were just standing there, watching the policemen... And that's when I knew it..." Gerald stopped, and took a deep breath, as he trembled... "My brother was dead."

"Shhhh...." Alexander whispered, and ran his fingers gently through the boy's curls. "Shhh..."

"I just want him back" Gerald was crying, "I want Stevie.... I want Stevie.... Why did you kill my brother?"

"Shhhh..."

"Why? ... Why? ... why?"

Alexander held his patient. The two sat huddled on the floor for a time. Gerald was sobbing and sniffling, and Alexander held him in his arms.

CHAPTER THIRTY THREE

"So what are the koumbari again?"

"Alexander and Page."

"Yeah, but what are they?"

"It's just like the maid of honor and best man. They are supposed to help with the arrangements, and bring the candles and the silver tray and the crowns, and I think they make some affirmation to the church that we are dedicated to one another, and they don't have to but usually become the godfather and godmother to the first child."

Susan was in the kitchen, mixing the warm stuffing in a large ceramic bowl. Michael and Alexander were at the table, examining the cornish hens. There was also bread and salad, and a sizable carafe of mead. "This stuff is great" Michael said as he tested it with his pinky. "Did you brew this yourself?"

"No, my friend Jim did" he said.

"I'm almost ready" Susan called from the kitchen.

"It's okay" Michael said, "take your time."

The two men sat down at the table, and Alexander placed the three cornish hens on the several plates before them. Michael dispensed the salad, and then poured Susan a glass full of mead.

"We should have invited mom and Helen" Susan said stepping into the room with a bowl full of stuffing,

and the smell of celery and butter and garlic and freshly
baked bread crumbs warmed the room. "I called her"
said Alex. "She is having dinner with Henry and
Martha, and Helen is eating at a friend's."

"How was dinner the other night?"

"Good" he said. "You would not believe how well
Helen is playing the piano."

"I heard her a few weeks ago" Susan said. "She's
incredible."

"And mom sold some more platters and vases."

"Really?"

"Yep."

"That's great" offered Michael, as Susan was asking
"to who?"

"I don't know."

"Her stuff isn't bad."

"I didn't say it was bad" said Susan (defensively),
"it's just not very marketable."

"Well, people buy them."

"I'm happy for her."

There was a brief silence at the table. Alexander
took a fork full of stuffing, and placed it beneath the
wing of the hen. "She'll be okay."

"So how do you make this stuff?" asked Michael.

"It's like beer" Susan explained, "but it's made with
honey and malt instead of hops and barley. Right?"

"Uh huh."

"It's really good" Michael said, taking another sip.
"Good libations."

"What are libations?"

"Wine."

"Originally it was choe, a liquid poured out to the
gods."

"Really?" Michael said. "That's interesting. I
thought it meant wine, but was really just a general
term used for anything with alcohol."

"Did you see the architectural prints that Michael bought for me?"

"Yes" said Alex. "They're nice."

"What are they, like lithographed, and then hand-colored?"

"Exactly" Michael said. "That's exactly what they are."

Alexander nodded dispassionately. He was eating from the leg of the hen, working his way to the center of the breast. Michael was eating from his salad plate, while Susan was spreading butter over her bread. "This is good" Alexander said standing, "but I think I'm gonna get a coke as well. Do you guys want any?"

"No thanks" Susan said, as Michael was saying that "new coke doesn't taste like old coke." And he took another sip of the mead. "That was both the greatest and the worst advertising campaign of the twentieth century."

"Um hum."

"Did you get Helen anything for her birthday yet?" asked Susan, as Alexander returned to the table.

"Yeah, I got her something pretty special."

"What is it?"

"It's a cross" he said. "I made it myself."

"That's nice."

"What did you make it out of?"

"All kinds of stuff. I'll show it to you after we're finished eating. Remind me."

"Susan and I were thinking about getting her that malachite and silver necklace from Tiffany's."

"That's nice" Alexander agreed.

"Do you still think that cop might be following you?" asked Michael.

"I don't know."

"You better be careful" Michael said. "Pretty soon this guy is gonna get tired of just following you around. I mean, I don't think they are ever gonna close the book on that case. I mean they had to let Raintree go, Stiles is dead, and they never found your father. And I think at some point, it's all going to come to a head. Especially with this crazy guy."

Alexander was finishing his salad.

"And cops can pretty much do anything" continued Michael. "They really can. I mean, all he has to do is shoot you in the head when you're not looking; plant a gun in you hand; shoot it; and say it was self-defense. Someone from internal affairs might ask a few questions, but nothing will come of it. And he knows it. I would be careful if I were you."

"I don't know" said Alexander. "I think Officer Simmons is harmless. I'm no real threat to him. It's just the fact that there aren't too many unsolved crimes around here. Especially high profile. So when you have one, they have to make the most of it. And that's the bottom line. To him, it's only a game."

"I used to care a lot about what happened to the Judge" interjected Susan, "and what happened to dad. But now I don't want to know. It's too painful. I just want to put it behind us, and move on."

Michael put his hand on hers, and gripped it affectionately.

"Did that lawyer Marvin Dane ask you about testifying?"

"Who's Marvin Dane?"

"He's a civil lawyer" Susan explained, "who tries to bankrupt hate groups like the nazis and the klan by holding the organizations and their leaders responsible for the actions of their members."

"That's cool."

"I don't know" Susan said.

"What?"

"I mean I respect Mister Dane for his intentions. And as a lawyer, as a person, and politically I support what he does. But, as a legal matter, I'm not sure how I feel about what he does."

"I don't see a down side to it" said Michael. "The law should be employed to hold those kinds of groups accountable."

"I don't know. I'm just not sure if that is really good precedent, for other things."

"That's crap" he said. "It's a war out there. And if you spend too much time protecting your enemies, you are going to discover too late in time that they have done everything but protected you."

"Maybe" she said, "but I'm not going to assist them, by fighting them on one front, and at the same time opening up a great big gaping back door."

"I don't know-" "the trial" she interrupted, "will not be about whether Raintree killed the Judge. And it won't be about whether the klan or the nazis played a part in that crime. It will be about sending a message. It will be about whether you like, or agree with, or accept, the organization. And when it gets down to it, they will be asking the jury to punish the defendants, or at least some of the defendants, for no more than simply what they believe. And any time that happens; any time the courtroom becomes a political weapon, for the purpose of stifling what people we don't like, or don't agree with, or are threatened by, say, or write, or paint, or think, or believe, then we are treading on thin ice. Because it's only a matter of time until someone doesn't like, or doesn't agree with, or is threatened by you."

Michael and Alexander sat back in their chairs with raised eyebrows. "You gonna marry this girl?" Alexander teased.

"I don't know" Michael said. "What do you think?"

"I don't know" he said, "she makes a hell of a cornish hen."

"Thank you" she said, standing, "why don't you two do the dishes, while I climb into a nice warm bubble-bath."

"No, because it's a conspiracy" said Michael.

"What are you talking about?"

"Marvin Dane" he said. "That's the difference. Anyone can sit around in the room and talk about communism, or devil worship, or how to make a nuclear bomb. But when a group of people sit in a room together, and plan to blow up a building, or have some child or animal sacrifice, or go out and lynch some black man, and then a few people go out and actually do it, then they are all responsible."

"Bubble-bath?"

"Sure."

"You two kids be careful."

"Wait, you have to show us your present."

Alexander stepped into his bedroom, while Michael helped Susan clear the dishes away from the table, and finished the last of the mead. Michael placed the carafe down into the sink and kissed Susan, who kissed him back.

"Oh Alexander" she then said when she saw him, "it's beautiful."

He was holding an ancient greek crucifix, which seemed large even in his hands. It was crafted of silver and onyx, with angels and trumpets and lions etched and sculpted about the several onyx stones. In the center of the cross was a crystal. It was round, and elegant, with a ruby red powder that fell in between the cut glass. All the light of the room seemed to focus upon it: swimming on the courteous edges of silver, drawn into the depths of the deep crimson powder, and reflected by the gracefully cut stones. Alexander shook the crucifix, and the red powder instantly melted before them into a burgundy liquid inside the glass. "It is the miracle of Saint Januarius" explained Alexander. "And this is his blood."

CHAPTER THIRTY FOUR

"Happy Birthday" said Alexander, and kissed Helen on the cheek. "Where is everyone?"

"Mom and Susan and Mike went to pick up Theresa from the airport. They should be back in about an hour."

"Do you want your present now, or do you want to wait for everyone else?"

"You can give it to me now" she said, and Alexander followed her back into her room. Blinky and Twinky, the turtles, were resting on the rock and in the water of the aquarium. There was a soccer ball and school books on the floor with dirty clothes, and a print of Klimt's The Virgin above the bed.

Helen picked up the stray clothes from the floor and threw them into the clothes hamper in her bathroom. She sat on the adjustable chair beside her desk, and Alexander sat across from her on the bed. Slowly, he revealed the crucifix from beneath his jacket. "Oh my god" she said, "it's gorgeous," and stood to hold it in her hands. "Thank you so much" she said as she kissed him, and lifted the silver and onyx piece into the light. "I love all of the angels - oh and the lions. This is so beautiful, Alex. Thank you."

"Shake it" he told her, and the powder turned gracefully into a crimson liquid inside the glass. "It is the miracle of Saint Januarius" he told her. "It has been passed down through the ages since the Emperor Diocletian sentenced four Christians to death at the hands of a wild beast, and Saint Januarius kept the beasts at bay."

"And that's his blood?"

"Yes" he said. "That is the blood of our Father."

"Our father, Jesus Christ?" asked Helen.

Alexander was silent.

"Or our father, Victor Thealah?"

"Our father, Saint Januarius" he said.

"You killed him, didn't you?" she asked him squarely, sitting beside him on the bed, and tucking her soft head into the center of his breast. "And the Judge, too."

"Sometimes I feel like a lonely marathon runner" he told her, "whose course has been wrenched and thrown outside the track. My whole life I have tried to be just, yet I could feel it in my heart. Preparing for some great and terrible violence, or pain."

"You killed him, didn't you?"

"Yes, I killed our father. Not without some right."

"How did you do it?" she asked him.

"It was a weekend" he said. "He was supposed to be going out of town. Susan was out with Mike; I knew she would spend the night. Mom had to stay in town for a meeting. That's how I knew she would not go to the lake.

"I was in the back seat" he continued. "And when he climbed into the car, I gripped his face and his neck, and soon he was asleep. I drove to Lake Croce. He stirred a bit in the car. And I wept. But by the time we got to the lake house, I had dried my tears. And I had broken his neck. He was dead.

"It was a long night at Lake Croce" he told her. "First I had to bleed him. And I had to do it carefully. You don't know how much blood is in a human body.

And it has this smell. This kind of metallic, salty, thick red smell....

"It took four buckets until he was dry. And each time I had to paddle out, slowly, silently, deep into the marsh. It was pitch black, no moon. And on the third trip, there were a few fishermen in a boat. I was lying as flat as I could, praying that they would not hear me, trying not to breathe. And yet my breath was so loud, it was pounding, because it was so great in my consciousness. They were three feet away from me at one time. I could see his orange vest, and I could hear the paddle brushing almost imperceptibly at the marsh.

"There was one vial that I saved, though." He nodded to the crucifix, saying: "That is the miracle of Saint Januarius, who saved us from the beasts, those many years ago.

"Next was the skin" he continued. "I had to boil it, in pieces, away from the bone. White flesh, like mutton, falling like a jellyfish through the water, and that stench. I had to use chili powder, and pepper and salt, and I made a chili next to the pot of boiling water on the stove. But you could still smell it beneath the chili powder, or above it, that smell of death and algae, that I remembered from medical school quite dispassionately. But I remembered it.

"When it was done boiling, I ran it through the meat grinder. It was so tender, and malleable. Like a soft, warm, pink clay. It's in the flowers now, and the grasses and the bird seed and the trees. But as our once father, it's gone.

"All that was left was the bone" he continued. "I put it in the kiln. Piece by piece. Until it was dry, and white, and brittle, and could be crushed. I got the hammer and I pounded, and pounded, and pounded, until there was nothing but ash and dust. It was easy to mix with the soil.

"I had these great bags of soil, that I bought from the Taj Mahal. I bought them the same day that I bought all the soil for your garden, so that there would naturally be soil in the car. And I mixed the ash and the dust with the soil. And I put it back into the bag. And I sealed them, as if they had never been pierced or opened at all. Later I placed the bags of soil back into the yard at the Taj Mahal. And I discreetly disposed of the bucket and the hammer and the pot, which have been washed, disinfected, and placed in a junkyard at the edge of the four-twelve service road. I cleaned the floors, and the everything - there was no apparent evidence, but I was careful. I cleaned the grinder, and I then grounded a fat juicy sirloin, and put the meat into the chili, which later I froze.

"The sun was beginning to touch the air with its fingers by this time. And when I came out into the morning, it startled me. I said a prayer for our father, and then I cried for him, and for me, and for mother, and for you, one last time."

Alexander was holding his sister, who gripped the crucifix tightly in her arms. Her body was shaking, and she sobbed, taking deep breaths, and crying in his arms. And it was then when Alexander's voice came whispering like a rush of thrushes and nightingales singing. "Down in the valley" he was singing, "the valley so low; hang your head over, hear the wind blow. Hear the wind blow, child, hear the wind blow; hang your head over, hear the wind blow...." Alexander touched her quiet forehead, and combed her delicate tresses gently in his hand. "Roses love sunshine, violets love blue; angels in Heaven, know I love you." And Alexander was holding her in his arms as she was sobbing quietly. "Down in the valley" he sang, "the valley so low; hang your head over, hear the wind blow. Hear the wind blow, child, hear the wind blow; hang your head over, hear the wind blow...."

Helen raised her head from Alexander's chest, and started to wipe the tears from her delicate cheeks and eyes. "I'm gonna go wash my face" she sniffled, "before the others get home."

"Okay" he said, and kissed her on the forehead. She wiped again at her eyes with her nimble fingers, and stepped into the bathroom, where the sink-water began to flow.

"Are you okay?" called Alexander.

"Uh huh" she said. "I'll be out in a minute."

Alexander placed the crucifix gently on the top of the desk beside her computer and next to her phone. He studied the photographs that she had pasted: Helen in her soccer uniform; Helen with Victor and Catherine; Helen with her friend Stacey Atwood at a slumber party; and Helen with Alexander and Susan and Catherine and Victor and Carol and the Judge.

The water was still running in the bathroom, and Alexander stepped away from the desk, where he ran his fingernails across the shells of Blinky and Twinky, who were unresponsive. He uncovered the small vial beside the aquarium, and dropped a small bit of food into the water below. Then he moved again to the bed, and straightened the stuffed animals and the pillows. He was studying the colour reprint of Klimt's Virgin. The water in the bathroom ceased to flow.

The bullet entered at his temple, and the echo sounded out like thunder against the doors and the walls of their home. Helen was standing in the doorway. She moved slowly to the center of the room. Her hands, still wet, were quivering at her side. She stood before her dead brother. His hair floated about his head, and like a halo circled his noble cheeks and lifeless smile. Helen looked into the hollow caverns of his eyes, and watched the blood, like the tide of some dark ancient tyrian ocean, spill out onto the floor.

Outside the crickets were scattered about the grasses, and the frogs croaked to their neighbors from the edge of the pond. The sun was setting in the west. All was rose and gilded in the trees. But there in Helen's bedroom, she cried alone in the corner with her ancient crucifix, as the dark blood was consuming the dust and the wood below.

Acknowledgments

I would like to thank everyone who assisted me with the creation of this book, particularly Alan Medvin, Jamie Ellsworth, Benjamin Coleman, Andrew and Lora Leyens, Sam Rubin, Christine Ferguson, Nancy Trichter, Joseph Bosco, Isaac and Lilian Kirshbom, MawMaw, Grandma, Penny, Liz, Mom, Dad, and, most of all, Karen.

[June 1999]

And thanks to my daughter, Alexandra, who helped me with the revised edition for e-book publication in August of 2018. Love you.